Alive for Now

Bob Howard

ISBN-10: 1945754095
ISBN-13: 978-1-945754-09-8

DEDICATION

This book is dedicated to my wife, Dawn, who always wanted me to write.

CONTENTS

ACKNOWLEDGMENTS

I would like to express my appreciation to all of the people who have given their suggestions, comments, support, and editing skills to create this book.

MUD ISLAND

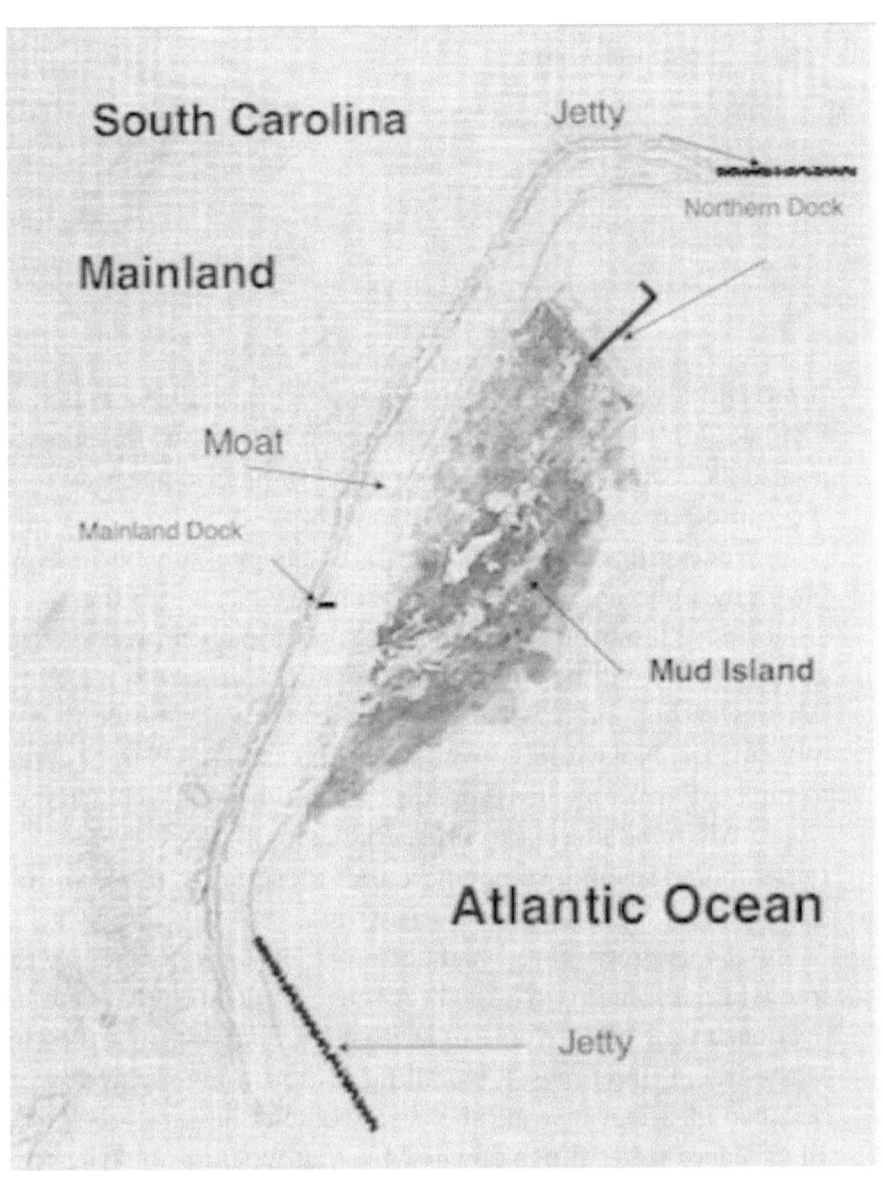

1 SURVIVAL

A mosquito got me on the back of my right ear, and it was itching like I couldn't believe. I wanted to scratch at it, but I needed to be as still as I could, and there are a lot of things far worse than a mosquito bite in this world.

Bee stings are bad. Spider bites can be really bad. Being bitten by a person......I don't even know what to call that.

So, I'll put up with the mosquito bite for now, and my guess is there will be a few more mosquito bites before dawn. Warm weather and a wet climate makes for some very big mosquitoes. Noisy too. Maybe when the sun comes up, I can get to my boat and a few less mosquitoes will be able to reach me.

My mind started to drift a bit as I got sleepy, and I remembered reading somewhere that mosquitoes never fly more than ten feet high. Someone was wrong.

I was pretty sure I had gotten at least twenty feet up the tree where I found two large branches I could straddle. One leg over each limb allowed me to at least lean back against the trunk of the tree. Killing myself by falling and breaking my neck would be a bad idea, but it would be even worse to be paralyzed and alive. There were things down there that wouldn't be near as unhappy about it as I would.

My head slid to one side, and I jerked awake. Something below the tree groaned, and I quietly cursed at myself for letting

1

my mind wander. If I wanted to stay awake, I had to do something besides remember trivia.

I decided to put my mind to work on what I would do when I reached the boat, but I was really tired, and it wasn't long before my mind started to wander again. This time my mind went to an earlier part of my life when things were more like they should be, and much simpler.

I didn't get the island because I needed it. I didn't really even want it, and I guess you couldn't say I would have bought it, either. It just landed in my lap, and I probably gave up a lot of money to keep it. Let's just say sometimes you get stuck with something whether you want it or not.

There are plenty of thirty-two year old guys who would think of a ton of good reasons to own an island, but I wasn't at that point in my life. Single, working on a career that was developing too slowly, and being constantly reminded by relatives that they had done better at my age. Maybe I just didn't have enough imagination to get excited about owning property yet. Then again, I also didn't know what I know now.

When the lawyers called me they said it was a good news, bad news kind of thing. I was supposed to ask which one I wanted to hear first, but I never really liked lawyers enough to take the bait.

After a few moments of silence, the 'suit' on the other end of the phone made the decision for me and went with what he thought was the good news.

"You own an island off the coast of South Carolina. It's undeveloped and hard to get to, but you own it."

I didn't say anything because I didn't really know if it was a prank call, or if it was the truth and maybe I should brace myself for the bad news. I didn't think the undeveloped and hard to get to part was really what he meant by bad news.

The good news sounded like a phishing email in person. You know, the kind that says you just have to reply to the email, and someone is going to give you a million dollars. They usually

2

include a bunch of bad grammar and are from someone with an email that begins with freakyhotlegs.

The suit was smart enough to realize I was waiting for him to deliver the punchline, so he went on with the bad news.

"You do, however, owe a large sum of money in back taxes on the property. Probably more than you can afford to pay, which means the island will go to auction, and someone will take it off your hands."

"You mean I own an island, but I'm not going to get to keep it. Is there really some good news here?"

I wasn't sure why they even bothered to call me if I was going to wind up with exactly the same thing after the call that I had before it.

"Well, uh." He cleared his throat and became so uncomfortable that I could literally picture him sticking one finger into his collar to loosen it up enough to breathe.

"Well, uh, it's sort of our firm's fault that there are back taxes due. We somehow neglected to tell you that you inherited the island back when it was left to you in a distant relative's will."

I've always been the kind of person who can't resist turning the thumbscrews just a bit more when I don't like someone, and since I don't like lawyers, and since I especially don't like lawyers who cost me money, I had to turn that thumbscrew.

"How does that sort of thing happen, Mr.......What did you say your name was again?"

"Uh, Mr. Weintraub."

Mr. Weintraub sounded young, said "uh" too many times for me to think he would ever be a good lawyer, and was probably getting stuck with making a phone call for a senior partner who had screwed up, so I eased up on him just a bit.

"Forget it, Mr. Weintraub. I don't really care how it happened, I just don't understand why it's a good thing that I own an island, but I can get rid of it just by letting it go to auction for back taxes. Especially if it was your firm's fault that I owe those back taxes. I may not be a lawyer Mr. Weintraub, but usually when something is someone else's fault, they have to face some consequences. Consequences like, oh I don't know, paying some kind of penalty. What's the word you lawyers would usually use?"

"You mean settlement, Mr. Jackson?"

His voice sounded smaller than before and I had the impression he had been told his career might be developing just a bit slower too, unless he could get out of offering me a settlement.

"Yes, Mr. Weintraub, I mean settlement." I mentally saw the thumbscrew turn, but before another "uh" could escape from the junior lawyer, a heavy hitter spoke up.

"Mr. Jackson, this is Amanda Lee. I'm a senior partner with this firm, and......"

"Ms. Lee, isn't it considered impolite to not tell people when they are on a speaker phone? Something tells me you've been hanging over Mr. Weintraub's shoulder for the last few minutes listening to every word."

I couldn't resist going on the offensive now that I had warmed up on Mr. Weintraub. It was clear from the silence on the other end of the phone that Weintraub was frozen in his tracks, and Lee was probably fuming. She wasn't used to being put in her place by anyone, and she undoubtedly had a pretty good idea she was talking to someone whose total assets were less than the cost of her weekly dry cleaning bill.

"Mr. Jackson, maybe Mr. Weintraub could have made better use of your time by getting straight to an explanation of how this is going to benefit you."

It wasn't exactly an apology, but it was a step in the right direction.

"Our firm is prepared to make arrangements for payment of the back taxes on the property in return for your consideration."

"Consideration for what, Ms. Lee? Not making a public spectacle of the fact that your law firm screwed up?"

"Something like that, Mr. Jackson," she said without being fazed at all. "As a matter of fact, we are prepared to cover the taxes and a few amenities that we believe you will find to be very attractive."

She said the whole thing as if the words were liquid gold, and each word was delivered slowly. She made "very attractive" into about ten syllables, and despite my better judgement, a small part of me hoped she was one of the amenities.

"Such as?" I asked.

"As Mr. Weintraub said, the island is undeveloped, but it isn't worthless. We could make you an offer for the island that I'm pretty sure would be beyond your wildest dreams. You could retire on what we are prepared to pay you to take this problem off your hands."

Up until that point I was seeing dollar signs, Ms. Lee in a tight dress, maybe my own business, or just retiring young. There was just something about the way she was acting...like she would be doing me a favor. It made me feel like she didn't just consider herself richer than me, but smarter.

She was right about the richer part, but sometimes money can make you think you're smarter than you are. That rich guy with the world's worst comb-over who ran for President was living proof of that.

A big part of me was saying, "Draw up the papers."

A smaller but more stubborn part of me said, "I think your firm is trying to take advantage of me, and I think I have a different settlement in mind, Ms. Lee."

Was I actually turning down an offer of money that hinted at a lifetime of luxury? Was I passing up on being rich just because I didn't like being talked down to by a successful woman?

I guess I was, and Mr. Stubborn went on to say, "Why don't you take care of those taxes for me and give me a call when you do? We can get together and get a notary seal on a deed to that island, and if I decide I want to sell it, I'll be happy to consider your offer…along with a few offers from other interested parties."

I hung up the phone and then just stood there staring at it. I think I was trying to will it to ring. I would answer, and a voice would say I'm forgiven for being the biggest idiot in the world. That I'm really a smart guy, and I didn't just turn down the opportunity of a lifetime.

The phone didn't ring. Eventually, I looked around my apartment from where I stood and realized I must have been dropped on my head when I was born.

******

Perched on my tree limbs, I looked around and my thoughts came back from that moment just a few months ago. I remember I even considered sitting down on my worn out, curb-treasure couch and playing some video games. I figured a few hours of war games or zombie bashing would make me feel just a bit more superior than I felt.

There was just something so unreal about the phone call that playing video games seemed to be the right thing to do. I could go from one unreal thing to another. It seems I didn't have a clue back then about the definition of unreal.

Something moved past the bottom of the tree, and I held my breath. There was a mosquito buzzing my right ear again, but it could abuse me until it got fat and fell off as far as I was concerned.

In the near total darkness, I listened and thought again about how I felt when I hung up the phone. I didn't know it yet, but I was one of the smartest men alive.

I dozed off before sunrise, and I was lucky I didn't fall out of the tree, but I needed to clear my head. You can only get so tired before you have to shut down. Going through so much combined with a lack of sleep will make you screw up in a perfect world, and this wasn't a perfect world anymore.

The sleep seemed to help because I felt hungry. Up until now, I had been too scared to be hungry. In my half awake, half asleep, very hungry world I remembered when the phone had rung, and when the whirlwind changes began.

******

The law firm had neglected to give me plenty of the details. The will specifically said I got the island and everything on it. The relative who had become my benefactor was the family nut. I called him Uncle Titus, but he was more like my cousin's stepbrother, and I was the only one who ever listened to his far fetched claims about survival.

Uncle Titus left me the island, but according to the will, a key left in a safety deposit box would fit a lock in Uncle Titus' fallout shelter somewhere on the island. The island was so overgrown and so bug infested that the law firm didn't even bother to inventory the shelter. They just made me sign paperwork that said I had to provide a list of all valuables for tax purposes. It was probably also because they couldn't even get inside.

The shelter...if you want to call it that, turned out to be more of an underground mansion as far as I was concerned. It was a modern day ark with an inventory worth far more than the island. Of course it wouldn't be worth a damn if I couldn't get to it again.

I surveyed the tree I was sitting in and realized I could see the ground better. That meant dawn couldn't be too far off. I was probably twenty feet up, which meant anything that passed by below wasn't likely to notice me if I stayed quiet.

I silently hoped there wasn't anything hanging around once the sun came up, because I didn't think my body could survive another day and night in this tree. Of course, I wouldn't have much choice if there were more than a few things hanging around. I had at least fifteen yards of dried brush to thrash my way through just to get to the beach, so I was going to make noise.

I would have to find the strength to run another fifty or so yards to my boat...if it was still there. There was always a chance that someone did what anyone would do under the right circumstances. They would steal the boat to save their own lives and say a quick "thank you" to the person who had done them a favor and left it there to steal. They would also be thinking the poor slob who owned the boat was dead and wouldn't be needing it anyway.

I started thinking about Amanda Lee and my visit to the law firm. She was every bit as good looking as I had expected, but she was ten times the witch. She held out her hand and dangled a key at me. As soon as I took it, she turned on her expensive high heals and left me alone with Weintraub.

He was also as young and nervous as I expected. He had me sign all the papers and told me the name of the island, Mud Island. Nice......there had to be a reason, but I had my suspicions.

I would have to look into how to go about changing the name of an island if I decided to sell it. I thought about asking Weintraub why it was named Mud Island, but he read the look on my face and volunteered the answer before I could ask.

"Mr. Jackson, your benefactor was...how should I put this, eccentric?" Weintraub was looking at me as if I didn't already know how Uncle Titus ticked.

"When he came to our office to write this will, he wanted it kept very quiet, so he said he had named the island Mud Island because no one would really think much of it. They would just see it as being a worthless sandbar with trees on it." Weintraub was giving me another look, as if his explanation was enough.

"Why would he do that?" I asked. "He had to know he was devaluing his own property."

I had already considered the possibility that Uncle Titus was going to use the island as a survival base rather than develop it, but it seemed like even he was going too far. Besides, I felt like it was a good idea to do as Uncle Titus had and act a bit naive.

Weintraub looked like he was searching for the right words. "Exactly, Mr. Jackson, he didn't want it to be worth anything to anyone, even if it meant life or death." Those were his exact words.

"Frankly, Mr. Jackson, your uncle made me a bit nervous. He asked me if I had made plans for what was coming, and when I told him I hadn't, he just looked sad and said to pray that the end is quick. What did he mean by that?"

Sitting on my numb rear end looking down from a tree, I wondered how Weintraub would have reacted if I had said, "Well you see, Weintraub. People are going to start dying and then they're going to start getting back up. Then they're going to start trying to eat you. Who knows? Maybe that hot senior partner of yours, Ms. Lee, will try to eat you."

I think Weintraub would have understood one thing...... why crazy Uncle Titus was leaving Mud Island to me. I was the crazy nephew. He would also feel safer knowing I was out on Mud Island and not running around out in public. I signed "Edward C. Jackson" in about a hundred places and initialed a hundred more then headed home.

*****

I saw Mud Island a week later. I flew down from my small but comfortable apartment in Charlotte to see what I had gotten into. I knew that there were plenty of small, uninhabited islands off the coast of South Carolina, but I was fairly sure that South Carolina didn't even know about this one.

It was an easy living sixty degrees in Charlotte when I got on the plane. Forty-five minutes later I was in Columbia, and it was close to ninety with one hundred percent humidity. I always thought one hundred percent humidity meant it was raining outside, but what it really means is that you sweat even if you aren't moving.

A charter plane took me to Myrtle Beach in about an hour, and from there I headed south in a rented Jeep. The map I followed took me through rich, full magnolia trees, green with leaves but heavily spotted with big white blossoms. Then there were oak trees covered with hanging moss, looking like they hadn't changed since the Civil War, and then through cypress marshes. Trees with no branches until their canopy blocked out the sunlight.

The water between the trees was black and didn't look like it was a great place for people. This was a spooky place, and the only sound was from the tires rolling over the gravel on the mostly dirt road. I saw an alligator and wished I had stopped at a bathroom earlier. Alligators…I wondered if they think people taste like chicken.

When I came to the end of the road, it just ended, and I mean that literally. It just stopped being a dirt road. There was a wire fence strung across the end of the road with a rusty sign on it that said No Trespassing. I laid my map out across the steering wheel and studied the route I had taken, pretty much sure that I had made a mistake and taken a wrong turn somewhere along the way.

On the map the road ended too. There was a wide stretch labeled as marsh, and then there was a narrow strip of beach. Across from the beach was Mud Island. I didn't see any way to get to it other than straight through the marsh. I thought about the alligator and decided Uncle Titus was more nuts than I had suspected.

I climbed out of the Jeep and walked up to the rusty sign. I don't know why……maybe because this was already totally weird, but I looked at the back of the sign. Taped to the back was a small package wrapped in plastic.

I pulled it loose and tore it open, certain that Uncle Titus knew I would be standing here at the end of this road. Uncle

Titus seemed to be right about a lot of things. Under the last layer of plastic was a compass and a note. The note was in Titus' scrawled handwriting, and it just said, "Stay straight to the East, and when the cypress trees end you won't see any more gators, but watch out for snakes and spiders."

Great! I like snakes and spiders much more than alligators. I got a small pack of hiking supplies out of the Jeep and aimed the compass to find the East. I thought I would get lost or have to wander around in the woods all day, but I was surprised when I made it through to the beach sooner than I had expected.

I hadn't realized that the cypress trees and black water had given way to oak trees that were large but not as ancient as the first oaks that had lined the road. They were spaced wider apart, and even though the ground between them was overgrown with a hundred years of scrub oaks and brush, I could almost picture someone living here long ago.

When I stepped onto the beach, the best surprise was the sight of a well built dock and a decent looking boat tied against it. I never bothered to learn much about boats, but this one I knew was called a Boston Whaler. Not big, but big enough to get me where I was going comfortably and small enough for me to handle. It wasn't too far of a walk from where I came out of the trees, and the only moving creatures were crabs and birds......no snakes or spiders.

The planks on the dock were so new looking compared to the old surroundings. I had the sense to stand and admire it and wonder how my crazy uncle had managed to get the materials for a new dock through the dense brush to this strip of beach without disturbing the surrounding terrain. I vaguely wondered if he hadn't done it from the air, but I let it go. The fact was that he had done it. The dock and spotless white boat told me I was in for more surprises.

******

I remembered that day standing at the dock and said another silent thank you to my uncle. I may be sitting in a tree now, but at least I had somewhere to go. The sun was just starting to peak over the horizon, and with any luck at all, I could make it to the dock in minutes.

I very slowly started to push myself up from a sitting position. My legs had joined my butt cheeks in the numb department, and I wasn't going to outrun anything until I got some circulation back. I had been sitting for so long that I actually looked at my left leg to see if it was still attached.

Having confirmed that it was still there, I started shifting from one foot to the other. The oak was pretty strong, so I wasn't moving the branches and attracting attention. I wasn't entirely sure what I had heard under the tree during the night, but I didn't think anything groaned, walked upright, and preferred a steady diet of living flesh except one thing.

If there was something down there that matched that description, I didn't want to give it advance notice that I was about to drop to the ground and make a run for it.

When I could feel my toes and there was no stinging pain as they regained their circulation, I turned to face the trunk of the tree. I needed to take a good look around the other side of the tree to see if I had any company.

I imagine if there had been another living person clinging to a neighboring tree, it would have scared them bad enough to make them fall, but I was only greeted by the sight of more trees and heavy underbrush.

It was quiet, and I was just going to be forced to put my big boy pants on and get to the dock. After all, I had already made it this far, and that was much better than a few thousand other people could say.

That reminded me......as connected as I've always been, I hadn't looked at my cell phone in hours. The thing had nearly scared me into falling when it had lit up and displayed a FEMA message. I'd had the good sense to turn off the volume to the ringtone, but the last thing I expected was to get any kind of connection this far out. I guess FEMA was able to do a little better than most mobile carriers.

Once I had gotten over my initial scare, I had checked the message. Carefully covering the phone inside my zip-up hoodie, I had read the warnings. FEMA said that everyone should stay home and not open the door for anyone except the military. The National Guard had mobilized, and they had orders to shoot anyone seen in the streets.

At first I had thought that was a bit extreme, but it didn't take long to figure out that the only people on the streets without guns were probably not in need of help......not anymore.

I pulled out my phone more carefully this time and checked it again. There wasn't any need for hiding it because there was enough sunlight coming through the trees.

The FEMA message was still on the screen, but it didn't say anything about getting shot if you go into the streets. Instead it said to go to a list of locations, mostly schools or military bases. It said to stay away from hospitals. It didn't say why hospitals were not a safe place, but I had a pretty good idea why.

It also said if you had been bitten, you should stay home and wait for help to come to you, but family members shouldn't stay with you. The message reassuringly said your relatives would be well cared for. Right.

I scrolled back and saw that there had been other messages through the night, none from anyone I knew. Maybe that was because of my location. I checked my internet browser, and the page wouldn't load. I couldn't get a connection with a server.

On a whim I tried the FEMA website and got a canned message that said to set cellphones to receive alerts. I went back to the alerts and scanned over them for anything I had missed. One caught my eye that might as well have said, "Edward Jackson, go to your island now."

What it actually said was, "If you have prepared for an extreme emergency and have a secure location where you can go, do so now. If you have provisions and the capability to take others to safety, please exercise generosity by assisting others, but under no circumstances should you attempt to provide aid to individuals who have been bitten."

That was pretty much what I had in mind as I once again began surveying my surroundings and began to climb downward.

******

One reason I had picked my tree was the lower branches. From my vantage point I could see around the bottom of the tree okay, but not great. Still, if I dropped to the ground and found myself face to face with company, it would be no more than a quick pull-up and a leg over for me to be back to safety.

I lowered myself to the branches below mine and went into a squat. I was listening for noise......any noise. This was way too quiet for me. On my first trip to the island, back when I had followed the compass taped to the sign, there had been plenty of sounds. Whether it was a woodpecker rapping on a tree or a splash somewhere out in the jet black water between the cypress trees, there was never silence.

I felt a tingle run up my back, and I didn't know if it was from the early morning chill, or if I would turn around and find that the dead could climb trees. There wasn't much chance that I could ignore the feeling, so I slowly swiveled on the branch until I could see what was there. Nothing, but the mind does some wonderful things when you're scared, so I jumped anyway.

So much for quietly dropping to the ground after doing a thorough check for trouble. I felt my feet leave the solid surface of the branch, and I went over. I landed with a loud thump that was only rivaled by the sound of the air being knocked from my lungs, and suddenly it wasn't so quiet anymore.

I was tangled in a mass of brush that had probably saved me from being really hurt. No more than a few scratches. The problem was my savior bushes were also keeping me from getting up, and something was in a hurry to get to me.

That 'something' was making a now familiar groaning noise that left little doubt in my mind what it was, and the best I could hope for was that it was alone. At least there wasn't a chorus of groans.

I managed to get one foot free from between two stubborn branches, but the other one felt like it was tied in place with rope. It didn't help that every move caused me to get scratched a few more times, but there wasn't a scratch out there that could kill me.

I listened as the groaning grew steadily louder but then seemed to stay the same, and I realized the creature that wanted me had the same problem that I did. The thrashing it was doing told me that he...she....it......was having to untangle itself from the thick brush just as I was.

Movement to my left caught my eye, and I could see an arm reaching out from some really nasty undergrowth. I at least knew I had a few minutes to work my way loose, and I set about solving the problem of getting free. I could also keep an eye on the progress of the "groaner".

Ten minutes later I had my other foot untangled and was able to start wiggling between vines and branches in the direction of freedom. Groaner had been quiet except for the thrashing, so I hadn't paid attention to his progress. When I did look in his direction, the gender question being answered immediately, he was close......too close. If I turned my back on him, he would be on me in no time, and I needed to be facing him to at least try to keep his mouth away from my body.

The smell was finally reaching me, and even though marshy, muddy swampland doesn't smell too sweet all by itself, this was worse, and I was already starting to gag and retch. If they had any thoughts at all, this one was thinking it was going to grab me with one more lunge. Its hand actually got close enough for me to push it away, and then I was falling backward trying to get my feet high enough to kick it in the face.

There was a snapping and cracking noise as my weight carried me out onto the sand and away from the undergrowth, but there was no time to celebrate my freedom or the fact that I was much closer to the beach than I had realized. Groaner was coming through the same path that I had made, and he was almost on top of me.

If he was capable of getting a surprised or confused look on his face, he would have. It was like everything stood still for a long time but was really only a matter of seconds. One moment he was about to drop out of some serious undergrowth and land right on top of me, and the next moment he was moving in reverse. I caught just enough of a glimpse of the slippery body to realize that an alligator had a good hold on the groaner's leg, and I would have at least a slim chance of living one more day.

I was on my feet and running toward the dock with something like a whimper escaping my lips. I remember thinking two totally separate thoughts…if the groaner hadn't been there, would the alligator have gotten me instead? The second thought was whether or not that alligator had ever eaten a chicken. One glimpse back over my shoulder was enough for me to answer both questions the same way……it didn't matter.

******

The boat was just as I had left it. On my previous excursion to the island I had cautiously untied the boat and jumped onto the deck. I had this irrational fear that it would drift away before I could even get on board, but it stayed where it was. I had started the engine and then eased the throttle forward while keeping a white knuckled grip on the steering wheel. I guess I expected it to take off fast enough to launch me out the back, but I learned quickly that giving just a little less throttle made the boat glide across the water.

I admit that on that particular day I was at least a little happier about having a boat than an island. This could be fun, and I spent a couple of hours touring the coastline before finally coasting up to another new dock on the northern tip of the island.

As islands go, Mud Island didn't look like anything special. It was separated from the mainland by a narrow strip of water that was much deeper than I would have expected it to be. When I stood on the dock looking at Mud Island I wondered why even bother with a boat. It looked almost close enough to build a longer dock or even a bridge. Then I remembered that Uncle Titus apparently felt like it would be a place to survive, so the water had to be like a moat. Not really wide, but it had to be deep.

When I was joy riding and getting to know the Boston Whaler, I had started out by heading south toward the tip of the island that appeared to be closer. I was new to boats, so my first reaction was to take it from point A to point B, and that was it. I didn't really think about which end would have a dock for me to use, but for some reason I thought it would be at the closest point.

The dock wasn't there when I rounded the southern tip of Mud Island, but by that time I didn't care. The boat was fun, and for the first time since the phone call from Weintraub, I felt like good things were happening. That this wasn't just some kind of crazy dream.

I stayed toward the middle of the narrow channel because I didn't want to scrape the bottom of the boat on oyster beds that seemed to be everywhere. As a matter of fact, it looked like the entire side of Mud Island that faced the mainland was nothing but sharp edged shells pointing upward. According to a boating guide I had picked up at a fishing supply store near where I rented the Jeep, high tide was just about over, and that meant I was just seeing the tops of the oyster beds. I wondered if the oysters were for eating or protection.

As I cruised the Whaler out of the southern mouth of the 'moat' that surrounded Mud Island, I had expected to be able to make a sharp left and head up the coast along the sea side of the island. I started the turn but spotted the huge rocks poking out of the water. There was a man made jetty that extended outward for at least one hundred yards, and I had to go straight out to sea to reach the end of it. Once I reached the end, I was able to turn left, and begin my trip north.

Once again, I was realizing just how smart Uncle Titus was. The jetty was there to keep silt from drifting across the mouth of the waterway that separated the island from the mainland. Without the jetty, the gap would need to be dredged, or it might fill in. Then you could walk to Mud Island.

This was a learning curve for me, but I was starting to think like Uncle Titus. It occurred to me that when I reached the northern tip of the island, I would find another jetty. This one would be from the other side of the waterway sticking out from the mainland, and it would prevent the northern mouth of the waterway from filling in. And that would also be the logical place to put the dock.

Sure enough, thirty minutes later I could see a long jetty in the distance, and a wide entrance to the "Mud Island Moat" on my left. As soon as I started my turn, I saw the northern dock. Uncle Titus was a nut, there was no doubt about that, but he must've been a talented nut, because this dock was much larger than the one on the mainland, and moored to one side of it was what looked like a houseboat.

Actually, it was a fully equipped houseboat, as I would discover while exploring, but it conveniently hid the real surprise from view. The dock was "L" shaped, and within the protected side of the L was a twin engine plane on pontoon struts. I didn't know Uncle Titus could fly a plane, but then again, I don't think you could have gotten me into the cockpit with him behind the stick. Still, I gave him credit for knowing how to fly the thing. I knew enough to call it a cockpit, and I knew the thing the pilot used to control it was called a stick, but beyond that, all I knew about flying I had learned playing video games.

I think I was starting to catch on to what Uncle Titus had in mind. I don't know what he was thinking of when he said we needed to be ready for something to happen, but so far I was looking at a remote location, separated from the land by deep water, oyster beds that could shred steel belted tires, and inhospitable terrain with alligators on the other side. Whatever happened on the mainland, it was likely to stay on the mainland.

******

When I reached the boat this time, I wasn't being a tourist. I was winded from sprinting to the dock, and I almost forgot to untie the moorings before trying to cast off. I started the engine and then dove back to the ropes. The thrum of the engine felt good under my feet, and I felt good for the first time in days. I got the ropes onboard and gave the dock piling a hard shove, then ran to the throttle.

The dock quickly receded behind me, and this time I turned north. In a matter of minutes I would be seeing the L-shaped dock, and minutes after that I would feel safe again.

The sun wasn't too far above the horizon as I made a sweeping curve to make the starboard turn toward the dock. The sea plane and houseboat were safe and secure where they had been tied off. I let the Whaler coast up to the dock on the opposite side from the sea plane, and I thought to myself, "I've never been so damned glad not to see anyone else in my whole life."

******

I was in a place called Surfside, South Carolina when the world came to an end. Or at least the world as I knew it. I had made my first trip to Mud Island, discovered the boat, the plane, the houseboat, and then the island itself. My head was still swimming with the wealth of the things I had found. I didn't think I could be surprised by anything more because of what I had already seen, but a quick inspection of the houseboat answered so many of the questions I would have asked Uncle Titus if I had spoken with him before he died.

There was a TV with an old VHS player sitting in plain view so I would see it as soon as I opened the door to the houseboat. To this point, I was thinking, "Okay, I have a Boston Whaler, a seaplane, and a houseboat, all tied up to an island that was pretty isolated." The VHS tape with my name on it had the rest of the story.

I slid the tape into the player and turned on the TV. The gritty, weather worn face of Uncle Titus filled the screen. If not for the sort of crazy eyes, he was ruggedly handsome, and could have been mistaken for "The Most Interesting Man in The World."

"Eddy, welcome to Mud Island! If you're watching this, I hope it's because those lawyers earned their paychecks, and the world hasn't gone to hell yet. Well, doesn't matter either way, does it? As long as it's you watching this video, it doesn't matter. If you're here, you're also safe."

"Now, let me explain something to you about how a survivalist has to think, and you need to start thinking like one from this moment on. Don't watch this tape and go thinking you can do it later."

Uncle Titus looked down like he was collecting his thoughts. When he raised his head it was like he was really looking at me as he recorded the tape, or he was looking at me now. He got a really serious expression on his face with just a touch of sadness.

"Eddy, a survivalist believes it's only a matter of time before all hell breaks loose. Whatever it is, nuclear war, plague, or a comet crashing into to the Earth, it's going to happen any minute. That's how you have to start thinking if you want to live. You need to believe that you are prepared for anything if it happens one minute from now, but you won't survive unless you act like you're already too late. If you don't start thinking that way, no amount of preparation will do you any good. You're going to be somewhere else when everything hits the fan, and you'll just be another victim."

"Now, Eddy, I've tried to think of everything, but after you're done watching this, don't leave the island unless you have to. Something is coming, and I don't know what it is. Call it a gut feeling, but every one of my survivalist buddies is saying they can feel it in their bones."

"Time is short, so stay on Mud Island, and hunker down for the long haul, but on the off chance I didn't think of something, I've left you some cash in the shelter. If you absolutely must go buy something, be quick about it, but if I'm right you should stay here."

I thought to myself, "Okay, I have a Boston Whaler, a seaplane, a houseboat, and now I have a shelter. Where's the shelter?"

Uncle Titus continued on the tape, "If I know you, you're saying you knew this couldn't be all there is. There's a path at the end of the dock. It is well hidden if you're looking from any direction except right at the end of the dock, but if you know it's there, you can find it."

"Follow it about a mile to the center of the island. You'll notice the farther you go that the ground gets a little higher. The island looks flat from the air, but there's a hill right in the middle, and the shelter is in the hill. Don't be fooled by the big door and the combination lock. I got it from a bank, and you won't open it without the combination, which I had reset to your favorite date."

I had jokingly told him my favorite day was the day a new game had been released, and the old sucker remembered it. He also knew no one else would know that date.

"That's all there is, Eddy. Like I said, I don't know what's coming, but it's big. A survivalist can feel it deep down in his bones. Go have a look at the place, and don't leave unless you have to." Uncle Titus gave the camera a weak smile as the tape ended.

******

I knew I had to return to the mainland for only two reasons. First of all, I couldn't just not return the Jeep to the rental place. I know Uncle Titus wanted me to start thinking like a survivalist, but I wasn't quite there yet. After all, he had died long enough ago for the island to almost go to auction. A few more days wouldn't really matter.

As for how I would get back to the island after returning the Jeep, the shelter was not a disappointment. It didn't need a safe, because no one could have opened that door without knowing my favorite date, but just inside the door was a wall safe with my name on it.

I felt for the key in my pocket then slipped it into the lock. Whatever the world was going to become, cash was still king in this one, and Uncle Titus had left plenty of it in the wall safe. The first thing I needed to do was to go back to civilization and buy myself a new ride.

The second reason to leave the island was Uncle Titus himself. I seriously suspected when I surveyed the contents of the shelter that there was one thing that was going to be totally missing. Uncle Titus had plenty of hidden talents and lots of imagination, but his idea of entertainment and mine were totally different.

With or without an apocalypse, if you were lucky enough to have too much time on your hands, you had to have something to do. Uncle Titus apparently felt like there would be enough to keep him busy, and his idle time would be filled by reading and watching old movies. I had to have video games and the internet. I wasn't sure about getting the internet way out here, but I could fix the video game problem.

I closed the big bank door behind me. I was sealed in by the total silence as the door separated me from the outside world. Then I began to take stock of the layout and contents my new home.

******

The front door and the safe full of money were right up front. I was just asking myself why someone would even bother with a safe if they were going to put it where anyone could find it. Then I saw the book sitting next to the stack of money. I took it out of the safe and opened it to the first page. Uncle Titus had left me his own handbook on how to survive the end of the world. There was a message in his handwriting:

"Eddy, these are the rules of survival. This place could get hit by a nuclear blast or a mile high tidal wave, and you would survive. You might be buried under a few tons of ocean bed or a few hundred feet of water, but this place would be able to take it. Rule 1, don't open that door for any reason once the hammer goes down. Rule 2, you have what other people will want, so don't break Rule 1. Rule 3, there is nothing that anybody could have that you need, so don't break Rule 1. If you are not getting my drift, let me make it clear to you. Eddy, don't open that damned door again!"

I mentally added, "Except to buy a vehicle, some gaming consoles, and a nice supply of video games."

The rest of the book was a catalog of the contents of each room and a folded map of the layout of the entire shelter. I spread the map out on the floor and whistled. I thought this was going to be a one floor deal, but this was beyond belief. The map showed floor after floor descending downward. I was on the top floor, and according to the map, there was a small room to my left.

I peeked around the corner into that room and I got the impression it was some kind of decontamination airlock. There were wetsuits for scuba diving, a hazmat suit, and something that looked like a suit of armor from one of my video games. I walked over and felt the material and guessed it was really kevlar.

There was also a shower stall and some benches. I guessed that Uncle Titus made Rule 1 with the intention that it shouldn't be broken, but he was a survivalist, and that meant don't open the door, but be prepared in case you have to.

I didn't see another real door, but there was a round, steel hatch with a big wheel in the middle of it. I consulted the map and saw that the hatch led to a stairwell, so I walked over to it and gave the wheel a hard spin to the left. The door was heavy, but I was able to swing it on its big hinges until it was wide open. I thought I would have to turn on a light or something, but as soon as I shoved my head through the hatch, the stairwell lit up while the lights in the decontamination room dimmed.

"Energy efficient," I said out loud. It made sense. I didn't know what the power source would be, and I didn't know how long the reserves would last, but leaving the lights on in an unused room was a waste. Uncle Titus must have put motion sensors somewhere.

I crawled through the hatch and pulled it shut behind me. There was such total silence as I spun the wheel into the locked position that I could sense the whole place was air tight and probably had a positive pressure. I wasn't the scientist Uncle Titus was, but I knew there was one way to keep bad air, germs, and fallout from getting in, and that was by pressurizing the inside higher than the outside. My ears popped about a minute later.

One flight of stairs downward, and I was thinking of one thing. "How did Uncle Titus keep the ocean out?" The air didn't feel damp, so I wouldn't have known if I was still surrounded by earth or if I had gone down far enough to be below sea level.

I had plenty of friends with basements in their houses, and some of them fought a constant battle with water. I decided that Uncle Titus had taken into account the fact that water needed to be kept out. How he had done it didn't matter, especially since he claimed this place could survive a nuclear blast or tidal wave.

As I put my foot onto the floor of the first level down, the lights came up in a circular room that was as comfortable looking as any apartment I had ever seen. The furniture, the decorations, the bookshelves, even the rugs all looked like a showroom in a model home. There was a TV hutch on the long wall to my left, but the obvious lack of a video game console was almost distressing. As I planned from the start, I knew I would have to correct that if I was going to stay here for any length of time.

The book I had pulled from the safe said this was the first room of the residence, and there was a complete list of everything in it. I scanned the list and confirmed that the game console was missing.

Across from the TV was a huge leather sofa that would be a great place to fall asleep, which is something I tend to do when I play video games until my eyes bleed. Behind the sofa was a dining room table that could seat eight people.

At the end of the sofa against the wall was something that looked like a computer workstation, but it wasn't just for the computer. There was also a shortwave radio set. Despite the lack of video games, there was plenty of tech to play with.

The map showed that the next room would be located somewhere behind me, and I found the entrance behind the stairs I had just come down. It was only one set of stairs down from the top floor of the residential part of the shelter, so I felt almost like I was in a split level ranch house. The lights dimmed behind me as the lights came up in a kitchen that looked like it had been designed for a master chef.

Uncle Titus probably had a good laugh when he pictured me walking into this room the first time, and if I knew him as well as I thought, I was probably going to find a large supply of Ramen noodles in the pantry. Not because they were great for survival, but because Uncle Titus knew I could get into trouble just trying to boil water.

Once when he visited my little apartment, he had nearly fallen apart laughing when he had watched me try to crack an egg. It seems like I have the same thought every time I crack an egg. I always wonder, "Exactly how many eggs do you have to crack before you feel like you're doing it right?"

I opened a few cabinets to see what goodies they held, and I figured I had better learn to cook because there was a large supply of ingredients I couldn't identify, but I also guessed that Uncle Titus was pulling my leg. He was a survivalist, and somewhere in this place I would find survivalist food. Things you didn't have to cook that probably came from some kind of easy open package but would last a hundred years without refrigeration. There was a refrigerator, but refrigerated foods don't last as long as packaged foods, so I knew that wouldn't be the main food supply, and I didn't even bother to look inside. I could save that for later.

I checked the guidebook to see what he listed in the kitchen, sure enough it said that the main food storage area was in a lower level of the shelter. There was a smiley face at the end of the entry.

The next level was located down a hallway with a sloping floor. It was the bedroom, but the guidebook said, 'main sleeping quarters'. I saw on the map that it was designed just like any normal master bedroom with a master bath attached to it, but there were several round hatches like the one at the top of the stairs. They were all labeled the same way......Emergency Exit.

I looked around the room to see where they were located and couldn't spot them at first. Then I realized they were so well made they were seamless, and the handles were recessed so that they were practically invisible. I figured it could wait for now, but it would be a good idea to find out where each one of them went.

I only took a quick peek in the bathroom because I was eager to see if there were any other big surprises. It occurred to me that I wasn't thinking like a survivalist yet, because I was already taking hot water for granted. With all this luxury around me, that really wasn't a surprise. My apartment in Charlotte was functional, but it would have fit inside the shelter several times over.

The next level was beyond belief. The stairs went down to a room that was labeled in the guidebook as the armory, and the inventory list was impressive. I had been to a shooting range once with a friend who had taught me the basics, but my knowledge of guns was pretty much limited to pointing and shooting.

I looked at each type of rifle and pistol and was amazed by the differences. Next to each was a manual that had a picture of the weapon on the cover. In cabinets beneath each weapon there were cases of ammunition. The inventory book had 'K' after the numbers of rounds, and any video gamer knows that means 'thousand'.

There was enough ammunition to fight a war in this one room. So far, I had to see where those emergency exits went, how to handle these weapons, and learn how to cook.

I picked up one of the pistols and just felt its weight. I felt a little sick wondering why Uncle Titus thought I would need so many guns, and maybe for the first time I took this whole thing just a little bit more seriously......But I still wanted some video games.

Across from the armory was a door with a big red cross painted on it, and a sign that said Medical Center. I expected a little room with cubbies and cabinets loaded with bands-aids, rubber gloves, and tissues. There would be a sink and an examining table. It occurred to me that I was picturing an examining room at my doctor's office, and I knew about the cabinets and other stuff because I liked to snoop around while I waited for the doctor. Experience told me I would have at least thirty minutes, so I snooped to ease the boredom.

As expected, there was an examining room where a nurse could take your vital signs and a doctor could have you sit on the examining table and listen to you take deep breaths. The cabinets, the band-aids, the tissues, and rubber gloves were all present. What was different from a normal examining room was the other door across from the examining table. It said Surgical Suite.

I stepped through that door into a room that had a long sink where a doctor could scrub up before doing surgery. There were lockers for changing clothes, and fresh surgical clothes in plastic wrapping. Beyond the scrub room was a totally stainless steel room that would be the envy of any hospital. Big lights, operating table, trays of surgical instruments, and cabinets full of supplies dominated the room, but the real shocker was the X-Ray machine that could be swung over to the table from above.

I thought out loud, "Let me see......master chef, gunsmith, or doctor. Which one do I want to be when I grow up?"

I figured I would get around to doing a complete inventory of the medical rooms when I had time, but I doubted I would ever need it for anything more than a band-aid or some aspirin.

A quick check of the map and guidebook showed that I was just about to drop down to a level that had several rooms all arranged in a circle under the armory. There were nine rooms total.

Two were smaller bedrooms and one was a bunk room that could sleep as many as six people, and one was like a dorm type locker room, complete with a community shower. This pair of rooms told me something about Uncle Titus. He may have been crazy. He may have written a rule that said you can't open the door for anyone, but he had provided for the possibility that someone else may need to be given shelter. Between the armory and the bunk room, the shelter was beginning to have a sobering effect.

One of the most impressive rooms so far was the exercise room. Uncle Titus obviously planned on being in here forever, because this was more than a serious home gym. There were heavy duty treadmills with TV screens at the end of each, weight machines, and free weights.

After a good workout, there's nothing like a recovery room so there was a large hot tub and a sauna, and of course there was a TV that could be seen from either.

There was a row of stationary bikes, and they faced TV screens too, but I noticed there was also large collections of music with the option to listen through headphones or by cranking up an awesome sound system.

I flipped through the titles of the music selection and saw a pretty good mix of tastes. There was a CD in a player ready to go, so I hopped on a bike just for the hell of it. The music started just as I started to peddle, and I had to laugh at my Uncle's ironic sense of humor.

Uncle Titus had always been fond of this really enigmatic TV show where a plane crashed on an island, and the survivors kept finding more puzzling problems and places than they did answers. One of the places was something like a fallout shelter located at the bottom of a long ladder, but they spent several shows just trying to get through the hatch at the top of the ladder. Anyway, in the fallout shelter was an exercise bike, and there was a guy riding the bike while listening to The Mamas and The Papas. The same song was playing on this CD player as I peddled the bike.

The remaining four rooms were massive storehouses of supplies. I went from one to the next reading the labels on the boxes and marveling at the contents. Uncle Titus thought of everything except video games.

There was enough packaged food to last years. There were hundreds of cases of MRE's, short for Meals Ready to Eat. The military had invested a fortune in meals that could be prepared while in extreme battlefield conditions, and while they didn't live up to the expectations of their names, they were at least edible. There were meals like chicken parmesan and turkey with all the trimmings. Uncle Titus probably figured I would starve to death before I learned how to cook, so it was a good idea for me to have something that only needs to be opened for it to be called food.

Uncle Titus must have bought everything they had at an Army Navy surplus store. There was spare clothing, medical supplies, personal hygiene items, and an endless supply of DVD's. The titles didn't give me that, 'run to the box office' feeling, but I wouldn't get bored.

The last storeroom was cooler than the others, and I found it had a large walk-in freezer. I looked inside and saw shelves of frozen food. A note on the inventory list said, "Eat frozen foods first. You never know if the power will last as long as you live."

That's when the gravity of this craziness really hit home. I hadn't even thought about what powered this place or how long it was going to last. As a matter of fact, I had just pictured myself living in the lap of secluded luxury, happily playing video games and not having to worry about bills. I looked at the map again and saw that there was one more flight of stairs, and it was labeled Physical Plant......also known as power.

If everything else was impressive, the physical plant was incredibly impressive. It hummed with energy, and I knew I that I had to figure it out before I learned to shoot, cook, or stitch wounds. Uncle Titus must have figured that I would be smart enough to come to the conclusion that power was vital because there were labels and instructions everywhere.

The main source of power was actually a landline......or more precisely a power cable that was buried under the island and was even deep enough to go under the 'moat'. An instruction card on the massive control cabinet explained that it was a high voltage cable that was designed to power a public school. In other words, I wasn't going to cause any breakers to trip by drawing too much current.

The rest of the room was a series of generators. Each one was described as fuel efficient, and each was capable of providing enough power to run all of the essential systems at the same time. There was also a chart that showed how long the fuel would last if fewer systems were in operation.

That chart made me start thinking again. "Where was the fuel?" I pictured fifty gallon drums of generator fuel stacked to the ceiling, but I didn't see even one. I wasn't surprised by the emergency generators because everybody knows power will fail in a major catastrophe, but it was starting to look like Uncle Titus didn't get around to finishing that little detail. As a matter of fact, "How was I supposed to gas up the boat if I needed to?"

I turned in a circle looking at all of the machinery, instruction cards, switches, levers......switches and levers. I saw that each generator had a main switch, and a big red lever. The levers had tags that said, 'Fuel'. After a stunned minute of staring at the big fuel line below each lever, I figured it out.

The shelter was sitting on top of buried fuel tanks, and there were so many that it was virtually a big gas station.There must be a pump somewhere out at the dock that can be turned off from this room too. It didn't take long to find it, and it made perfect sense. Uncle Titus didn't want someone else to gas up at the pump, and even more importantly, it couldn't be used to blow up the shelter by igniting the fuel line. The shut off valve also served as a pump to drain the line back to the fuel tank or prime it up to the pump. Uncle Titus was a genius.

The last thing I considered important was listed in the book with the rest of the physical plant, but the equipment was located in each room. The ventilation units were distributed throughout the individual levels so no level was effected by the loss of ventilation on another level.

"What did Uncle Titus do, win the lottery?" I asked myself.

I made my way back up to the food storage area and found a packaged meal to eat. I know Uncle Titus said to eat the frozen food first, but the world hadn't ended yet.

******

A quick trip up to a mall and a car dealership in Myrtle Beach was all I had in mind. I stopped at the safe in the upper level and made a sizable withdrawal that should cover a Jeep of my own and my entertainment needs.

The trip back in the boat was much faster than the trip out, and I felt like I was on top of the world. I had money, property, and most importantly, independence. I didn't need my job anymore, and I didn't have any personal ties to keep me from disappearing down my own private rabbit hole.

As I drove back to civilization, I thought about nothing else. Average job, average height, average weight......hell, I was so average I could disappear anywhere.

Just under six feet, 175 pounds on the nose, and brown hair with average looks didn't get me a lot of dates, so I didn't have a girlfriend. I couldn't invite a girl back to the shelter because any girl in her right mind would think she was being kidnapped by some kind of serial killer by the time we would reach the island. She would probably start asking me to turn the car around long before we reached the island.

As for family, I grew up mostly in the homes of relatives that didn't want me around to start with. That's how I got hooked up with Uncle Titus. He paid attention to me, so I listened to him more than the others.

My parents were out of the picture before I was even old enough to remember them. Everyone always said that was a shame, but you don't really miss what you never had. I learned to spend time by myself and not feel alone, so this rabbit hole was perfect for me. There was a big smile on my face as I passed a sign that said Welcome to Surfside.

******

Traffic was light because it was a weekday, and most of the tourists were trying to find room on the beach a little further up the coast in Myrtle Beach. Strip malls, fast food places, and motels dotted the landscape, and it wasn't long before I spotted a store that specialized in video games. I didn't even need to drive all the way to the main shopping areas to get what I needed, so I navigated the turn lanes to get to the other side of the highway and found a parking spot.

When you don't have to worry about the cost of the games, it doesn't take long to find what you're looking for...... one of everything. I went down one aisle after the next like a little kid. The guy working behind the register got me a cardboard box and told me if there was something I didn't see that I wanted to be sure to say so. I smiled and gratefully accepted the box.

I decided not to limit myself to one platform, so I asked him to get the three best consoles and a variety of controllers. He didn't bat an eye, and he didn't seem at all surprised by the size of the purchase I was about to make. He didn't care as long as I had either the cash or a credit card with a high enough limit. Neither of us paid much attention to the police car that screamed past the strip mall with its blue lights on even though it practically slid into the entrance of a fast food place across the highway.

Another customer came in and started looking at the new releases. He glanced our way and got a look of obvious envy on his face when he saw that the guy behind the counter was scanning one game after the next and had long way to go. He was a stereotypical gamer who was seriously trying to reinforce the belief that all gamers wear thick framed glasses, don't wash their hair, and don't know how to dress. This guy was destined to live in his mother's basement forever.

The cashier and I exchanged a few comments with each other about different games, which ones he liked, which ones were going to have a new version soon. He looked past me and stopped scanning. I looked over my shoulder and saw that he was looking at the gamer by the new releases.

For some strange reason, the gamer was still staring in our direction. I almost said something, thinking he was getting a little too far into my business, but I noticed his eyes weren't on my pile of video games anymore, and his mouth wasn't set in a permanent look of awe. It was more like a slack mouth......like he didn't know what look he should have.

He was looking past us and out through the big window on the front of the store. The guy behind the register looked to his left and followed the gaze of the other customer. I saw his expression change, and I looked too.

Across the four lane highway with the wide grass median was the Surfside Police Department car with its blue lights on. The officer was standing outside the car and pointing at the ground with one hand while reaching back with his right hand to his holstered weapon.

He was yelling at someone and continually pointing toward the ground. Gamers are all familiar with the stance the police officer was assuming. It was the one where the gun comes out of the holster. It wasn't hard to figure out that he was telling someone to get on the ground.

The person who was the subject of his attention was a girl who looked like she might work in the fast food place. She was wearing an apron and a baseball cap. She also looked like she had spilled something all over herself. She was a mess, and I wondered if she hadn't gotten sick and thrown up. From the mouth down, she needed to clean herself.

She took a step in the direction of the officer, and the ball cap fell off of her head. She didn't seem to notice or even care. I glanced at the cashier and at the other customer and saw that they were glued to what was happening. None of us were reaching for our cell phones to get it all on video. Even though we didn't know it at the time, it wasn't going to be a novel scene by the end of the day, because it would be happening everywhere. It wasn't like we would be able to sell the video to the media.

We couldn't hear what was happening, but the officer was still shouting and pointing downward as he pulled his weapon free of the holster. Another police cruiser slid into the exit of the fast food place, and the officer quickly drew his own weapon as he jumped out of his car and moved into a position to be ninety degrees from the first officer.

Both were shouting at the girl, but she never acknowledged the presence of the second officer, nor did she seem to be aware of his arrival. She just took a second and then third step toward the first officer. I wasn't sure, but from our distant vantage point, it looked like she might be hurt, but neither officer was acting like they were dealing with an accident victim.

The gamer by the new releases said, "Whoa man, if this was something like Undead Zombies, I would think someone is just about to score some points."

It was my turn to get a dumb look on my face. We were watching a real-life stand off happening across the highway. Guns were being pointed, and it looked like someone was about to die, and the basement dweller was talking about which shooter was about to get bonus points.

The guy behind the game shop counter was still frozen in mid scan. I looked outside and saw there were people on both sides of the highway who were watching to see how it was all going to play out. Some of them were holding up their cell phones and jostling each other for better angles.

There was a popping sound, and my head snapped back to the action in the fast food driveway just in time to see the body of the girl jerk backward. The force of the bullet hitting her in the upper left side of her chest caused her to flip over onto her back. She fell out of my view because of the position of the police car, so I moved to where I could see better.

The cashier and the basement dweller squeezed up against the window with me, and I asked, "What's that on the ground? Is that someone else?"

No one had a chance to answer before we saw the girl roll over onto her stomach and push herself into a sitting position. She was facing toward the second cop now, and he didn't seem to be trying to talk to her anymore. He was just slowly advancing toward her and taking aim.

"Do you think it has to be a head-shot?" asked he gamer. He was still thinking of this as something you could forget about after the TV gets turned off. I, for one, didn't want to ever see a head-shot in real life.

A fire engine with sirens blaring and red lights spinning coasted to a stop between us and the drama across the highway. The crowd outside, which had grown significantly, surged left and right to be able to see again.

We reacted too, and went out the front door. I didn't say anything, but I saw the basement-dweller slip a game case from the stack of games the cashier had already scanned for me. That meant the security device had already been deactivated. He slid it into an oversized pocket, and pushed his way outside with us all bunched together.

Without the plate glass windows between us and the other side of the four lanes and grass median, we could hear the terrified sounds coming from the crowd. We also heard the next pop and the cries of people who couldn't believe they were really seeing a girl who couldn't have been more than twenty years old getting shot. We had a clear view, and we saw her fly backward for a second time. This time, she didn't get up, and the gamer said, "Whoa, someone just leveled up!"

I was almost ready to shut him up by mentioning the game he had stolen from my pile when the cashier said, "Hey guys. That does look like someone else laying on the ground."

"Where?" I had a feeling he meant the dark shape next to the girl's body, but I was catching on fast that seeing something unreal could make you question the obvious. We were seeing it happen, but we didn't believe it was really happening. When you got right down to it, we were no better than the basement-dweller acting like it was all a game.

"Right there by the girl. Isn't that a guy?" He pointed, but it was a useless gesture because we were across the street at least forty or fifty yards from the action.

The two officers were moving slowly toward the girl and whatever it was on the ground. They still had their guns drawn, but they were gradually lowering them as they advanced. They were still ninety degrees from each other, one approaching from the front and the other from the side. I wondered why they were still being so cautious since the first one had obviously put the second shot straight to the forehead.

The game store cashier said, "Am I imagining any of this?"

"I don't think we're in each other's imaginations, man. This is real." My voice sounded like it was coming from somewhere far away. Nothing seemed real, and everything seemed like it was straight from a movie set or from one of my video games. "On second thought, I hope we are imagining this."

As if on cue, the dark shape on the ground that the cashier said looked like a body sat up, and both officers raised their guns again. This time they were pointing at the guy on the ground.

At the same time, two emergency medical technicians were moving into position between the two cops. They had a stretcher ready and were obviously thinking the guy on the ground needed their help. When the guy on the ground sat up and the cops raised their guns again, the EMT's stopped moving.

A collective scream went up from the crowd as the guy on the ground pushed himself to a standing position and started walking toward the open door of the fast food place. Someone from inside had opened the door and stepped outside to get a better look at what was happening. At least we weren't close. That spectator was practically on top of the girl who had been flipped backward by the bullets.

We could see that the guy who had stepped outside was frantically pushing back at the people who had pushed out behind him. There was a log jam at the door because people behind those in front couldn't tell what was going on. The guy who had been laying on the ground a minute ago was slowly advancing toward the door.

Realization dawned on the log jam and everyone started pushing back inside, closely followed by the guy who had come out first, and he was pulling hard on the door to get it closed. The door opened outward, so he had a firm grip on the bar across the door. He didn't need to bother because the guy who had gotten up off of the ground shambled into the door like he didn't have a clue that the door was even there, let alone that he needed to pull the door outward.

The way the man inside was leaning backward and pulling as hard as he could on the door. I don't think anyone could have opened it, but shambling guy walked into the glass, bounced off of it, and walked into it again.

By this time the two cops had closed in on the man from behind. They grabbed him as they were trained to do and spun him away from the door. As they guided him to the ground, they pulled his hands behind his back and put handcuffs on his wrists.

We got a good look at the man because he was turned straight toward us as they spun him away from the door. He didn't look any better than the girl did before she was shot. His face and clothes were covered with something dark, and all I could think of was that looked like blood.

The EMT's had resumed their slow advance forward, and as soon as the cops had the man cuffed and face down on the ground, they were in position to take over. They got the stretcher in place and moved to his knees and shoulders to fit him onto the stretcher.

The EMT who had tried to get a grip on the shoulders jumped back and was holding his own right hand in his left. He looked surprised, and I could see that he was trying to stop the flow of blood from the big veins just above the wrist.

The second EMT dropped the cuffed man's knees and went to help his partner, but he never got there because he had to pass too close to the man's head. Like a rabid dog on a short leash, the man lurched as hard as he could to reach the right leg of the EMT with his teeth. He clamped firmly onto it just above the ankle.

The EMT went down hard, and we could hear his screams above the sounds of the crowd. His partner went to his knees, still holding his right hand with his left. The whole thing was crazy.

The two cops had backed away to process what had happened, and several more had joined them. They had holstered their guns and were turning and pointing at various things, including the dead girl. They were interrupted by the new screams coming from the EMT's. When the second EMT went down, the cuffed man kept his mouth gripped to the back of his leg.

The cops dove onto the cuffed man, and it looked like they were trying to pull his mouth open. It looked just like it would look if it had been a big dog trying to hang onto a victim, but it was a man in handcuffs. The EMT was screaming at the top of his lungs.

The struggle to free the EMT suddenly ended when one of the cops barked a command to everyone else. As one, they all cleared out as ordered, and the cop that shouted the order shot the man who was biting the EMT.

The first shot was clean through the middle of the cuffed man's back, dead center between the shoulders, but he kept his grip, and the EMT kept screaming. The cop hesitated for only a split second and fired a second shot about a foot above the last and straight into the back of the head. The biting man stopped moving, but the EMT was still screaming.

A second pair of EMT's rushed forward to give aid to their friends, and were quickly joined by several others. The first EMT who had been badly bitten at the wrist had gone quiet. He was on his back while fellow EMTs were getting a temporary dressing onto the wound. Another was getting a bag of something hooked up to the left arm while a third was getting a blood pressure cuff around the upper arm. Several others were doing pretty much the same thing to the second EMT, and our view became blocked by uniforms.

The crowd's screams dropped to a murmur as people turned to each other and began telling late arrivals what had happened. Many of them stopped taking videos and made calls to tell friends or relatives that they wouldn't believe what they had just seen.

It all reminded me of a fireworks show. First everyone was quiet, then everybody was screaming, then everyone was noisy, then the noise tapered off as people turned their eyes back to the sky for the next skyrocket to blow up.

This time was no different. Just as the noise dropped to something like a vibration, it escalated into screams again. The screams were accented by several pops, and the crowd surged in all directions. Even though we were across the street in relative safety, there was no mistaking what had happened at the fast food restaurant after the cuffed man had been shot in the head.

The cops spread out and had all assumed shooter stances. The EMTs were pulling back with their wounded friends, people were literally stepping on each other trying to get out of the door of the fast food restaurant. The log jam that had almost kept the one guy from getting back in was now trying to get out. He was last seen trying to reverse his direction and had disappeared under people who were either trying to get away or were being attacked by people trying to bite them. In my typical warped sense of humor, I thought it gave new meaning to fast food.

The cops were shooting at anyone who was trying to bite someone else, but there was no shortage of targets. I was pretty sure they couldn't exactly be positive about which ones were which, and as people went down from head-shots, the log jam got worse.

Eventually the shooting stopped. On my side of the street, the screaming and running were both at a peak. We hung back at first, but the store cashier came out of his trance first and turned toward the store.

"I don't want to be here anymore," he said.

I followed him back inside, but even I wasn't thinking about the videos games anymore. I actually wasn't sure why I had followed him. It just seemed like I was supposed to. It probably didn't feel right to be leaving right in the middle of a big purchase. The gamer had disappeared with the rest of the running people outside.

The game store cashier looked at me as if he was expecting me to do something, and then I caught on that he was also holding the door open, and he was waiting for me to leave so he could lock up.

I snapped out of the confused disbelief I was experiencing and went out the door. The cashier couldn't shut it fast enough, and I heard the lock slam into place. There was no sign of him when I turned and looked back at the door, remembering for the first time that I needed the video games and consoles. A quick glance across the street put that stupid thought out of my mind for good.

It was total mayhem over there. I could see uniformed people wrestling with practically everyone, including other uniformed people. I didn't see anyone who didn't have blood on them. I decided there was only one place for me to be, and that was on Mud Island.

******

I never gave another thought to returning the Jeep to the car rental place. From what I was hearing on the radio as I drove south, they would not be waiting for me to bring it back, and they would not be calling the police to report it as stolen.

I turned on the radio to see if I could find out how widespread the problem was. I remembered the number of times that Uncle Titus had told me to think like a survivalist, and to expect it to be big instead of isolated. I felt like Chicken Little at first and wondered if the sky was really falling, but then I had a really awful thought. I was glad I didn't stop for some fast food before going to the video game store.

The first reports on the radio were more cautious about what they reported. They said there were confirmed reports of sick people attacking people who tried to help them. They said that all police departments were responding to multiple calls to 911 asking for help, so everyone should stay calm and be patient if you couldn't get through to 911 on the first try.

I tried another station, and the reporter was saying it was happening up and down the area known as the Grand Strand. I didn't know how long that was in miles, but I knew enough about the area to know it was likely to be in front of me as well as behind me. This station was saying to stay home and not to open your doors for anyone except the authorities.

Listeners were advised to stay away from anyone who was showing abnormal signs of sickness or had been bitten by someone who appeared to be sick. If relatives or loved ones were sick or bitten, it would be best to isolate them, and it would be a good idea to restrain them.

I couldn't help but be amazed by the stupidity that could come out of some reporter's mouths when they got really excited.

"Stay away from people who had been bitten by someone who appeared to be sick?"

I thought. "I'm staying away from anyone who had been bitten by someone whether they look sick or not."

There was more of the same on every station. Hospitals that had originally taken in sick people who were either biting other people or had been bitten, started closing their doors and placing armed security guards at entrance and exit. They were all full and couldn't take in more people.

At first the radio stations were telling people to go to the hospitals and small urgent care clinics to get immediate treatment if bitten. The messages gradually changed to stay home and wait for help.

Blue lights came up in my rearview mirror, and I thought I was getting pulled over. As I slowed and moved to the shoulder, the police car sped by me. I resumed speed but he disappeared in no time. I also saw police cars responding to calls in the other direction. I wondered how long it would be before they stopped responding to new calls.

I made it back to the turn that would take me to my shelter, but I had my doubts about getting there. I didn't think I would feel home free until I made that turn, and just when I was starting to think I was safe, I came over a small rise in the road and saw two police cars blocking the way. They had the big badge on their doors that told me they were with the county sheriff's department. There were a few cars ahead of me already in line, and there were some that had passed through that were accelerating like they had just left a toll booth.

A deputy stepped out from behind one of the cars and held up one hand while he used his other hand to brace a shotgun against his hip. I could see other cars already had armed deputies looking inside and talking with the drivers. One of them was waved through, but the second car was directed to the side of the road. The driver looked like he was arguing with the deputy, but when the deputy stepped back from the car and began to lower his shotgun, the driver unhappily complied.

My deputy walked cautiously to the driver's side of the Jeep and made a circular motion with his hand. I took it to mean roll down the window, so I did it immediately. The last thing I wanted was to be kept here. All I could think about making it to the shelter.

The deputy approached, and I expected him to ask for my license and registration. Instead, he asked, "Are you alone?" He leaned in closer to get a better view off the back seat. "Are you injured, or have you been bitten by anyone?"

I said, "Yes sir," and two quick, "no sirs."

"Where are you heading?" The deputy asked without skipping a beat.

I answered, "I don't live very far from here, sir. The radio stations are all saying to stay home and don't open your doors. That's what I plan to do."

Without a word he turned from me to the car coming up behind me. He only glanced at me long enough to point at the opening between the cars forming the roadblock.

I started forward at a roll and navigated the opening. As I was about to enter the gap I checked out the car that had been told to pull over. Two deputies had joined the first, and it sounded like they were telling the driver to turn around or to have someone in the back seat get out of the car. The driver was yelling something about his constitutional rights being violated, but the deputies were not going to bend.

I passed between the parked cars and lost sight of the exchange, but there was no mistaking the sound of a shotgun blast followed by the screaming. I didn't know if someone had been shot, and I doubted if I would ever know. I hit the gas like the cars ahead of me and didn't look back.

I reached the turn that would take me to the safety of Mud Island, but I only drove until the road entered the trees. I wanted to stop to see if there was anything new on the internet or the radio stations. The cellphone connection was a bit slow when I opened the web browser, but it eventually connected.

It was no surprise to me when I saw the headline banner on my home page. I tapped the screen to go to the website and saw that the police had teamed up with FEMA and Homeland Security. There was a nationwide alert warning everybody of what I already knew. I skimmed through the warnings looking for something new.

The National Guard had been mobilized, and the headlines were saying that the military forces had gone to the highest alert status. The Navy had put all ships to sea that were in port and could muster enough crew members. The Air Force had ordered all planes to go to the most remote bases. Ground forces in the Army and the Marines were told to report for extended duty.

The first reports were saying to stay calm and order would be restored, but other reports followed those by saying that the police would not be able to send help. Hospitals weren't a safe place to go. Shelters were open at most public schools, but communications were being lost between the shelters and the Red Cross. There were reports of widespread looting, and fires were burning out of control because people were shooting at the fire fighters.

One report said that the hardest hit areas were populated places where more people were being either bitten or shot. The one report that was missing was any kind of explanation for why people were biting other people.

There was nothing about how they got sick in the first place, and after they got sick what would happen. There just wasn't any information that was being passed along through the media, and maybe that was because no one who knew what happened was living long enough to tell others about it.

There were three things that seemed to be facts. If you got bitten, you were going to die, if you died you were going to get back up, and the only way someone could put you down and keep you down was to deliver some serious head trauma. Having seen it all first hand, I would add a fourth fact to the list...when you got back up, you were going to try to bite someone else.

They were calling it a mystery virus, but they weren't sure where it had come from. Research centers, especially those run by the government, were claiming they could stop the spread of the virus. People just had to give them the chance.

A radio broadcast out of the Middle-East said that several groups were claiming responsibility for the outbreak of the mystery virus, while here at home, local reports were claiming the likelihood that the virus had escaped from a research facility, and that's why they were so sure they could stop it.

The most frightening report was the one that said this wasn't isolated to South Carolina or even to the East coast. As a matter of fact, there were plenty of news sites from other countries that were reporting the same scenario that I saw play out in Surfside. England was evacuating the Royal family, just as the President of the United States had gone to a secure bunker at an undisclosed location. There were no longer any official reports coming out of European countries, and the Chinese mainland was in total chaos. One astute reporter pointed out that it was unlikely to have originated in the United States because the progress of the virus was so much more widespread on other continents.

I knew that South Carolina was home to several military installations. The Army was in Columbia at Fort Jackson, the Marines were near Beaufort at Parris Island, the Navy was in Goose Creek near Charleston, and the Air Force had bases in Charleston and Sumter. If any state could mount a military effort to push back the spread of the virus, it would be South Carolina, and I found myself wondering if I could reach any of the military bases before things had gone too far.

I had just started to get into the mental grip of a day dream when there was a thump against the side of the Jeep. I looked across at the passenger side window and saw my first infected person close up.

This person had once been a local elderly woman. She looked like the old black lady who wove sweetgrass baskets and sold them to tourists out along the highway. I had stopped out of curiosity on my first trip to Mud Island. I didn't need a basket, and I didn't really want one as a gift for someone else, but I was curious about how someone could sit under a little shade all day and weave baskets.

She didn't look like she was going to sell any more baskets. There was a huge gash on the side of her face that caused her jaw to be unhinged on one side. It was hanging down at an angle, and it was my guess that she had been hit by a car.

Despite her inability to close her mouth, she was doing her best to bite the window on the passenger side. I was grateful for the fact that I needed the air conditioning more than fresh air, so the window was all the way up.

I put the Jeep in gear and drove forward. There was a little guilt as I watched the forward motion throw the old lady into a spin, ending with a face plant in the road. I slowed just a bit and saw her getting back up and half walking, half falling in my direction. I didn't need to see more to know she was beyond help, and I drove into the thicker trees. I hoped I would make it to the island before she got to where I had to leave the Jeep.

She was nowhere in sight when I reached the end of the road. I also didn't have the expected burden of carrying what I had originally set out to buy. No video games and no game consoles were going to slow me down. I ducked under the rusty sign and dove into the brush. All I wanted was to be back in the safety of my shelter.

My long night in the tree was the result of first getting lost, and second making so much noise that I drew the attention of what was probably the only infected person for miles other than the sweetgrass basket weaver. This one looked like he had been bitten right on the side of the neck. He was missing a chunk where the artery had been and had probably bled out in under a minute, but that didn't stop him from closing in on me.

It was his constant groaning that gave him away. He saw me and moved in my direction. I heard him and immediately began trying to increase my speed through the dense brush. If I hadn't already gotten turned around in the wrong direction, I probably would have found my boat in five more minutes, but I didn't see anything familiar that would tell me which way to go.

I originally planned to climb a tree just to try to see the beach or the boat, but the "groaner" showed up under the tree before I could get high enough to see. I didn't realize that my view would get worse as I went higher, but my stupidity probably saved me. The infected groaner didn't see where I had gone, so I carefully pulled myself higher into the tree. I didn't know at the time that I was going to spend the night in the tree feeding mosquitoes.

2 MUD ISLAND

As I tied the Boston Whaler to the dock on Mud Island, I
thought about the warnings Uncle Titus had given me. I did
need to start thinking like a survivalist. If I didn't, I was
going to end up like the fast food worker and the basket
weaver. He had thought of so many things in advance. He
may have run out of time, but if he had been able to hang
around a little longer, he also would have been able to
appreciate just how ready he was.

The boat, the shelter, the incredible inventory, the
seaplane, the wonderful isolation of the island, the
houseboat...what was the houseboat for? Okay, it was a
good place to put a VCR and a message for me to find, but
it was completely stocked just as if it was a survivalist's
hideaway, and I was wondering why.

I walked the few feet across the dock from the Boston
Whaler to the houseboat and stepped onto the narrow deck
that ran the length of the cabin. At each end was a foredeck
and afterdeck. Both ends looked like a great place to relax
and pass the unlimited time I was going to have on my
hands.

As soon as the thought of free time and relaxation crossed my mind, I put it aside. That wasn't thinking like a survivalist, and Uncle Titus was right that I had to think like one to live. The houseboat couldn't be for relaxation. It had to be for something else.

I opened the door and stepped into the main cabin. I didn't know what I was looking for, but I had a feeling Uncle Titus didn't put a houseboat next to a remote island as a big, floating TV stand. "Now, I'm thinking like a survivalist."

The cabinets were stocked full in the kitchen, but there was far more food in the shelter. The toilet and sinks were functional, and the stove was connected to a full propane tank. "I must be missing something." It was almost like you could live on the houseboat if you had to, but I would be safer in the shelter.

There were sleeping quarters for six, and there was a supply of clean sheets and blankets. I searched the entire houseboat and couldn't escape the thought that it was better than my old apartment. Even the location was great with or without an apocalypse. Unless the dead groaners could swim, it looked impossible for them to reach the dock where the houseboat was parked. Judging by the depth of the water and the current, a live person would be crazy to try to swim across. If not for the shelter, I would be happy to live out here instead of inside the shelter. The fresh air wouldn't kill me......or would it? "Think like a survivalist!" I scolded myself for the slip.

Just when I was ready to put the puzzle of the houseboat aside for another time, I glanced upward. In a corner where the overhead of the main cabin met with a piece of decorative trim I spotted something gamers appreciate......tech. Any kind of technical equipment, or 'tech' as we call it, is worth playing with and is appreciated for what it does. Gamers just seem to have a natural attraction to tech. In this case it looked like a tiny glass lens.

I climbed up on a tall chair and studied the little circle of dark glass that was just barely visible. It looked exactly like what I expected it to be, but, "Why is there a camera in the houseboat?" I said out loud. A camera could only mean one thing, but there were too many variables to consider. Someone would be or had been using the camera lens to spy on someone else, but there had to be a power supply to send the images to wherever the 'watcher' would be located.

"Who was the watcher?" I thought.

One thing was certain. If it was here, Uncle Titus had something to do with it. Another thing was also certain, and that was Uncle Titus would have solved all of the variables. There would be a power supply. There would be a transmitter. There would be a receiver, and that receiver was probably somewhere inside the shelter.

A smile crossed my face when I finally had an idea of why the houseboat was here, because it meant I was starting to think like a survivalist. It didn't matter if I was right or wrong. It only mattered that I was finding answers, and I thought Uncle Titus would be proud. I still had to find the receiver to be convinced I was right about what I was thinking, but I was willing to bet the houseboat was a decoy. If someone found it, they were likely to think there was nothing else to find.

I remember seeing a TV show once about survivalists building shelters. This one guy had put his life's savings into a buried shelter only to have someone steal the ventilation system he had above ground. This houseboat was the equivalent of leaving the ventilation system outside for someone to steal.

I searched more carefully through each room but didn't find more cameras. There was an obvious risk that the camera would be discovered if there was more than one, but this one was so strategically placed that one was enough.

Using survivalist thinking, I took it one step further. If someone was using the houseboat, and someone else came along, they might try to take the houseboat from the occupants, but each new occupant would serve as a buffer for the shelter. There was only one thing to verify in order to test that theory. I climbed up into the wheelhouse and found the engine starter. I pressed the button and saw an indicator light up that said Check Engine.

Using the survivalist premise that the houseboat was a decoy, I decided that it wouldn't be a very effective decoy if someone could leave with it. So, Uncle Titus had sabotaged the engine.

The best thing I could do was find the receiver on the other end and to use the houseboat the way Uncle Titus would have. Now......what about the seaplane? Somehow, I thought that would be overkill. The best use for the seaplane was exactly what it was intended for, and that was to get a bird's eye view of what was happening to the rest of the world.

A quick check confirmed my suspicions. The plane powered up easily. I couldn't fly the thing, but I was betting I could at least drive it around like a boat. I powered it back down and checked for supplies. It had a small cache of provisions stowed in the passenger compartment, and there was an inflatable raft in a big yellow bag. From what I had seen so far, I figured it would be a way to get back to the shelter if the pilot had to land the plane somewhere further up or down the coast.

If someone stole the plane, they were welcome to it. Since I couldn't fly it, it would just serve as another way to distract people from the shelter. As long as I didn't lose the Boston Whaler I could come and go from the island as I pleased, but I didn't see a way to hide it. I decided at the last minute to drag the big yellow bag out of the plane onto the dock. I had everything I needed on the island, but I was not going to be stuck out here.

A movement out in the water caught my eye. It was there and then gone. I watched for a few moments, but the next time I saw movement, it was further into the strip of water I called my moat. A dorsal fin broke the surface, but instead of going back down, it skimmed along in clear view. The pointed shape was not something I would want to see if I was trying to swim to the beach. A second and a third fin broke the surface. They were moving toward the South in the direction of the part of the beach where my mainland dock was. I couldn't see the dock from this end of the island because it was too far around the bend.

I hurried over to the Boston Whaler and grabbed a pair of binoculars from a hook over the steering wheel. The best view would be from the top of the houseboat, so I ran back over to it and climbed the ladder to the roof just outside the control room.

I focused the binoculars on the water and scanned back and forth until I found the fins. They were circling. That usually means there's something in the middle of the circle that is about to be eaten. I was fascinated by the way the sharks were patiently waiting instead of moving in for the kill. There was a dark spot in the middle of the circle that was bobbing up and down, but I didn't see any other movement.

When the first shark turned and struck, it was with lightning speed. The victim of the attack was lifted clear out of the water, and I got an unobstructed view of the basket weaver. She was looking directly at the shark that lifted her above the surface, and I was mesmerized by the look of indifference on her face. She was about to be eaten, and it didn't matter to her. Somehow she had followed my trail from the road all the way through the dense undergrowth and past the alligators, but the last hurdle would prove to be more than she could survive.

Before the first shark could begin its death shake, the other two moved in with jaws stretched wide. I watched as the former basket weaver was ripped into several pieces, but there was only one thing on my mind. "What if the sharks hadn't come along? Would the current have carried her out through the southern exit to sea, or would she have been able to float far enough to reach Mud Island?"

I felt like the odds were really in my favor that Uncle Titus had put enough barriers between Mud Island and this particular kind of apocalypse, but I would have to be careful. Live people would be lucky to survive all of the obstacles to get here, so it would be unbelievable for me to run into a mindless, groaning flesh-eater, but the survivalist way of thinking would be to expect it. I made a mental note to try to find a way to measure the depth of the water that ran between my island and the mainland.

******

When I closed the door to the shelter, I felt an incredible rush of well-being. I felt safe for the first time in the last two days. I had seen people die. I had seen people get back up again and kill other people, and I had seen them close up. The safety of the big door closing behind me washed over me, and I knew I had work to do.

The first thing I had to do was take a closer look at some of the rooms. There had to be something I missed because the camera on the houseboat had to be sending an image to a monitor somewhere. The living room seemed like the best place to start, so I looked for the remote to the TV. I didn't get it at first, but the TV was a really nice flat screen mounted to the wall, and I thought about the ratty little portable TV and VCR in the houseboat. This was Uncle Titus making people think there was nothing but low-tech around the island in order to better disguise the high-tech. If someone did find the houseboat, they wouldn't expect anything sophisticated to be nearby.

I sat down on the sofa across from the TV and discovered it had one of those fold down middle sections where you could put your drinks and snacks, but instead of a cup holder, there was a keyboard, a mouse, a bunch of controls, and the power button. I pressed the button and the monitor lit up. My cell phone may not have been able to locate a server, but this setup could, and I got my first real look at what was happening on the mainland.

I used the mouse to bring up the sound on the TV and listened as a tired and totally defeated sounding reporter tried to explain what I was seeing. At first it was like a movie. Someone had just lowered the lights and the first previews were starting. It was unreal because I hadn't heard a live voice since yesterday. It seemed like a hundred days ago, and I was glad to hear it. I wondered how I would feel when it was really one hundred days ago.

The reporter was saying the military had ordered all of its forces to pull back from the populated areas and to establish safe perimeters where they could. He said the TV station where this broadcast was originating was one such secure perimeter. That's why he was still able to get the word out to any survivors who might be watching. He went on to say that anyone lucky enough to be watching should try to stay where they were. Once the military had established secured perimeters around key sites, they would begin trying to locate and rescue survivors.

Someone was showing some common sense. I had to admit it. Every book I had read, and every TV show or movie I had ever seen about this kind of craziness made the military look pretty bad. Mistakes were always made, and the infected got inside the perimeter. Someone always gets bitten, and then they start biting other people, but whoever was making the decisions knew that communications was the key. They got to the TV station and made it a safer place to be.

The reporter was getting some camera feeds from people in the real world, and he was doing his best to describe their locations and the events happening near each camera while he still had live people operating those cameras. He had a large screen behind him that had multiple views. Most were moving in jittery bursts, first running and then panning back and forth. A couple of the views were from cameras laying on theirs sides on the ground. Their operators were not alive to run and pan.

One camera was down a main street somewhere. It could have been anywhere. I wasn't sure because nothing looked familiar. There was smoke, fire, and total chaos. I saw people trying to escape mobs of the injured, wild-eyed groaners like the few I had seen. Each time someone looked like they were going to get away, they would run head first into another. The dead, flesh-eating mobs outnumbered the living, and it wasn't long before the scene changed from chaos to an eerie slowness. As the living disappeared, the dead began wandering aimlessly. Then they noticed something, and for a moment it was like they were looking straight at me. Then they began moving in my direction.

I heard the reporter on the anchor desk saying something about getting out of there. He was saying over and over, "Chuck, leave the camera! Run while you can! Get back to the station!"

The camera stopped moving around, but this time it wasn't on its side. Chuck apparently knew there would be no Pulitzer for this story, so he had put the camera down. The dead kept moving in the general direction of the camera but not straight at it. I could tell which way the cameraman had run by the direction the infected were going. I could also see groups of the dead gathering around unlucky people who couldn't get away but didn't die quickly.

"This, Mr. Weintraub, is what Uncle Titus was talking about when he said he hopes the end comes quickly." I said out loud. "You don't want to be one of the people out there who weren't lucky enough to die before those things started eating you."

One of the dead shambled into the camera and knocked it over. The screen went blank, so I focused my attention on another screen. This one must have been from somewhere inside the TV station perimeter. It showed armed soldiers standing guard while other soldiers rapidly built up fortifications inside a tall fenced in area. These soldiers were stringing the modern day version of barbed wire along the bottom and the top of the fence. I knew it was called concertina wire from some movie I'd seen. It had razors spaced out along the wire, and the wire itself seemed to resist being pulled straight. It was like watching someone pull on a dangerous slinky, and I couldn't imagine anything getting loose from it once they got tangled in its grip.

A soldier raised his rifle and took a few random shots through the fence. I couldn't see what he was shooting at, but the soldiers who were pulling the concertina wire into place doubled their efforts. They kept glancing at something out of view from the camera, and more soldiers came up to join them. Some started shooting while others grabbed the wire and started pulling.

The reporter at the anchor desk asked someone about the view, and the camera started moving to the left of where it had been located. I was glued to the screen when the view to the right became clear. All I could see was a crowd of people, and they seemed to be moving as one toward the soldiers inside the fence. They walked with a swaying motion, not hurried, but focused on the living, breathing bodies who were gathering inside the fence to meet them.

The soldiers all lifted their weapons and let loose a withering burst of fire. The mob went down quickly, and I noticed the soldiers were aiming for the heads. Someone had apparently spread the word. You could shoot for the heart all you wanted, but the only way to stop these things was to shoot them in the head.

The reporter kept saying, "Oh, my God. I can't believe this."

I answered the TV with, "You don't have to believe it. You just have to accept it." I sounded a little like Uncle Titus.

The first few rows of infected dead went down, and for several minutes the crowd couldn't advance because the bodies piled up to block their advance. The next few rows fell over those bodies and began crawling toward the fence. I watched the soldiers take down more of the standing dead, but it was one soldier who saw the mistake in the making and ordered the others to begin shooting the ones who had fallen but were still crawling over the bodies.

They just kept coming and coming, but the smart thinking of the brave soldiers inside the fence was starting to pay off. It became more and more difficult for the dead to crawl over the pile of bodies in front of them. The tide of movement on the other side of the fence began to shift to the left and right. I couldn't guess how many there were, but the soldiers were forced to split into two groups, following the sea of infected dead as it tried to surge around the piled up bodies instead of over them.

One group stayed in the field of vision while the group on the right once again moved out of sight. I could tell by the hand signals between the two groups that they were trying to build a 'body fence' outside of the wire fence, but they had to drop the shambling, stumbling corpses at a steady pace, or a group would eventually reach their perimeter.

I watched in stunned disbelief along with the reporter as the numbers of dead trying to reach the fence gradually dwindled, and the shooting stopped. The soldiers had won this round, but as they reloaded their M-16's, I could see them exchanging looks. They weren't sure if they could keep it up as long as they had to.

I didn't know how many soldiers were inside the fence, but wherever this scene was being played out, I didn't think they were going to run out of things to shoot. I also couldn't help but wonder how anyone who had survived outside the fence was supposed to reach safety inside. It was supposed to be a place where people could go for protection, but they were under siege, and throughout time people under siege had to be prepared to outlast whatever it was that was trying to get to them. This was like watching someone shuck an oyster. Sooner or later the oyster always loses and gets eaten. I would have to keep that in mind and not become the oyster.

Another camera view came up on one of the blank screens. This time it was the pandemonium at the cruise ship terminal in Charleston. I recognized the view of the Holy City as the camera panned toward the historic buildings. The cameraman was somewhere high up on the cruise ship and was able to get a clear view of the wide pier that was the only way to get to the terminal.

In the near distance was a beautiful city that had survived earthquakes, hurricanes, and the Civil War. Black smoke was rising from an area that I knew was beautiful historic homes along White Point Gardens. The locals called it The Battery. On a typical day, tourists, joggers, horse carriages, and Charleston residents flocked to The Battery just to enjoy the breeze coming across the water. It was sad to see such a beautiful place facing yet another tragedy, but judging from the way this thing was spreading, it could be the last tragedy the city would have to face.

Natural disasters kill people and destroy property, but this was what I would call an unnatural disaster. It was killing the people first and then destroying the property because there was no way to stop the spread of the fires that were ravaging the city.

There was a red and white ticker running across the bottom of the monitor that said the fires were already spreading in all directions outward from Tradd Street, which literally bisects the peninsular city. The ticker message said fire departments that had responded to the spreading flames had come under attack from citizens who were attempting to bite the firemen. Their thick protective gear had saved them from the vicious bites at first, but unknown to the firemen, their truck sirens had drawn the infected like flies. The trucks had weaved through already crowded streets at a crawl just to reach the fires, and the slow moving dead had no trouble following them. They had become Pied Pipers for the infected.

The firemen, not knowing why they were being attacked, were eventually dragged down by the shear numbers of the infected. A few were able to gain the safety of their trucks, but just like any good fireman would do, they pulled their wounded comrades to safety with them. It was much too late to stop what happened when the firemen began to die and then turned on their friends. The ticker said there were reports that there were no longer any fire stations capable of responding to calls asking for assistance. While the fires burned unchecked, the brave firemen joined the infected dead looking for more victims.

Above the ticker, the camera had gradually panned back to the terminal and was capturing the decks of the cruise ship from its vantage point high above. The ship looked huge, and I wondered how many people could be safely carried on it. I was sure that they would put more than the normal number on it for this last cruise, but I couldn't help thinking about supplies. If they could get safely out to sea, maybe the Navy could help with that problem. When the time was right for military ships to return, they would come back with a plan.

The camera panned downward toward the rest of the ship. People who had already boarded were being directed to the left and the right in an orderly fashion, being told how to get to each deck and which room to look for. This was an entirely different scene than the ones that were playing out in the streets and at the TV station where the soldiers were shooting through the fence.

The camera panned one more time down the length of the great ship and then came back to the left toward the area where the gangway stretched from the ship to the dock. There were armed guards at the top and the bottom of the gangway, and I could see a group of people dressed in hospital clothes checking everyone in line. They were checking for bite marks and taking vital signs. They were moving from one person to the next as quickly as possible, but the boarding dock looked like it had well over a thousand people squeezed onto it. The space between the ship and the terminal was like a large parking lot without spaces marked, but somehow they were maintaining order.

The terminal itself was probably full too, and those waiting inside were probably being told there was room on the ship for everyone, so behave if you want to be allowed on board. On the other side of the terminal there was a smaller crowd waiting to get inside. They were likely to be more afraid than the lucky ones who were already inside because they could see what was happening in the city behind them.

People inside the terminal and on the boarding dock were relatively safe at the moment because they were between the ship and the front of the terminal. There were a lot of people packed into a small area, but someone had been smart enough to park a large number of cars at the end of the pier on the street side of the terminal.

Whoever had the idea was a genius. The cars were parked right up against each other so close that the drivers had to get out before the next one was put in place. After about ten rows of cars were in place, a couple of big container trucks were jockeyed into position across the pier.

Any infected that could possibly climb over the cars would have to climb over the container trucks at the end. That was something they just couldn't do.

As a final security measure, a narrow strip was left open on the left and the right side of the pier. The strip on each side was only wide enough for one person to barely be able to walk the length of the barricade, and that was another thing the infected couldn't do. The dead would make it as far as the second car before they would get pushed from behind or trip and fall. The end result was always the same. They would drop over the side onto the slope below and tumble to the mud and oyster beds under the pier. Those who were able to climb over the growing pile of bodies below would eventually reach the water and drop out of sight. Some would float, and some would sink. The current was causing a steady stream of heads to occasionally bob to the surface as the infected were carried away into the Cooper River.

The reporter who was still manning his post at the anchor desk in the TV station was trying to describe the scene, while he kept one eye on the monitor that showed his own predicament. I guess I couldn't blame him for feeling like he had to tell his viewers what was happening. It probably took him years to reach the anchor desk, and this was his chance. I didn't know if this had been his position before, or if he had inherited the job because someone didn't make it to work today.

From the safety of my shelter I watched along with him as he described the scenes on the different monitors. I was surprised when he actually paused from his commentary and announced that the broadcast was going to be commercial free, and that his station would stay with us throughout the crisis. Normal programming would not resume until the crisis was over.

I thought to myself, "I've got a news flash for you. The crisis is going to last for a long, long time, and your viewership is steadily decreasing. They won't care if it's commercial free or not."

The reporter returned to his description of the situation at the cruise ship terminal and the genius behind using the cars to block the pier. He identified a local police officer named Kathy McGinley who was assigned to work at the terminal as the architect of the plan. She was a young rookie who wasn't even on the force long enough to be assigned a car, but when people started streaming to the terminal to escape the increasing numbers of infected dead who were getting back up and attacking the living, she organized enough people to seal the terminal.

They were able to get the cars into place because there had been a tall chainlink fence and sliding gate around the terminal parking lot. Once they got the gate closed, the rookie had people park their cars up against the fence to strengthen it. Then she had them retreat to the pier where they put the container trucks and row after row of cars.

With everyone safely behind the container trucks they watched as the parking lot fence was breached at the weak sides, and the dead began pouring through. At first they reached the pier and tried to just push against the cars, but as their numbers increased, they spread toward the edges of the pier.

The plan wouldn't have worked as well if the original builders of the pier had put guardrails along the length of the pier. Instead they just put a raised area of concrete that was about a foot wide and only a foot high, so any of the infected dead who tried to walk its length met with the same fate.

As added insurance, armed soldiers who had made their way to the area had joined in and stationed several shooters on each side. When it looked as if an infected dead was able to get further than the others, they would be shot, and if they didn't fall over the side, they would become a trip hazard to those pushing from behind.

I wondered what had happened to the rookie cap and hoped she was safe on board the cruise ship. She deserved to be safe, because it looked like she had made a few thousand other people safe.

The crowd outside the terminal on the barricade side had dwindled to nothing, and it was just a matter of getting everyone on board the cruise ship. Soon the only people left on that side were the soldiers who were stationed along the sides of the pier, and they were beginning to pull back. The reporter commented that he had communications open with a reporter who had managed to board the ship and then reached the cameraman who was perched at one of the highest points on the starboard side of the ship.

The reporter stepped in front of the camera, and the anchorman gave her the go-ahead to begin talking.

"This is Maegan Kennedy for WCHS TV in Charleston, reporting to you live from the cruise ship Atlantic Spirit." She looked a bit shaken but was getting the chance to do the broadcast of her life, so she was going to deliver it like a pro.

"What you are seeing below is an attempt to save as many people as possible by getting them onto this beautiful safe haven and getting out to sea as quickly as possible. We have been told that a Charleston City Police Officer was responsible for sealing the terminal. We have reports that she is safely on board and hope to find her for an interview. I'm sure our viewers would like to meet this extraordinary person. In the meantime, let me tell you what's happening below."

The cameraman dutifully aimed his camera back down to the area where the doctors and nurses were screening passengers to make sure no one got on board if they had been bitten.

"The medical staff of this ship has been checking everyone for bite marks, and they were told that anyone who had been bitten should be escorted to the tent at the end of the dock. We saw some people being taken to the tent, but fortunately the number of bitten has been small. We don't know anything about their fate, but it is not likely they will be allowed to board."

As Maegan Kennedy did her job, I watched as the last of the people waiting on the dock started up the gangway, followed by the medical staff. No one was coming out of the tent, and as soon as the medical staff started up the gangway the soldiers at the barricade quickly retreated to the terminal and then followed the crew onto the ship.

As soon as the last person was on board, the gangway began to rise, and the huge ship was pulled away from the dock by a trio of tugboats. By some miracle, people were keeping their act together long enough to escape. It wasn't a shelter with an impenetrable door, but they were all alive......for now.

******

Across the harbor from the cruise ship there was a similar scene of desperation unfolding at the Patriots Point marina. Boat owners trying to save their families and friends were escaping from their slips as quickly as they could. Some were successful while others found themselves either trapped by other boats or overflowing with unwanted passengers, both living and dead. Total strangers were pleading for space on boats. Some were offering money while others just boarded. More than a few used deadly force to take the boats from others.

Sometimes the living were infected and going to die, but they either didn't know that, or they didn't care. They still weren't going to tell anyone. Literally hundreds of boats from large to small, power boats and sail boats, were trying to at least pull away from the floating docks separating the slips to keep more people from jumping onto their decks.

The cameraman on the cruise ship zoomed in on the USS Yorktown moored at Patriots Point as a tourist attraction and then to the right in the direction of the marina. A microphone must have been open nearby because it caught the shocked voice of the cameraman when he said, "Oh, my God."

Boats that were at least getting away from the mayhem at the marina were being capsized by the weight of the people who had forced themselves on the boat owners. As many as thirty to forty people were crammed onto the decks of single masted sail boats that were intended for four to six people, and engine powered boats sat so low in the water that the slightest wake caused them to list then sink, throwing their passengers into the river. Some immediately gained holds on other boats and tried to board, but the occupants more often then not beat at their hands to make them let go.

Cabin cruisers that had the largest slips had been able to pull away because they weren't blocked by other boats, and they also seemed to have the smallest numbers of people on board. Gun shots could be heard all the way across the harbor as angry people fired at the escaping cabin cruisers and as their occupants returned fire from the relative safety of their decks. It was unreal to watch as people fell on both sides of the guns.

One of the smaller power boats that had been overwhelmed by people managed to make it to Castle Pinckney, a tiny island in the center of the harbor that had housed a small fort during the Civil War. The camera followed them as they chose to jump off onto the island rather than to sink in the Cooper River. As soon as they were ashore, they began helping other groups of people out of the water to keep them from being pulled under by the strong current.

Their heroic efforts didn't last long as they at first were pulling people ashore and then running from them. Bodies that had fallen face first in the sand were getting back up and following their would be rescuers at a lurching, stumbling gate. Those who were too slow were pulled to the ground and then mercilessly bitten by their attackers.

Boats that had been drawn toward the shore of Castle Pinckney by the current were trying to steer back toward the open water, but infected dead that were in the water were also pulling at the safety rails or the arms and legs of the people who didn't quite fit into the boats. Only a matter of yards from the relative safety of open water, boatloads of people were dying, and I watched as the population of Castle Pinckney became more dead than alive.

The water beyond the marina and Castle Pinckney became dotted with hundreds of white sails as they found their wind and tried to reach the mouth of the harbor. In their haste to reach open water, too many failed to pay attention to the channel markers and wound up stuck in the mud banks on the Mt. Pleasant side.

Those who were more careful and able to reach the part of the harbor where the Ashley River met with the Cooper River only had to avoid collisions with the other boats. Some were not lucky enough to avoid colliding with others because there were infected passengers who had begun biting people, including those who were doing the steering.

The scenario that was unfolding at the Patriots Point marina was also being played out at the Charleston City Marina located just around the bend on the Ashley River. As a result, the boats that did escape joined the melee where the two rivers converged with each other just south of Castle Pinckney. The end result was that many of the boats that weren't overcrowded and carrying the infected were lost anyway. There were just too many of them trying to reach safety at sea.

When the massive cruise ship was escorted from its berth by the tugboats, their preference would have been to have a clear path, and they did at first. The tugs guided the ship past the bloody scene on Castle Pinckney by staying in the western channel of the Cooper River, then it began a slow turn to the East that brought it directly into the path of the unlucky boats that had been too slow escaping from the city marina. The fastest boats were able to maneuver clear of the Atlantic Spirit, but many were pushed out of the way and then caught by the tremendous wake.

******

I watched different camera views for several hours. Some of the screens went blank and stayed that way. The cruise ship stayed on camera until it cleared the harbor and then escaped beyond the jetties. Maegan Kennedy interviewed the captain and several survivors, but she never located the rookie cop. The captain told anyone who was watching that their plan was to sail up the coast. Most of the US Navy ships that had been in port at the big eastern naval bases were at sea off the coast, and his information was that they were concentrating their forces near Washington DC.

If I was correct, they would eventually pass by my location, but I didn't think there was a chance of seeing them. They would probably be happy to stay well offshore.

As the big ship had slipped past Fort Sumter, the fort where the Civil War began, the cameraman zoomed in to see if survivors had managed to secure the old fort as a safe haven. At first the reporter and other passengers went silent as they watched only the infected dead walking along the walls.

Some of the infected were drawn by the living who watched from the cruise ship. They blindly attempted to walk over low places in the ramparts as if they could fly or walk on water. People watching from the decks of the Atlantic Spirit started to cry and scream as bodies dropped over the edge and became entangled in the sharp shells of the oyster beds. They didn't die as they landed but continued to try to reach the ship. Those that managed to get back to their feet staggered to the water and disappeared just like they did back at the dock.

I hoped if anyone tried to reach Fort Sumter, all of the infected dead will have already fallen over the walls. I couldn't imagine what it would be like to land there thinking it would be safe, only to discover it was certain death.

As the broadcast from the cruise ship went blank, it occurred to me that I hadn't eaten in a long time. I made my way to the next level into the kitchen and checked the refrigerator first. I didn't have the appetite for a real meal. I just wanted something I could carry back to the living room. I found a generous supply of frozen sliced meat and bread and a well stocked section that was full of one of the real essentials......beer. I thawed the meat in a microwave oven, made several sandwiches, and returned to the TV.

When I was situated, I remembered that I still hadn't found a way to see what was happening in the houseboat. Moving the mouse connected to the console in the center of the couch caused a menu to appear in the corner of the TV screen. I clicked on the menu and was rewarded with a list that included the news broadcast I had been watching, the Internet, entertainment, and the best find of all, Island Security.

I dragged the cursor to Island Security and clicked, and was happy to see another grid of screens, this time the view was of the outside of the shelter. The views told me it was getting dark outside, so I must have watched the news broadcasts longer than I thought. No wonder I was so hungry.

I checked the views one at a time and found that I not only had a camera in the houseboat, they were everywhere. I could see the front door from one, which I thought made perfect sense. If the shelter was discovered, I would have some idea of what I was up against. If the infected dead managed to stumble up onto Mud Island, I would be able to see them at the door, the northern dock, and even on the empty beach at the southern tip. There was also a camera in the seaplane, and I figured that there had to be pretty good wifi on Mud Island for me to be able to see through cameras that weren't connected by cables.

That reminded me of the other menu items on the TV, so I switched to the Internet. I wanted to see what other countries thought of our predicament. I found a Bluetooth keyboard in the console and turned it on. It was powered by a rechargeable battery, but it also had a solar panel across the top. I'd have to remember to sit it under a florescent light if I couldn't take it outside to charge.

I started surfing through all of the news websites and consistently got the same stories. Each site described chaotic scenes, horrible deaths, and heroism, but they all mentioned foreign countries as if they were nothing more than a footnote. That told me one thing......there wasn't much contact with foreign countries.

Mexico and Canada were in big trouble, especially Mexico. The infrastructure wasn't capable of slowing the spread of the infection at all, and the drug cartels began shooting on all civilians. Coastal resorts became bloodbaths as the infection spread through the thousands of tourists.

Canadians were evacuating into their vast wilderness and cooler climates, but the infrastructure in Mexico didn't give the average person many options. South American jungles were probably going to be safe havens to those who could reach them, but only because there are so many natural predators there. That was an 'out of the frying pan and into the fire' situation because the predators were just as likely to kill a living person as they would the infected dead.

Europe was blacking out from contact too fast to get a really clear picture of what was happening, but the stories were too similar to ignore. The United Kingdom may be a big island, but a small island is safer than a big one, because sixty-four million people were all stuck on it together. There were still plenty of isolated pockets that were too inhospitable for the infected dead to reach, but the reason this thing was spreading so fast was obvious. Plenty of living people were infected and carrying it right along with those who managed to escape.

There were warnings about that on every site I visited. Our own reporters had said the same thing.

"If someone you love is bitten, do not bring them to a hospital, and do not bring them into a safe zone. They will not survive, so you must leave them behind. It will be hard for you to do, but for the sake of those who have not been infected, you must do as instructed."

Despite the warnings, people continued to hide their bitten and torn flesh until it was too late, and another safe haven would fall. I thought about the cruise ship and the sheer numbers I saw getting on board. I didn't see how they could screen everybody well enough at the end of the gangway without stripping everybody completely naked.

Even as they were escaping with their lives, modesty and civility were more important than survival. Uncle Titus would have been standing at the bottom of the gangway with a gun and yelling, "Strip! And I mean now!" Time may have been a deciding factor, but I wasn't sure which would be worse, running out of time on land or getting trapped on a crowded ship with the infection running rampant.

I did a search for news from Asia and got the same stories. Japan has almost twice the population of the United Kingdom and far less places to go. The news reports from Tokyo were grim, saying that the estimated rate of the spread of the infection was so high that over ninety-five percent of the population would be infected within one week.

When I switched back to the US mainland, the reports were similar to Japan. The naval bases along the West coast had all put their ships to sea, and the Marines, Army, Air Force, Coast Guard, and National Guard units were all mobilized. The President was reported to be safe, but the reports ranged from alleged bunkers to confirmed locations. One station reported that the Nuclear Regulatory Commission had ordered all nuclear reactors to be powered down, and judging by the reports of entire cities without electricity, it was a fair guess that they were getting it done. Since I still had power, it meant I was getting my power from either a reactor that was still up and running, or it was coming from one of the big hydroelectric dams in the state.

I switched from the internet back to the TV station and saw that most of the screens were still on. The anchorman looked like he could use some sleep and was sipping from a big mug of coffee.

He was talking about most of the same things I had found on the internet, and there wasn't any really positive news to report. A young lady came into the newsroom and walked up to the anchorman. They exchanged a few words, and he enlarged the screen that showed the perimeter of the TV station.

It was dark outside, but the soldiers had set up flood lights aimed at the fence. On the other side of the fence, the infected dead were so deep that you couldn't count them or see past them, and the fence was shaking so much it was only a matter of time before it collapsed. The soldiers weren't bothering to shoot anymore even though they all had weapons pointed outward. They were just waiting for the order to go inside and begin trying to fortify the doors. I hoped the doors at least opened outward.

A sense of guilt washed over me. I was sitting in a very heavily protected room eating sandwiches and drinking beer, and it had taken on the same unreality of a movie. It felt like I could turn it off at any time, go to bed, get a good night sleep, and then watch some more tomorrow. All of that was true. It was just like watching TV, but this was the reality show from hell......and I couldn't stop watching yet.

The fence around the station went down and disappeared under bodies. Most of them were trampled by other infected dead pushing from behind, but already there were hundreds pouring into the station perimeter and staying on their feet.

I was so mesmerized by the sight of so many infected that I hadn't noticed when the soldiers left the field of vision. The camera began moving with a slight jerk and then winked out. The anchorman turned to face his camera and explained that the outside camera was being moved to the top of the building, and we would have a live view soon. He went on to say that he had received information, probably from the young lady a few minutes ago, that the station had lost all contact with its network. The live feeds they were receiving would be able to give them some information about what was happening around the country and the world, but the network had been passing them live information and updates until the contact was lost.

I hoped I could keep the internet for a long time, but if the TV station had lost contact with their network, that also had to mean they had lost their own internet connection. They were blind except for the camera shots they were getting, and it was not likely that they would keep them much longer.

It was probably around midnight when I dozed off. It had only been since the night before that I had slept in a tree, and I was exhausted. When I woke up, it was probably because it was too quiet. The anchorman was gone from his desk, and most of the monitors behind him were dark. The others were too badly focused or pointing at nothing in particular. I turned off my own TV and went back to sleep on the couch. For some stupid reason I felt like I had to guard the door.

* * * * * *

I woke up the next morning to the sound of soft music coming from the TV. It had turned on by itself, and there was a message across the screen in closed captions.

A SURVIVALIST NEEDS A ROUTINE TO KEEP FROM GOING CRAZY

I looked at my watch and saw that it wasn't an unreasonable hour. Eight o'clock in the morning was a pretty good time to get up, and I needed a shower in the worst way. I was almost to the kitchen when it dawned on me that I was acting like this was just another day. It was less than two days from the end of the world. There were still people being chased down and eaten by infected dead people, and I was thinking about what time it was and that I needed a shower.

I only stopped in the kitchen long enough to find the coffee maker because that was one thing I had to have. The dull headache I felt behind my eyes was probably caffeine withdrawal. Two days since the end of the world, and two days since I'd had a cup of coffee.

With my cup of steaming hot coffee in hand I returned to the living room and turned on the TV. I found my news channel and was surprised to see the anchorman was back. He didn't look so good, though. He was also drinking coffee, but he was sitting it down between sips because he was shaking too much to hold it the way I was cradling mine.

There were only a few monitors on behind him, and I turned up the volume to hear what he was saying to the camera. He was telling his audience that the lower floor of the building had been breached by the sheer weight of the infected dead pushing on the glass doors. The soldiers had found it to be easier to secure a stairwell because they could drop barriers down the stairs until nothing could get through. They had gone through the offices on the second floor of the TV station and carried the desks back to the stairwells. When the exits were filled with desks from the first floor to the second, they finally stopped.

The anchorman explained that they felt safe for now, but they were worried about food and water. The soldiers had carried in large amounts of supplies when they had arrived only two days before, but they were already rationing what they had. It wasn't that they were really in danger of running out yet, but they were beginning to doubt that help was going to reach them any time soon.

I watched as he gave updates based on what was being seen on the monitors. The camera that had been moved to the top of the building was feeding a live picture to one of the screens again, and it was a pretty ugly scene. There were infected dead everywhere within the field of vision. The only time I saw any living people in the area was when a car went weaving through. The driver was trying to avoid hitting the stumbling infected because there were just too many of them. He couldn't miss them all, though, and a trail of still moving bodies was left in his wake. He passed from view, and eventually the dead went back to just wandering in all directions. Now that they couldn't see any activity around the TV station, they weren't adding to the numbers already inside the downed fence.

I finished my coffee and with that same guilt I had felt the night before, I headed for the shower. With the hot water turned up as high as I could stand it I started thinking about what to do next. Like most people, I could lose myself in a shower so well that it had become a place where I did my best thinking.

There wasn't much sense in going outside for any reason I could think of. Even after it reached a point where I wouldn't be able to get any information from TV or the Internet, it wasn't like I had to know what was happening. People were either going to stop the infection from spreading, or people were going to keep dying. There was a third group of people, and those were the ones who had a safe shelter where they could ride this out.

Feeling somewhat revived by my shower, I got a second cup of coffee. I found some frozen bacon and powdered eggs in the kitchen and decided to give cooking a try since no one was around to laugh at me. At least I didn't have to crack the eggs.

I managed to get everything cooked without hurting myself. I held up my coffee cup as a mock toast to myself for being lucky to have a crazy uncle and for finally learning to cook breakfast instead of ordering at a drive through place.

With clean clothes on and the need for a routine, I sat down and started working on a schedule, but I didn't really have a clue about how to schedule free time, especially since there was nowhere to go. The logical thing to do at this point was to keep trying to gather information until there were no more outside sources, so I wrote on my schedule that I should check the TV and internet at least three or four times per day.

******

Despite my earlier hesitation about trying to schedule a routine, I found myself establishing exactly that. I got used to going to bed and getting up at the same time every day, courtesy of Uncle Titus who had the bedroom lights on a hidden timer. They came in nice and bright every morning at 8:00 AM. I gave up looking for the timer after three days. Meals were at the same time, showers were at the same time, and updates from the outside world were at the same time. There was also time in between for the armory, even though I usually had my face buried in the tech manuals for the weapons while eating meals and going to sleep. Each morning I would wake up and find one open near my pillow.

While I watched the news updates, I got to know the guns by field stripping them, cleaning them, and putting each one back together. I loaded clips and magazines, unloaded and reloaded them. I couldn't exactly teach myself to shoot inside the shelter, but I was considering breaking the number one rule as decreed by Uncle Titus. I needed to go outside, so I reached the conclusion that I could take the Boston Whaler far enough offshore and shoot at targets in the water.

So far, I was heeding the rule, but the outside cameras were showing nothing but trees and water day after day, and I was already getting a bit stir crazy, even after only a few days.

The updates from the only TV station I could receive were getting more and more grim. I felt sorry for the anchorman who looked worse every time I turned on the

TV. He had less news from the outside that was any different from what was already known, so he gave frequent updates on their status. They were getting low on food because they had twenty-four mouths to feed, but the water supply was critically low. I noticed his coffee cup was gone.

The first floor of the TV station was still full of the infected. The anchorman said as far as they knew, there wasn't a city in the world that hadn't suffered to some extent. They had reestablished contact with their network office when someone managed to get their email working, but they didn't know how long that would last.

The news about New York was particularly disturbing because so few people got out alive, and the place became a hotbed of infection. There were large pockets of people holed up in buildings just like the TV station, but no one had planned for this, and the essentials for survival were running out.

The anchorman said they had received word that a well armed gang had tried an all out assault on the infected in order to break out of the city, but they had been overwhelmed quickly. Thirty or forty gang members with automatic weapons who didn't know what they were trying to kill found themselves surrounded by thousands of hungry infected. Even if every bullet was a head shot, they wouldn't have even been able to carry enough ammunition to make a dent in the never-ending wall of the dead. The sound of their weapons firing was replaced by their screams before they made it two blocks.

On the fourth day of my new routine, my anchorman friend said they had received information that the military was successful in evacuating large groups of people with helicopters. Unfortunately, they had also learned that too many of the rescued had already been bitten and had caused widespread infection throughout military bases and even the ships at sea.

They had confirmation that an aircraft carrier was adrift and not responding to hails from other ships. A flyover of the deck of the carrier was all anyone needed to see. The pilot described the scene as the worst thing he had ever seen, even in combat. There were infected dead crewmen wandering around the flight deck until they reached the edges of the huge ship. Then they simply dropped over the side into the ocean.

There were probably pockets of survivors on board, but the likelihood of gaining control of the ship were terribly slim. There were over five thousand crew members on a carrier, and they had taken additional people on board when they left port.

The military announced that they were suspending all rescue efforts in the United States because they didn't have the facilities for mass care available in secure areas, but the real reason was probably related to the number of secure areas that had been lost due to families not disclosing that a loved one had been bitten. It also wasn't just loved ones who didn't get reported as bitten. It was the military, too.

News stories were plentiful about military units establishing secure zones only to be overrun from within.

I asked myself, "Would you tell the guy next to you that you had been bitten by an infected dead if you knew the guy was going to react by giving you a head shot?" I didn't think so. I'd probably just keep telling myself it was only a scratch, and it would get better.

I sat down the Glock I had just finished cleaning and thought about how many times I had cleaned it already. I had a nagging feeling that Uncle Titus was wrong about one thing. It wasn't enough to think like a survivalist. You had to demonstrate survival. It wasn't enough to be able to clean a gun. Eventually you had to be able to shoot the gun.

I knew my mind was made up to violate Uncle Titus' rule before I even decided to do it. I had been thinking about going outside for no other reason than to just go out and breathe the fresh air, but I could also teach myself how to survive by shooting guns at floating targets.

It only took about an hour to get myself ready. I used one of the large cases I found in the armory. It was made of some kind of durable plastic that would float if something went wrong, and it went overboard. It was also light enough for me to carry without help even after loading it with several weapons and an assortment of ammunition to match the guns.

For targets I gathered a collection of water jugs, bottles, and cans from the food and water I had already consumed since taking up residence in the shelter. There was a disposal area in the kitchen that would compact the containers when I was ready to do so, but I had put it off. It was a good thing I had, because there would be enough garbage for me to use as practice targets.

I had considered shooting on the island so I could position the targets at various heights on trees. I figured if I used the side of the island that faced the ocean, the sound wouldn't attract anything stumbling around in the woods. The problem was that I wouldn't know if my plan worked until the damage was already done. Even though I could shoot an infected dead before it even left the beach, and even though it would most likely be eaten by sharks if I missed it, there was still a chance that the gun shots would attract the attention of living people.

If the living people were just decent folks trying to escape the infected dead, I wasn't so sure about who I should take in. I had the space for at least six more people, but I had a feeling that I should choose carefully. Then there was the possibility that the people were infected but not dead. I wondered, "Could I order people to strip naked on the beach so I could inspect them for bites?" I wasn't so sure I wanted do that even if they turned out to be uninfected.

Then there was the other possibility......the people who would try to take what I had whether they had been bitten or not. The woods were crawling with predators on four legs, but the two legged predators would be a bigger problem if they were also armed and were able to slip up on me while I was doing target practice.

So, the floating targets would have to do, and I would enjoy the time out in the boat while I became a better shot. The prospect lifted my spirits, and I pictured the satisfaction I would have cleaning the guns later. The smell of gun powder would make it all real, while up until now the only smell was cleaning oil.

I strapped on a shoulder holster and slung one M-16 across my back, and then I towed the crate up through the rooms and out through the hatch that led to the bank vault door. All together I had a dozen different weapons in the crate, and I had a huge plastic bag full of targets. I checked the security camera views around the island, saw that it was all clear, and headed for the big door.

In a matter of minutes I had the crate and bag in the Boston Whaler and was happily casting off the mooring lines. I gave the key a turn and the engine purred to life.

The sun was shining so bright, and the air felt wonderful as I steered the boat straight out to sea. I pulled the throttle back as far as I could and felt more alive than I could remember ever feeling in my life. It felt so ironic that the world had to come to an end for me to feel this free.

When I was far enough off shore, I throttled back and brought the Boston Whaler into a smooth turn facing Mud Island. It looked small enough from where I was that I didn't think the sound would carry back to shore. I began dropping targets and then idling the boat gradually away until I had dropped all of them.

I looked back along the line of targets and decided I would shoot at the closer ones with the pistols and the others with the rifles. I had to be reasonable about what I could hit, and if I did well enough, I could always try to hit something further away.

I chose the Glock from my shoulder holster first and sighted in on the first target. When I pulled the trigger I was surprised by the flat pop of the gun firing. It wasn't like the sound in movies or in my video games. The sound seemed to surround me and hit me at the same time. No one ever told me you could feel the sound of a gun shot.

I looked in the direction of the target expecting it to be gone, obliterated by the bullet. It was still there, gently bobbing in the water, and the worst part was that I didn't even know where the bullet went. It could have clipped a tree branch on Mud Island for all I knew. I sighted in on the target for a second time. This time I exhaled and squeezed the trigger and was rewarded by the sight of the target being shredded. I must've shut my eyes the first time, expecting to be some kind of natural expert at this.

The second target took three shots, but I was satisfied with the results. I was getting comfortable with the gun and was ready to switch to the next gun already. It was while I was sorting through the ammunition for a revolver that I heard someone yell, "Hey, you! You in the boat!"

3 ATLANTIC SPIRIT

Most cruise ships have a maximum capacity of just over four thousand people, but that was under the best of circumstances. Before taking on that many passengers, there would be plenty of provisions in the storage compartments because there would be another eight hundred to one thousand crew members.

As the Atlantic Spirit slowly pulled free of Charleston harbor, rookie police officer, Kathy McGinley, was wondering what she could have been thinking. She only wanted to save as many people as she could, but as she looked around at the frightened, crying people she wondered if she hadn't just saved them for a worse fate. She couldn't imagine the crew being able to find a place to put everyone, and when everything had gone crazy the ship wasn't nearly done loading provisions for the next cruise.

Patrolman McGinley had heard there was a reporter looking for her so she could interview the hero who had taken charge at the cruise terminal, but she wasn't in the mood for a talking head asking her what it was like to be a hero. She didn't feel like a hero. Some of those people trying to get around the car barricade were still people, but she knew they couldn't take the chance of having someone who had been bitten make it through to their side.

She wasn't an imposing person. She just had a way of getting people to listen to her. At five feet five inches and one hundred and twenty pounds, she looked good in her uniform and had to work hard to be treated as an equal. The blonde hair and nice features also made it easy for her to get the attention of men around her, so when she started giving orders, everyone just started listening. The more she directed them, the more people joined in.

It seemed like no time had gone by at all when she boarded with the last of the passengers. A ship's officer with gold epaulettes on his shoulders was waiting for her at the top of the gangway, and he asked her to accompany him to their security center.

"I've been asked to find you as soon as possible," the officer said as they went deeper into the ship.

They went through some doors that were for crew only, and he led her to a cabin with a sign on the door that said Master at Arms. It was a bigger cabin than she expected, and it was manned with about a dozen people and a considerable amount of technology.

"This way, Officer McGinley," he said. "There are some people who need to see you. I am Ensign Reeves, by the way. If you need anything, just tell a crewman to find me, and I'll take care of it."

A burley man about twice the size of Officer McKinley stepped up to her and shook her hand.

"Chief Barnes, Ma'am. That was a good job you did on the docks. You ready for another job?" The Chief had a way of looking kind and gentle but all business at the same time. Kathy had been told by her father that every ship had one 'old salt' on board who kept the ship from sinking. This was probably the old salt on the Atlantic Spirit.

Chief Barnes had red hair and a full beard, and he seemed to fill her whole field of vision. She couldn't imagine what this mountain of a man would want her to do, but she needed to keep busy. The last thing she wanted to do, besides get interviewed by the reporter who was looking for her, was to have someone stick her in a cabin to get some rest.

"What can I do for you, Chief Barnes? Can I help with organizing the passengers or something?" she asked.

"Oh, I have something much more important for you to be doing, Ma'am. We have almost five thousand people crammed onto this ship without anyone in charge of security. Our Master at Arms didn't make it back to the terminal. We don't know if he was even trying to get back to the ship. The way you took over on the docks to keep those raving maniacs from tearing everyone to shreds was just genius. You think you could put some of that genius to work on this ship and help us get organized?"

"Me? You want me to take over security?" she asked. "Look, I'm just a rookie, and something had to be done out there. Someone had to do something, or we were all going to die."

She wondered if she sounded like she was whining, but what she felt was exactly what was coming out. This cruise ship was as big as a small town, and she wasn't really experienced with something this big.

Chief Barnes gave Officer McGinley a big, wide smile and said, "We won't be conducting interviews for the job, and the pay is not so good, but I doubt there's a more familiar face to the people on this ship. They know you saved them, and those who don't know surely will find out soon enough. Now, we could use your help, and it would be good for morale for them to see you're still here with us. What do you say?"

McGinley rotated to look over the operation and thought it resembled the 911 call center at the police station. She saw people in uniform with various insignia showing rank, and they returned her look with appreciative smiles.

"I guess I can't say no, Chief, but I would definitely need your help." She looked up at him and liked him instantly. Unlike the police station, she wasn't going to have to prove herself to this man. She knew he was really in charge, but his ego wasn't bruised at all by enlisting her because of her superstar status.

"You've got it, Ma'am." He flashed that big smile again. "Now, let's get down to work. What are your first orders?"

She hated to admit it, but she knew exactly where to start. There had been too many people on that dock for her to believe no one had been bitten. She had seen some people taken into the tent after being identified as a risk, but the number was just too small.

"Chief, I need to meet with the head of the medical staff. I need to see how the crew is prepared to respond if anyone on board was bitten before boarding."

Chief Barnes furrowed his brow in thought and said, "But we had a medical team on the dock examining people before they boarded."

"You had a team of twenty medical workers who checked a few thousand people who were desperate to get onto the ship. How many people were already in their cabins before they started screening people? How many crew members were already at their stations? Would they have told someone if they were infected?" McGinley shot her questions at such a rapid fire pace that the Chief began to see the gravity of the situation.

"Chief, if I was one of those medical personnel on the dock, I might have even let somebody slip by just because I was in a hurry to get back on the ship myself."

Anyone watching would have become worried, because it looked like the Chief was angry at first, but Kathy McGinley saw his expression for what it was. If there was one person on board who was infected, it could become uncontrollable fast because there was nowhere to go except overboard.

She softened her voice and lowered it so no one else could hear, "Chief, there's no such thing as quarantine for this infection. From what I saw, you can't just put someone under observation to see if they get better. We have to be ready to make the hard choices, and I can't make them by myself. I need medical and security staff, but more than anything we need to start screening everyone again."

"And if we find someone who has been bitten?" he asked.

"You tell me, Chief. Are we going to be able to let them stay on board? We need to be prepared for entire families to defend each other. What if it's someone's child? Do we let infected children stay with their parents and hope they don't get bitten?"

Officer McGinley was saying one thing but thinking another. "I am so far over my head here." What she didn't know was that Chief Barnes was thinking the exact same thing about himself. This was an entirely new problem for him, too.

"Officer McGinley, you're saying we won't be able to let people stay on board if we find they have been bitten.

How do you propose they be put off the ship? We won't have places where we can stop. If we pull into a port to let people off, there will be people trying to board. We don't have enough lifeboats as it is, and I don't think the Captain is going to let you just dump people overboard."

Now that he had laid it all out there, McGinley knew two things for sure. Like it or not, they would have to find a way to quarantine anyone who had been bitten, and it was only a matter of time before things got out of control.

"Chief, let's get together with the medical crew, and I need to know more about this ship. What's the most secure compartment where we can quarantine people? Is there a hold or large storage area that can be entered from above?"

"I'll have the Chief Medical Officer paged to meet us in one of the dining areas. It's large enough, and all of the large compartments can be accessed from above."

Chief Barnes spoke with a crew member who began trying to locate the medical staff. He and the new Chief of Security then began weaving their way through passageways and people. Kathy tried to memorize their path because she knew she wasn't going to be able to stop and ask for directions, and the maps all looked like maps of New York City. Being a police officer, she was pretty good at learning directions, but the ship was just too massive.

They eventually came to a large dining area that was crowded with people, most of whom were doing nothing more than waiting for instructions. Crew members with iPads were circulating through the crowd collecting names and other identifying information.

There were going to be hundreds of people who had left home without daily medications. Kathy wondered how many would need insulin, blood pressure prescriptions, or other drugs they needed just to stay alive. If statistics held true for this floating city, ten to twenty percent of the passengers would be smokers, and they were going to be in a great mood.

She saw an officer approaching with a small group in tow. His demeanor was immediately superior and arrogant as he stormed up to Officer McGinley.

"I'm a busy man, and I want to know who the hell you think you are having me dragged down here." He put his hands on his hips and leaned forward and downward into Officer McGinley's face.

Looking up at the officer's face would have been easier if he wasn't standing so close, and she could feel pressure on the front of her shoes where his feet were up against hers. He was tall, skinny, and had pale skin. He had a patchy black beard that was probably his attempt to look the part of the Chief Medical Officer.

Without backing up or turning away, she said in a calm voice, "Chief Barnes, as the new Chief of Security, I need this man detained on charges of assault. Please see to it, and then get me the next member of the medical staff who would be in charge if this man wasn't on board."

Chief Barnes didn't hesitate. He stepped forward, spun the surprised doctor around, and cuffed him as if he had done it every day. Officer McGinley was impressed by her new friend.

The loudly protesting Chief Medical Officer was handed over to a crewman who took him away without ceremony. Kathy saw a few of the medical staff with grins on their faces. It wasn't hard to figure out that Dr. Self-Important wasn't very popular with the staff.

Chief Barnes motioned to the second in command of the medical staff to step forward.

She extended her hand and said, "Jean Mitchell at your service, Ma'am. What can we do for you?"

She was a cute brunette who was not more than five feet tall, but the important thing was her open respect for Kathy.

"Thank you, Jean. I need all the help I can get, and right now I need help setting up this dining area as a quarantine site. Any suggestions about how to proceed would be welcomed, but I can see that our biggest problem is going to be clearing these people out of here."

Kathy didn't want to offend her new friend, but she had to bring up the examination process she had seen on the docks.

"Jean, I know we were in big trouble back at the cruise terminal and had to move fast, but do you think the passengers were screened well enough before they boarded? I mean, what if someone bitten is in a cabin right now?"

Jean looked around and said, "Well, maybe we can kill two birds with one stone, Ma'am. We could start by setting up an examining area in one corner of the dining hall and move these people to cabins. At the same time, the people in cabins already can be examined by separate teams."

"Those are the kinds of suggestions I'm talking about, Jean. Keep them coming, and please call me Kathy. How many people do you have, and where can we get more?"

Jean turned to a couple of the people behind her and gave some rapid instructions. They took off through the crowd while talking into small communication devices that looked like cell phones or walkie-talkies.

"They're contacting security teams. They need to send people to go with medical teams. If they find someone who's been bitten, we don't expect them to come willingly," said Jean.

Kathy turned to Chief Barnes and said, "Chief, the Captain has to sign off on what we're doing. Can we get him to do a ship-wide announcement asking everyone to stay in their cabins? We should also find a way to verify who has been checked. Do we have enough iPads and cell phones to be able to create a database of their pictures?"

"That's why we wanted you to be the security officer, McGinley. I'll get someone from I-T to start collecting the information." He gave her his trademark smile and started making his own calls.

While Kathy was talking with Chief Barnes, Jean was getting the dining hall separated into sections. She had partitions brought in for privacy because this was going to be more than just a check of visible extremities. She was also giving instructions in a low voice to the medical staff.

"Ok, people, we aren't doing physicals. We aren't looking at rashes, we aren't checking blood pressure, and we aren't saying ahhhh. We're looking for bite marks. If you see a bite mark, don't make a big fuss about it. Just direct the individual to the section on the starboard side away from the exits. Make sure the person gets there. We can't have anybody leaving once they've been identified. Any questions?"

Jean surveyed the faces of her staff and was satisfied with what she saw. They were a good group, and McGinley saw that they were already getting the passengers lined up at the appropriate area. They had ten cubicles partitioned off, and the first ten people were already being ushered in for examination.

Before they even came out of the examining rooms, crewmen brought in by Chief Barnes were standing by to get names and photos, and then they were turned over to the crewmen who escorted them to cabins. The only slow downs were created when families had to wait for other family members to finish their examinations.

Kathy McGinley watched with some small satisfaction, but she realized she was holding her breath. She estimated that the dining hall probably only held about one-tenth of the number of people on the ship, and if they found even one person who had been bitten in this group, she could only hope it didn't mean there were nine more out there who hadn't been found yet.

Crewmen escorted by armed security began arriving with people coming from the cabins. Kathy overheard bits and pieces of conversations from passengers, some of whom weren't happy about giving up their cabins, and some complaining that they were already examined. Kathy heard one man asking a crewman for information about how to file a complaint, and that this was the worst cruise he had ever been on.

Kathy stepped over to the man and asked him to come away from the line of passengers for a moment.

"You are not on a cruise, Sir. You are being rescued," she said. "Do you understand the difference?"

When the irate passenger was returned to his place in the line, Kathy was both amused and amazed, because the man had asked for her name, as well. He informed her she would have a hard time finding a job as a night security guard at Walmart when he was done calling in his favors from influential friends.

She gave him her name and simply said, "I'm sure you're correct, Sir." When she thought about it for a moment, it occurred to her that if she lived, she would have plenty of nights as a security guard, but for a very different reason than what this pompous ass was thinking.

The first five hundred came and went without incident, and that was a good sign. The Captain made the ship wide announcement asking all passengers to stay in their cabins until they were summoned and escorted to the dining area.

Part way through the passengers who had already been in the dining hall, ship service crew began passing out emergency rations to passengers who were being taken to cabins. One of them assured Kathy that rations were also being taken to the cabins where the first examined passengers had been placed. He told Kathy that Chief Barnes had given the order because passengers in cabins were also in need of a meal, and it was one way to get them to come peacefully.

McGinley was a bit lost in thought when she saw one of the medical personnel give a signal to someone by the quarantine area. It was subtle, but there was no mistaking that she had found a bite wound. It was a young man who had an embarrassed look on his face. He kept apologizing to the medical staff about not telling anyone.

The nurses turned him over to the quarantine staff and reassured him that he would be fine. Kathy walked over to the quarantine area and watched as they got the man situated just as if he was checking into a hospital.

Chief Barnes came up to Kathy with a grim look on his face. She patiently waited without asking what was wrong. He would tell her what it was in his own way.

"Officer McGinley, the Captain asked me to fill you in on what's happening ashore," he said.

They stepped out of earshot, and the Chief gave her a horrific description of what they had left behind. Not just every major city, but every country had reached the point of no return and was overrun by infected dead that were swarming into survivor strongholds by the hundreds and thousands. He told her they were monitoring a TV station in Wilmington, North Carolina that was still broadcasting, but they didn't know how much longer they would be on the air.

When the Chief was done, she asked if there was any good news, and she could see that the Chief was trying to find a bright side of this situation he could share with her. He leaned in and whispered, "I want to show you something."

Chief Barnes led her to a door that was discreetly placed in a corner and entered a long passageway.

"There's a corridor like this on every deck. You'll notice they are along the side of the ship, and no matter which deck you're on, you'll come to a ladder that goes down to the next deck. When you are low enough to the waterline, there are lifejackets next to doors where you can jump from. If you don't have time to make it to a life raft, don't hesitate to find one of these jump doors."

As he explained, he led Kathy to the first ladder and down to the next corridor. She saw the jump door and a cabinet full of lifejackets. She looked out through a window and saw how high they were above the water.

"The jump won't kill me," she asked?

"No, not if you do this with your arms." He demonstrated by hugging himself tightly across the chest. "You don't want your arms flailing around when you hit the water, and this will also keep you from hitting yourself in the face or from getting hit if there's something already in the water. Remember, if you're jumping you probably won't be alone."

They went back to the quarantine area and found that another bite mark had been found. This time it was a whole family that was in the quarantine area watching as a woman was being made comfortable. She was a wife and a mother, and her family didn't want to leave her.

Jean walked over to Kathy and the Chief and told them she felt like it wasn't worth making an issue of the family staying together until there was a reason. As she was saying it, another family was being escorted into the quarantine area. Kathy didn't see the point in watching to see who it was. Sooner or later it would be a child, and then it would start to get to her. She knew she had to stay objective if she was going to make the right decisions.

She motioned for the Chief and Jean to step outside. "I know it depends on how many there are, but do we have a secure area in case one of them dies?"

The Chief said, "We have a small brig, but it can only hold about six people, and not separately from each other. The only thing I can think of is being prepared to drop the dead overboard."

"We could monitor closely in quarantine, and if someone looks like they are getting critical, we can tell the families their loved one is being moved to a medical treatment room. Then we can secure the infected with restraints in the medical bay," said Jean.

"It's worth a try," said Kathy. "I can't think of any other way. In any crisis crowd control can make or break you. How about we also tell the families we will announce visiting hours when we're finished with the exams? That will at least stall the inevitable."

"Sooner or later the Captain is going to be forced to tell everyone just how bad things are," added the Chief.

Fatigue finally caught up with Officer Kathy McGinley, and Chief Barnes saw it before she did. After some coaxing he got her to a cabin on the level reserved for officers. He told her they needed her thinking with a clear head, and he had a steward bring a tray of food. She managed to not cry until he pulled the cabin door closed. Then she had to cry it out before she could eat the food.

She wanted a shower, but she figured she could do that after she shut her eyes for a few minutes, but the food and the crying had drained her. A few minutes turned into eight hours.

It probably would have been longer if not for the knocking on her cabin door. She opened it to find the steward with coffee and breakfast. She felt a little guilty about eating breakfast served in a private cabin, but the smell of the coffee made her stomach growl, and she couldn't resist. Guilt was okay, but going hungry would be stupid.

She found Chief Barnes in the dining hall where he was keeping an eye on the quarantine area.

"How's it going, Chief?" She noticed he looked tired and more serious than the day before.

He scratched at his beard and nodded toward the quarantine area. "We've examined about seventy-five percent of the passengers and crew, but the number of bitten really jumped. One thing we didn't think of was that whole families would have bites."

"What?" She couldn't believe her ears.

"Yeah, we had families that must have been caught in swarms of the infected. Some were bitten more than once. We had to move some to the medical ward to be restrained.

They weren't looking too good. As a matter of fact, we had one family that didn't even need to be brought to the examining area or quarantine first. They were so far gone that they were taken straight from a cabin to the medical ward. I can't help but wonder what would have happened if we hadn't started going door to door. Someone would've gone there sooner or later, and after the door was open, it would've been loose."

Kathy was about to ask the Chief if anyone had died when she noticed something under her feet. It felt like a gentle swell of the deck, unlike what she had been feeling since they left port.

"What was that?"

The Chief looked at her like he didn't understand the question at first, but then he realized he was taking for granted that others knew what it felt like to be at anchor.

"I think you just felt the ship roll a bit. We dropped anchor a couple of hours ago," he said.

"We dropped anchor? Why?"

"Like I said, a couple of hours ago, right after the Navy showed up. They hailed us and asked if we had any infected on board. When we told them that was affirmative, they ordered us to drop anchor. Apparently they were afraid we would try to make port."

"Did you tell them what we were doing? You know, quarantine then restraint?"

The Chief let out a heavy sigh. "Yes, we did, but we didn't have a plan for the next step, so they think we're planning to keep the infected alive."

"Who or what gave them that idea?"

"Officer McGinley, the Captain apparently didn't share our feelings about the doctor you took an instant liking to yesterday, and he let him talk with the Navy when they asked for the Chief Medical Officer. He wasn't exactly supportive of you. Instead of leading them to understand that you had taken measures to control the spread of infection, he made it sound like you were trying to help the infected."

"How long do we have to stay here? Do you know?"

"I have an idea," he said. "I think they want to see if we can keep the infection under control. If we dispose of the infected as they die, and no one new becomes infected, then they will let us resume our trip, but I have to ask you Officer McGinley, were we going anywhere in particular, anyway?"

When Kathy thought about it, it made perfect sense. The Navy couldn't do anything more for the people on the cruise ship than watch and wait, and even if they kept moving, there was nowhere to go. They might as well save the fuel for when they needed it......whenever that might be.

"So, Chief, has anyone died yet?"

"No, but it won't be long. There are several who are restrained and their vital signs are getting worse. Maybe we should go down to sick bay and see if we have to face that decision yet," said the Chief.

Kathy looked around and spotted Jean. She looked like she hadn't gotten any sleep, but she smiled warmly when she saw Kathy and the Chief looking in her direction.

"Jean," Kathy called out to her across the room. "Can you go with us to sick bay?"

Jean weaved her way through the people still waiting to be examined until she caught up with them.

"Good morning, what are we doing, Kathy?"

Kathy gave the tired looking nurse a quick hug and asked, "Have you gotten any rest or even food?"

"Oh, I've got time for that later. We're almost done. I'll get some rest after we're finished examining everyone."

"Nurse Mitchell, as the new Chief of Security, I'm ordering you to get some food and then some rest, but first we need for you to come to sick bay with us. It may be time for us to take the next step after restraint."

Jean Mitchell got the same look on her face that Chief Barnes was wearing. The question they couldn't answer was whether or not they would have enough time between the death of an infected person and when they came back.

Kathy felt like she had known these two people her whole life, and she could read the concern they had on their faces.

"We need a plan," she said. "I think we should leave them restrained as we remove them from sick bay."

"I agree," added Chief Barnes. "While we're at anchor we have a floating dock in the water on the starboard side. Sick bay has a direct exit onto the floating dock as a precaution. Under normal circumstances it would allow for rapid evacuation of passengers under a medical emergency. Ironically, we will be using it for rapid disposal of the dead."

The trio was somber as they navigated through the ship and down to sick bay. The atmosphere was even worse when they arrived. There were several armed guards standing by outside the door, and they took a few moments to brief them on their plan. They stepped through the door to the sound of several crying people. Most were infected and restrained, but the crying was from loved ones keeping vigil.

"I thought we agreed we would keep uninfected family members from coming to sick bay with the ones who need to be restrained," said Kathy.

Jean and Chief Barnes exchanged looks, and the Chief answered, "We did, but we also thought the Chief Medical Officer would stay in the brig longer. It could be worse."

"How could it be worse?"

Jean answered this time, "He could be down here. He's so busy kissing up to the Captain that he doesn't have time to be down here bothering us. Besides he can't stand to be around this many sick people."

Together they moved to the bed of a man who looked very pallid, and his eyes were closed. Jean listened to his breathing with a stethoscope and then used a pen light to check his pupils. She silently nodded toward the starboard exit to indicate the time had come for the final step. The Chief had security guards move partitions into place, and they quietly wheeled the bed to the exit.

Without a word, they removed the restraints, rolled the man onto his side and put a tie-strap around his wrists behind his back. The exit was made for rapid evacuation, but it was still a chore to get the man onto the floating dock. They were just letting his body slip into the water when his eyes popped open and he began snapping his teeth. Jean had a close call but got her arms out of the way with only a torn shirt sleeve. She was visibly shaken and kept saying, 'no' in a low voice. Kathy immediately inspected her arm for her and couldn't find a scratch.

"Oh, my God that was close," said Chief Barnes.

The three of them watched as the man slowly sank below the surface. His eyes still seemed to be on Jean, and his teeth were still snapping at her. Kathy couldn't tell if he was really breathing or if he was just filling up with water, but it didn't matter to her. She found she wasn't even thinking of him as anything but a danger to her and the others, just like the people back at the cruise terminal.

Jean was the first to speak. "He shouldn't have gotten on the ship. He should have stayed behind and not put everyone else in danger."

"Not much for eulogies, are you Jean?" asked the Chief.

"I guess I don't have much sympathy right now. If he had bitten me, I would have sunk with him to the bottom before I would've put everyone else in danger," she answered.

"Too bad everyone doesn't feel the same way," said Kathy. She didn't know if she would have tried to stop Jean, but she hoped she could be as brave if it came to that decision.

They walked back in single file and were met by one of the nurses working the ward.

Jean asked as she approached, "What is it, Carrie?"

"We have two more who look like they've expired. I checked their vitals, and both are zero." Carrie was an experienced trauma nurse who had seen death before, but she looked different this time. "One is just a kid," she added.

The trio of McGinley, Mitchell, and Barnes filed into the room and went to the beds indicated by Carrie.

Jean asked her, "Any idea which one went first, Carrie? We may need those few seconds."

"It was close, but I think his father was first." She pointed at the man restrained in the bed across from the little boy. As she pointed at him, his eyes opened, and he immediately began fighting against his restraints.

This time there was no attempt to restrain the arms behind the back. As if they had discussed it beforehand, they let the brakes loose on the bed and wheeled the man away. Chief Barnes was in the lead with one end, and Carrie was at the feet. As they were going out the door onto the floating dock, Kathy and Jean were right behind with the second bed. By the time they were going through the door, Chief Barnes and Carrie had dumped the entire bed over the side with the man still restrained. The added weight made it sink like a rock despite the buoyancy of the mattress.

They pushed the second bed into position and removed the restraints while tipping the bed to one side. The body fell freely into the water and sank, mercifully before the boy had a chance to come back as one of the infected dead.

This time they stopped for a moment of silence. The father could have told someone he had been bitten, but the boy had probably stayed quiet because he had been told to. They all understood hope, and hope that your child was going to live is one of the most powerful forms of hope they could think of.

Before going back inside, they had a quick discussion about what they had done. They didn't want to throw beds over the side, but the alternative was too risky.

Kathy was the one to make the hard decision, but putting it into words to the others made it sound like the words were coming from somewhere else.

"We should start restraining the hands behind the back in advance, and I think a mouthpiece should be taped into place."

Carrie asked, "Can't we sedate them?"

"We know sedatives will work while they're alive, but I doubt they would do anything after they come back," said Jean.

Kathy added, "I had wondered the same thing at one point, and I even thought about euthanizing them, but we know what would happen after they die. The only thing we would be doing is speeding up the process."

Chief Barnes said, "Maybe that's not such a bad idea."

No one answered him, but each quietly acknowledged to themselves that they had all been thinking the same thing at some point.

Over the next hour they made the trip outside a dozen more times. Twelve more bodies sank out of sight, and it never got easier for them mentally. Maybe it was easier to accomplish because they were getting practice, and maybe they lacked sympathy for those who had selfishly put everyone in danger, but they felt like it was a never ending funeral.

The Chief was the first to notice that their Navy escort had pulled away. He guessed that the crew of the destroyer had watched them and decided they were doing what they had to in order to survive. They also knew there was nothing they could do to help without placing their crew in harm's way.

As they entered the sick bay after making a trip outside like some sort of grim reapers, they were greeted by a crewman who was carrying a message from the staff in the dining hall. The breathless crewman managed to tell them there was some sort of problem with the Chief Medical Officer.

Carrie gathered together a new team to help her with the gruesome chore of removing the dead, and the trio that had become inseparable went to the dining hall. They didn't know what they were going to find, but if it involved the walking ego with the title of Chief Medical Officer, they knew it wouldn't be good. As soon as they walked into the large hall, he charged in their direction. Behind him work crews were dismantling the examining and quarantine areas.

"I need to talk with you," he shouted as he closed the gap between them. "You work for me." He jabbed a finger toward Jean. "And I out rank you," he directed toward Chief Barnes. His glare turned toward Officer McGinley, and he practically spit on her when he shouted, "And you have no authority on this ship. The Captain said so."

He had no sooner finished the sentence when chaos broke out behind him. Having said his piece, he was satisfied that he had put everyone in their proper place, so he charged back to the disruption in the far corner of the dining area.

"Can't you morons take down a simple partition without causing such a racket?" He disappeared into the quarantine area yelling something about people following orders, but the yelling turned into an unnaturally high scream. Medical staff and passengers alike began streaming out of the quarantine section, and they were closely followed by at least four infected who were biting victims who hadn't been able to get away.

The Chief Medical Officer was only able to get as far as the entrance to the partitions that created the quarantine section. Kathy saw him go down with huge patches of blood spreading across his white uniform. His screams were from the agony of being bitten by two of the infected.

The first impulse of both Chief Barnes and Officer McGinley was to pull their side arms from their holsters, but so many people were being bitten, and so many were already blindly rushing out of the exits that they knew what was about to happen. They could already hear the screams in the passageways as infected living and infected dead were being forced further away from the dining hall, carried away by the river of those fleeing behind them. What little success bringing the infection under control was lost in just a matter of minutes, and the feeling of defeat was palpable.

Jean stood helplessly behind them watching the carnage spread in all directions except theirs. They had their backs to the escape door on the side of the ship, and she managed to somehow get the Chief to look at her without getting shot. He flinched, but he saw where she was pointing.

"McGinley...we have to go. There's no stopping it now." He stayed calm, but his voice boomed in Kathy's ears. She kept her gun aimed in the direction of the infected, but recognition crossed her face.

They knew it was over. There would be no way to stop the spread of infection now that there were infected dead moving throughout the ship, and if they had been able to see beyond the bulkheads of the great ship, they would have seen how right they were. There would be pockets of survivors locked away in cabins, staterooms, and probably the bridge, but whoever tried to venture beyond their safe area was going to die.

The number of infected was just growing far too fast, and even as they entered the escape corridor, they would never know that a bitten crewman had already made it onto the bridge with the Captain before it was sealed and without revealing his bite.

They ran together to the ladder that would take them to a lower deck and scurried down it like rats trying to get off a sinking ship. The Chief kicked open the escape door on that deck and Jean grabbed three life jackets. She pulled a big yellow bag from the life jacket locker, and towed it over to the Chief.

He told the others, "I'll jump first and swim a short distance away to inflate the raft. After you see it inflate don't waste any time jumping. Whoever jumps first, get out of the way so the next one doesn't land on top of you. Are we clear?"

They both acknowledged with nods, and Chief Barnes didn't wait another second. He threw the big bag out and jumped right behind it. It seemed like the raft inflated as soon as he hit the water. Kathy felt Jean give her a shove from behind, and she was falling through the air. She thought about crossing her arms as the Chief had shown her, but before she could give it a second thought she was hitting the water. She was surprised when she was immediately tugged over the side and dumped into the middle of the raft. She was also surprised when she sat up and saw Jean already pulling herself over the edge using a handle.

Above them in the escape door they could see a crewman trying to jump, but there was another crewman firmly biting him on the side of the neck. It looked like they would fall together, but they only fell enough to block the door. Anyone who tried to use that escape exit was going to run into the infected.

There were gunshots and screams coming from everywhere, and there were splashes as desperate people jumped from too high up, only to be knocked unconscious when they landed awkwardly.

Chief Barnes shouted, "We can't pull anyone in. We don't know if they've been bitten."

With the unbelievable scene happening right before their eyes, they pulled out the paddles stowed in the raft and started pulling away from the ship. They couldn't help but watch as bodies fell, sometimes in pairs as the infected were pulled over with their victims. There were some who hit the water and started screaming for help, but most just floated briefly before slipping under the surface.

As they slowly put distance between themselves and the big cruise ship, they could see people higher up who were trying to climb out of windows onto the broad wings that extended outward from the bridge. The wings were intended for observation along the sides of the ship, but now it appeared to be a dead end for the bridge crew. It was far too high for anyone to survive the fall, but the infected dead were forcing them to make the decision.

Chief Barnes watched as he paddled and said, "It's much better that she's at anchor now. I wouldn't want her to be steaming up the coast with that many infected on board. It's too bad we can't put up a warning buoy or something."

"I think the Navy will figure it out, Chief," said Kathy. "They would have sent out a call for help, wouldn't they?"

"True," said the Chief, "and if the SOS included the ship was being overrun by the infected, I wouldn't expect there will be ships falling all over themselves to come to their rescue."

Jean asked, "What will the Navy do?"

"Most likely sink her," said the Chief. "There will probably be people hiding throughout the ship, but I would be surprised to see the Navy sending rescue parties. It would take weeks just to clear out the infected dead, but then they would face the same problem we had."

"Figuring out who was bitten and who wasn't," said Kathy, finishing the Chief's sentence for him. "Will the Navy pick us up?"

"Maybe, maybe not," answered Chief Barnes. "If I was in charge of protecting a crew on a fighting vessel, I would probably think twice. At least we have something to offer with Jean being a nurse, you being a law enforcement officer, and me being a seafaring type."

******

They stopped paddling and drifted in silence for a while. It was a long time before they were far enough away from the cruise ship to not hear the screams. There were still the sporadic bursts of gunfire, but they were becoming heard less and less often.

Chief Barnes did an inventory of the emergency kit that came with the raft. They had some of the basics, but there wasn't near enough for three people.

"Ladies, while the seas are calm, I suggest we begin finding our way to shore. We won't last long out here if we get pulled further out to sea by the current."

Kathy asked, "How far out do you figure we are, Chief?"

"The coast was just over the horizon when we put the anchor out. We're on the wrong side of the ship, so we should go north while we can, and then we can paddle toward shore and let the current carry us south at the same time," he answered.

"Why not head south with the current now?" asked Kathy.

"Charleston," Jean answered for the Chief. "If we go south, the current will just carry us right back into the

Charleston harbor. You may be thinking that's a good thing, but we couldn't expect a welcome home party when we get there. The chaos is probably still going on."

"Is there some place better?" Kathy asked. She hated that it came out as a bit of a whine.

"Well," said the Chief, "I would prefer somewhere less populated, but not so far out that we couldn't at least try to reach other survivors. What do you say, ladies? Ready to get to work?"

They nodded in silent agreement and started paddling. The Chief and Kathy went first with Jean working to get the built-in sunscreen into place. It ran down the middle of the raft so they could paddle from the sides, and if the weather got bad, it could enclose the entire raft while they ride out the storm.

Thirty minutes later they were passing to the north of the now quiet ship they had escaped. There were no more gun shots, and the only movement they could see were the infected wandering around inside large windows. They saw one walk off the stern and drop into the water.

As they paddled well clear of the ship, Kathy said, "They aren't people anymore, you know." It was more of an observation than a question.

"What do you mean?" asked Jean, "We know they aren't people. They're dead."

"I know," said Kathy, "but what are they? If they're dead, why are they able to walk? Why are they trying to bite people and eat people?"

"I think Kathy wants to know what we should call them," added the Chief. "I've spent some time in Haiti and New Orleans, ladies, and no matter what you think you should call them, even people who practice Voodoo wouldn't call them zombies."

Kathy stopped paddling and stared at the Chief with an expression that said she expected more, but with a lot of time on his hands and a captive audience, the Chief was a typical man of the sea. If he was going to tell a story, he was going to tell it right. She had to ask.

"Ok, Chief, I'll bite, why wouldn't they be called zombies?"

As soon as she said it, she knew what was coming because her choice of words was the absolute worst. She received a chorus of "boos" from both of her raft mates, and all she could do was cover her face.

The tension had been high for so long. The escape from the cruise terminal, the collapse of their safe haven on the ship, and then their escape for a second time had all caused their nerves to be twisted into knots that had to unwind sooner or later. The three of them fell apart into fits of laughter that seemed to go on forever. They had a right to laugh after everything they had been through, and the laughter was far more therapeutic than crying.

The laughing finally started to wind down with all three of them gasping for breath and holding their sides. Kathy and Jean both had tears streaming down their cheeks, and the Chief was rubbing the back of his hand against his eyes.

When they were finally able to get back to serious paddling, they all felt stronger and more lighthearted than they had in a long time. They paddled with renewed energy and started to make good headway. It wasn't long before they could see the South Carolina coastline on the horizon.

"So, Chief, you never answered my question." There was another burst of laughter as they were all reminded of how Kathy had asked the first time.

Chief Barnes was still smiling, but he gave them both a serious answer. "Control...you can't control them. Zombies in the traditional sense are reanimated dead, but not because they're infected. They get reanimated by dark magic, and the person who brings them back from the dead has control over them."

"So, calling them zombies wouldn't be right," said Jean.

"That's the whole idea, Jean, whatever we call them, we can't say they're under control."

Kathy said, "I don't think it really matters anymore. I've been thinking of them as infected dead long enough to be used to it already. Besides, zombie seems even more unreal than things are, and I think the only thing that's keeping me together is a feeling that someone can do something about this virus."

Jean added, "We can't help feeling superior to viruses because we've put so many in their place, but the only good place for a dead person is right where they're supposed to be, and that's under a gravestone. They aren't supposed to be walking around and trying to spread infection. Infected dead sounds right to me, too, though."

"So be it, then," said Chief Barnes. "Infected dead they are."

Kathy and Jean traded places to give Kathy a break, and they dug deep with their paddles.

******

Their first reaction to gunfire was to duck. Their second was to look back in the direction of the ship. They couldn't see it anymore, so they knew the sounds had to be coming from somewhere else.

"There," shouted Jean. She was pointing toward land, and the first thought shared by Kathy and Chief Barnes was that someone on shore was shooting at them, but that would be crazy because land was too far away. Then they spotted the Boston Whaler. There was a man wearings navy blue coveralls standing in the stern with his feet spread wide, and he was shooting at something in the water.

Kathy cupped her hands around her mouth without worrying about the consequences. He would either be a good guy or a bad guy, but she didn't think he would just shoot three people in a life raft.

"Hey you! You in the boat!" she shouted.

4 RESCUE

I thought I was hearing things, but knew it was real at the same time. My ears were still ringing from shooting without ear protection, but not so bad that I couldn't tell I had heard a voice somewhere. I looked at the radio that was fastened just above the steering column thinking it might be on but saw the channel indicator was blank. I hadn't bothered to even try it, because I was not so sure that I wanted to talk with anyone or give away my position.

Turning in a circle in the Whaler, I saw a yellow life raft. It looked to be about a hundred yards away, but the water was calm and the day was clear, so I could make out that there were two people paddling and one standing in the bow. I was busted, and I was going to have to deal with people whether I wanted to or not. I could just start the engine and speed away, but it wouldn't be long before they spotted Mud Island and the house boat tied to the dock.

Part of me said to do that, but a bigger part of me said I needed the company. Even though I had always been someone who was okay with being alone, I was not someone who would pass up on opportunities to be around people. The fact that I didn't have a lot of friends didn't mean I didn't want friends.

The better part of me also decided they didn't need to paddle a hundred yards, and I could go to them. If they were that far out, there was no telling how long they had already been paddling.

I hadn't dropped anchor because I wanted the target practice to be more real, and the gentle bobbing and turning of the boat made it more of a challenge. I had also left the engine idling in case I needed to adjust my position, so all I needed was a short burst of throttle and to point the Whaler straight at them.

In a matter of seconds, I was coasting within a close enough distance for me to tell my decision to meet them head on was going to be interesting if nothing else. Something was ringing a bell.

They were all in uniforms of different types, and I couldn't help thinking, "This isn't something you see every day."

The one standing in the bow was a pretty blond wearing a police uniform. The big guy with the red beard was wearing a white uniform with some kind of patches on his sleeves and anchors on the lapels of his shirt. I could see a smile as broad as my shoulders on his face. As big as he was, you could tell even from a distance that he was a likable guy. The third person paddling from the opposite side of the raft was a pixie sized brunette, and she was also pretty. She had her hair cut in a short but cute style. She also appeared to be wearing hospital scrubs with a torn sleeve.

I felt a chill run up my spine all the way to the back of my neck. From what I had seen of hospitals, wearing scrubs was like wearing a sign that says, "Bite me." This is what I had been dreading. If they had been bitten, would they tell me? If they were the kind of people who just took what they wanted, I was out numbered. The police officer was wearing a gun, and there wasn't any doubt in my mind which of us was a better shot.

The Whaler coasted and then turned easily to give them the broad, starboard side. The pretty police officer immediately grabbed the railing and started to come aboard.

"Hold up just a second, Officer," I said.

I didn't have to raise my weapon toward her, but she froze in mid motion anyway. She continued to hold the rail with one hand, but she raised the other out from her side as if to show me she didn't have anything in it.

"It's okay," she said. "We're okay, I mean we're not going to be any trouble to you. We're from a ship."

She trailed off like she didn't know what else to say, or that she didn't really know where to begin. The other two sat with the paddles across their laps, and as big as the guy was, he couldn't have looked less dangerous. He and the brunette looked helpless.

Even though I had been thinking about this moment when I would come face to face with other survivors, I wasn't prepared at all. I was such a softie myself that I felt bad about taking the smiles off of their faces.

"I......I'm sorry," I managed to stammer out. "I didn't mean you couldn't come on board. I just have to know, have any of you been bitten?"

It looked more like relief than anything, but it was also recognition. These people knew what I was asking.

The cute little lady in scrubs leaned around to where she could see me better and said, "Mister, I don't know how else to prove it to you, but if I have to get naked to prove I haven't been bitten, then so be it."

She stood up and pulled her shirt over her head before I could object. I felt more like a pervert than someone who was being safe. I wasn't the kind of person to expect anyone to undress just because I had a gun.

For the second time in a matter of minutes, I heard myself saying, "Hold up just a second." Not a shining moment in my life, but it probably earned me a measure of respect from the three strangers.

"If you're willing to prove it that easily, I'll take your word for it. Besides, I doubt the others would have stayed in a raft with you if you had been bitten, and if I made all three of you undress, then you might want me to get naked too."

Talk about an awkward silence. That had come out wrong in so many ways.

The big guy broke the silence by adding, "Thank God. If you would've told me to get naked, I don't think we could've ever looked each other in the eyes again without getting, you know, just a little excited."

I have to admit......he had me at first. I was like a deer stuck in the headlights of an oncoming car. A small grin crossed his face, and the ladies fell apart laughing. It was contagious, because I had tears running down my cheeks before I could stop laughing.

I reached a hand out to the police officer to help her over the rail. Something was definitely ringing a bell. Next on board was the lady in scrubs. She had put her shirt back on first, and I was glad I had stopped her. I was able to look her in the eyes, but I did get a little excited.

The big guy came over the railing on his own. The broad smile had returned to his face. He shook my hand

and thanked me for rescuing them, then he moved to the center of the Whaler. He was so big that we had definitely listed to one side when he put his full weight on the deck.

I said to all of them, "If you don't mind folks, I feel kind of conspicuous out here for some reason. We can do introductions and swap stories when we get to shore." They all nodded in agreement and found seats on the built in coolers.

The blond police officer asked, "Shouldn't we bring the raft? It might come in handy."

I smiled and said, "I think we have more than we need," and pushed the throttle forward until we were cutting a pretty good path through the water.

I glanced at the police officer and for a second I felt like I knew who she was, but the idea was too ridiculous.

It only took a few minutes for me to spot the inlet that led around to the dock on the northern tip of Mud Island. As the house boat came into view, the brunette came up next to me at the steering wheel and said, "Is that where we're going? Is that really yours?"

She had a look on her face like the one I had the first time I saw the house boat. I had thought it was great until I saw the shelter.

"Yes, that's where we're going, and yes, it is my house boat," I said over the sound of the engine.

I held back and didn't tell her there was more because I wanted to enjoy the reaction she would have when she saw the shelter. When I throttled back on the speed and turned the wheel to the left so I could swing around the house boat, she had to hook her arm through mine to keep her balance, and I have to admit again......it was nice.

When I coasted up to the dock, my three new friends jumped onto the dock with the mooring lines as if they were my crew. None of them was shy about being useful.

"Wow," they said almost as one.

The ladies were admiring the houseboat and the seclusion of the dock. The big guy was already admiring the plane.

"I haven't flown one of these in years, but it looks like it's in mint condition," he said. "Is this all yours? Do you really fly this thing?"

The brunette had gone to the far end of the dock up by the shoreline. She turned back toward me and called, "Did you know you can't see this place until you're practically on top of it?" They were like kids in a toy store.

The blonde police officer was already going inside the house boat. I just sat down on the dock and leaned against one of the pilings. It was kind of fun to watch them explore everything, and I would enjoy showing them the shelter even more after watching them play with the toys outside.

I guess I also wanted to see if they were just putting on a show for my benefit before they just took it from me, but I wasn't leaning in that direction. I liked these people, and I guess I didn't know how much I needed someone like them around. I had only been on my own for a few days, but I could feel the sense of loss on them. They needed me even more than I needed them, but I was discovering that I didn't resent them for it.

The police officer came back out of the house boat and called to the others. When she had their attention, she motioned with her hand for them to come to her. The three of them met at the door of the house boat and exchanged a few words while glancing in my direction.

I thought to myself, "Here it comes."

They walked back down the length of the dock to where I was sitting, and one by one they sat down cross legged facing me in a bit of a semicircle. If someone was watching, it probably would look a little strange to them.

"I'm Kathy, this is Jean, and this is Chief Barnes," said the blonde police officer as she pointed at each of them.

"I'm Ed Jackson," I answered.

We all nodded and said hello, but the question was still hanging in the air like a sign over their heads. It said, "Can we stay?"

"Got a first name, Chief?" I asked.

It was kind of funny the way the other two looked at him. Kathy hadn't asked when she was introduced to him, and Jean had always known him as Chief. It looked like they were waiting to find out his name too.

He answered with that big smile, "Joshua, but my friends call me Chief."

He extended a massive hand for me to shake. I shook his hand and returned the smile.

"I know this would sound like a line if we were in a bar or a grocery store, but why do I feel like I know you?" I asked Kathy.

Jean sort of giggled and said, "It sounds like a line on a dock in the middle of nowhere, too, Ed."

That got me to blush and I was just about to try to defend myself by claiming I really felt like I knew Kathy when she rescued me.

"We were on a cruise ship that escaped from Charleston. I avoided the reporter from WCHS News, but I'm pretty sure they managed to get a few pictures of me as we boarded."

I thought back to that desperate panic at the cruise terminal and searched my memory banks.

"McGinley...Officer Kathy McGinley, is that right?" I asked.

"In the flesh," she said, "but I have far fewer super powers than they claimed on the news."

"I watched it all on the news," I said. "From where you were could you see how many of them were trying to get past your barricade?"

"You mean the infected?" she asked. "We couldn't really see too far past the barricade ourselves, but I think the whole population of the city was over there trying to open the ship like a big can of tuna. It sounded like it anyway."

"Is that what you're calling them? You're just calling them the infected?" I asked to all three of them.

Jean answered for the group, "It's a long story, Ed, but the Chief explained to us why we can't call them zombies."

"Isn't that what they are, though? Aren't they zombies? I mean, they follow all of the zombie rules."

Jean started laughing so hard she fell over onto her back. The best part was that I didn't feel like she was laughing at me. Besides being really cute, I found myself completely captivated by her, and when I looked at Kathy and the Chief I saw that look people get when they catch you admiring someone. Neither of them looked as if they objected.

Jean sat back up and said, "There are zombie rules?"

I started to say, "Ask anyone who reads zombie books," but Kathy rescued me for a second time.

"Ed, we call them infected dead, but that's not so important right now. I think we need to get something out in the open. You see, we were caught up in that mess in

Charleston, and then we barely escaped with our lives when things fell apart on the ship."

"The ship didn't make it?"

I knew the answer to that question was obvious, but that meant thousands more people died.

"What went wrong?" I asked.

"People tried to protect their family members by doing exactly what you were worried we were doing, Ed. By not telling others about bites they got in Charleston, we wound up with a bunch of infected dead all over the ship, and when they started dying, we lost control," Kathy explained.

Jean added, "And the situation was made worse by a pompous ass who happened to be my boss. The Chief Medical Officer could have benefited by knowing a few of your zombie rules, Ed."

The Chief had been quiet and watchful, but he stepped into the conversation with a soft but firm question.

"Ed, can we stay here? We won't make you let us stay, but this looks like the safest place in the world right now, if not at least the safest place around here."

Kathy said, "We can tell you everything you want to know about what happened on the ship if you want to know, and we can do it now or later. If I were you, I'd want to know why only three people survived out of five thousand, but what you see is what you get, Ed. We three are good people, and we'd like to stay if you'll let us."

I looked from one to the other and realized they really didn't know for sure. Whatever hell they had been through was stopping them from seeing I was also a good guy, which is what I was thinking they were.

"Kathy, Chief, Jean…I'd be really happy if you decided to stay," I said.

I could see the tension fall off their shoulders, and the best was yet to come, but they didn't know it.

"All we need to do is figure out how to sleep all four of us in the house boat," said Kathy. "I looked it over pretty good, and there seems to be enough room and supplies. Do you have a fresh water source? I saw a lot of bottled water, but I didn't want to take any because I didn't know if we would be allowed to stay, and you're probably already rationing."

I couldn't help smiling since I knew life was about to get much better for them. If not for what was happening to the rest of the world, this was an ideal setting, but from what little I had seen first hand and the things I had seen on the news and Internet, I knew that being out here on this dock was still pretty dangerous. It suddenly dawned on me that I had slipped out of my survivor thinking by keeping them sitting out on this dock enjoying the pleasant day and their company. We were even in the shade as the sun had moved behind the tallest trees on the mainland.

I looked around toward the beach and the trees and got serious.

"Chief, I wonder if you could give me a hand with that big crate in the Boston Whaler. The four of us need to take a little walk, and I have a feeling that you could speed up the process a bit."

Chief Joshua Barnes looked as smart as he was big, and he was probably good at reading people. Just as he had read Kathy McGinley right from the start, he was reading me and my sudden caution. Without a word he quickly stood and jumped to his feet and then into the Whaler. He was already climbing back onto the dock with the crate of guns on his shoulder before the rest of us were even on our feet.

I was happy that Jean accepted my hand when I offered to help her stand up, and I saw Kathy get that look again.

"Kathy, I'm sorry to keep you waiting for that water just a bit longer. You three are probably all thirsty and hungry, too. I didn't even think to ask how long you had been out there in that raft, but that can wait a bit longer too. In the meantime, I have something else to show you."

They traded looks with each other, but they fell in behind me when I started to walk the length of the dock. It was a seriously good feeling to have the trust of this little group so quickly.

Kathy looked longingly at the door to the house boat as we passed it, and Chief Barnes was looking at the plane. I thought it was pretty good karma to have a survivor show up who could actually fly the plane. If I had thought it was possible, I would have accused Uncle Titus of arranging it.

Jean made me feel even better when she came up and walked along side me rather than behind me. I was rewarded with a pretty smile when I looked down at her.

I glanced again at all three of them as I stepped into the foliage of Mud Island. As Uncle Titus had described, the path at the end of the dock wasn't immediately visible until you were actually stepping off of the dock. Jean had a look on her face like she thought I was going to go straight through the bushes, but then she saw where I slipped in between the thickest patches, and I got to see that smile again. Kathy and the Chief followed, and the four of us disappeared from the view of anyone who might have been watching from the mainland. I immediately felt much safer for all of us.

We walked in silence, turning sideways at the thinest parts of the path. Not having to carry the big crate helped us make good time. A mile was much shorter with the Chief doing the heavy lifting, and after only fifteen minutes we were standing at the entrance to the shelter.

Being dramatic can be fun sometimes, and if I could have gotten a drumroll for this part, I would have. As it was, I got to enjoy the expressions on their faces, and I wasn't disappointed.

I reached up and twirled the combination on the big door lock. Just before I pulled the door open I turned and faced Kathy and said, "Yes."

Kathy looked between me and the door and asked, "Yes, what?"

As I pulled open the big door, I said, "Yes, we have a fresh water supply."

******

I offered to let the ladies have the master bedroom, but both declined saying they had put me out enough already. I wasn't sure why they felt like they were putting me out at all, but it was probably just a case of being totally overwhelmed.

The Chief didn't seem to mind sharing the bunk room with two pretty women, and I couldn't say that I blamed him. They could have taken separate rooms, but they all seemed like they wanted to be near someone else. I also think the Chief was still in shock over the armory. He picked up the weapons one at a time, handled them with loving expertise, then moved on to the next one. Every time he would pick one up, he would quote the specs as if he was reading the manual.

He also found the ample supply of different adult beverages that Uncle Titus had generously stocked and was sipping a glass of Scotch whiskey with no ice.

While the Chief was in his toy store, Jean was in hers. When she saw the medical center, she immediately started to do a complete inventory of the supplies. Not only was it fully equipped to do major surgery, it had a complete pharmacy. She was reading off the names of the drugs in the supply cabinets and was in awe of the variety.

"We won't have to worry about garden variety infections," she said. "There's an unbelievable supply of antibiotics in here. I should do health histories on all three of you so I'll know if you're allergic to any of these things."

I was standing between the armory and the medical center watching the Chief and Jean have the opportunity to enjoy their own private worlds. Jean started laughing about something, but I couldn't imagine what it might be in the medical center.

"Ed, would you have considered your uncle to be an optimist or a pessimist? I mean, I would consider a survivalist to be a pessimist, but I think your uncle was an optimist."

I was confused about what had generated the question until I saw what she was holding in her hands. It was the biggest box of condoms I had ever seen.

Jean was giving me that smile again, and she had her eyes looking straight up into mine. I didn't know what else to say, so just like an idiot, I said, "Those aren't mine."

Jean walked past me toward the kitchen level and was doing her best not to fall apart laughing. The Chief and I made eye contact with each other, and he was having a hard time keeping himself together too. All he could say was, "Smooth."

The ladies each had a sandwich and drank a bottle of water and then headed for the showers. The whole time they were eating they kept marveling at what I had in my hideaway. When I told them to consider it all theirs too, the three of them just stared at me for a long time. They looked like they were ashamed to have been so lucky, but while I thought I was being generous, I didn't realize they were going through survivor's guilt. They were the only people to escape from a ship with five thousand people. I guess if they weren't feeling the effects from that, they wouldn't be good people themselves.

Kathy was the first to break the silence by saying, "We'll earn our keep, Ed. I'm sure we can do something to help around here."

Not immediately sure how to answer the offer, I had the sense to remember we were still in danger. The outside world had become a place where death was not only likely, it was a certainty.

"There's plenty of clothes in the closets by the bunk room. Apparently my uncle cleaned out a military surplus store that was selling uniforms that had never been worn, and they're in all sizes. There are coveralls that the Navy wears on submarines, and I think everyone will find them comfortable, even you, Chief. I've already gotten used to wearing them."

While the ladies showered, I showed the Chief the closed circuit TV system and all the views of Mud Island. I told him about the layers of safety from intruders, whether they were living or dead.

"So, Ed, for something to reach us, they have to watch out for alligators, snakes, thick undergrowth, deep water with a strong current, and sharks. Is that all?" He had a big grin on his face that was probably as much relief as humor.

"Chief, when Kathy said you guys could earn your keep, I started thinking maybe we should have a rotating watch schedule. It can get a bit boring, and there are alarms to let us know when something has entered the field of one of the cameras, but I think we need to know what's outside at all times, at least until things get better."

The Chief looked down at his big hands, and I thought I'd said something wrong at first, but he said, "Ed, I hate to be the one to break it to you, but I don't think this will get any better in our lifetime. From what we saw out there, no ecosystem can survive this. All it can do is spread. As strongholds fall, the infected will just replace other infected. For every one of those things that walks off the edge of a building or gets shot in the head, two more people will get bitten. It's not like the world will run out of people any time soon."

"Chief, I know I got away really fast when it started, but I've been watching the news, and reality set in pretty fast. I'm under no illusions of how bad it is, but I do think it will get better. I mean, if every living human being out there dies in the next year, the infected dead must have a shelf life. Right?"

"You mean you think these things are going to die off? I might agree with you if they weren't dead already. For all we know, if they freeze they'll just thaw out and start looking for victims again," said the Chief.

I thought about what he was saying, and the grim truth set in. If the whole human race ran out and let themselves get bitten, then this thing would be over fast no matter how long the infected dead would last. The problem was that there would be survivor pockets everywhere, and there would be isolated places that hadn't even been touched yet. One by one they would be added to the infected dead population, and the number of uninfected areas would decrease, but they would remain a source for the future infected population.

"Chief, I guess I wasn't saying that I think things will get better. I was really saying that despite the security we have in this place, we could use a live set of eyes looking out on the island at all times."

"What about at night? Do we have night vision on these cameras?" He asked.

"The switch is on the console." I checked my watch and said, "It should be dark outside by now. The sun was already in the West when we came inside."

The Chief looked around on the console and found the night vision switch. He flipped it on, and then tuned the TV to the closed circuit cameras.

Every screen turned a bright, eerie green. There were nine screens in a three by three grid, so you could watch them all at one time or zoom in on one if you needed to examine the view in more detail. I switched to the first screen and could see the southern tip of the island, but the green light ended at the water, and it was pitch black from there on.

"Any idea what the range is on the cameras?" asked the Chief.

I thought for a moment because I really had no idea, but then I remembered that we could use some of the cameras for a frame of reference because there were known objects within view.

I switched to the grid and then selected the one that showed the houseboat. I had spotted that camera from the Boston Whaler when I went out for target practice. I knew it was there somewhere and wanted to see if it was visible to strangers. What I found was that I wouldn't have been able to spot the camera unless I had known it was there. I mentally pictured the location of the camera and the length of the dock and guessed that the range was only about twenty yards on a dark night.

I told the Chief my guess, and he said, "That's better than nothing, but it isn't great. I think you're right that we should have someone keeping watch around the clock."

We cycled through all nine views, and I showed the Chief another control that would allow the person on watch to keep track of news broadcasts at the same time. They might not last much longer, so I suggested that we have someone watching them until there were no more stations broadcasting the news.

The station I had been watching from the start came up on the screen. The anchorman wasn't at his desk, and the monitors in the background were blank. The chief and I both sat there watching as if something would happen, but it was just quiet.

I said, "That's probably why we need to watch. We need to see if anything happens that we didn't know about."

The big bearded face rotated in my direction. I felt like I was looking at a Viking in a white uniform. The Chief had not tried the coveralls yet because the ladies were still in the shower.

"Ed," he said in a low voice, "please don't tell me that you think these things are going to change, or that things can get worse."

"Well, no, I didn't really mean it that way, Chief. I wasn't trying to say these things were going to mutate and start running or learning to use weapons, or form a union. I meant that I'd like to know what happened to the people at the TV station. Maybe they were rescued or something."

The Chief smiled that trademark smile of his and laughed at himself. "I was seriously spooked for a moment, Ed. Just think about it for a second. Do you even have a clue about how tall the pedestal is that we've got you up on right now? You must really have your ducks in a row to be this safe while the rest of the world is in Hell, and if you told me the infected are capable of resuming the news broadcasts, we'd be inclined to agree with you. I thought you were going to predict something else since you seem to have predicted the end of the world already."

"Do me a favor, Chief. Take me down off of that pedestal. I'm not comfortable up there. As a matter of fact, change channels and see if you can find The Three Stooges or something. I could use some serious TV right now."

The Chief let out a hearty laugh that was really reassuring, and it felt good to get that scary serious look off of his face. The problem was, it stopped like someone flipped a switch. He just stopped laughing and froze.

"Did you see that?" He asked.

"See what?"

He switched to the security camera view and zoomed in on the screen that showed the mainland right about where the dock should be. The green light didn't illuminate the dock or the beach because its range was far too short, but it didn't have to reach that far to see light on the beach.

I hit the switch that changed the camera back from night vision to normal, and all we could see was total blackness. We stared at the screen for what seemed like an eternity until we both saw the unmistakable beam from a flashlight. It was right in the area of the dock, and it could have even been on the dock. The infected didn't use flashlights.

My mouth felt dry as we watched the beam move around as if the person with the flashlight was exploring the dock and maybe the footprints I had left around it.

As if the Chief read my mind, he asked, "Did you leave any clues that you were out here on this island?"

"No, nothing but footprints, and that would only tell someone that somebody has been at the dock recently. That spot where you see the light is where the mainland dock is located. Whoever that is, they would be just as likely to assume that someone had a boat here and escaped with it. The northern tip of the island where the houseboat is tied to the dock isn't visible from that part of the beach, and the part of the beach that would allow you to see the dock is pretty inhospitable."

"Something's happening over there," said the Chief.

I watched and could tell he was right. First the flashlight aimed back toward the trees and then toward the sky. We couldn't see anything except the light changing directions, and that didn't make sense. It seemed like it was moving in circles at one point, and then it was moving closer like it was out at the end of the dock. Then it went down to ground level and stopped changing directions. It was just a little white star in the blackness, and it was pointed toward mud island.

"Some poor slob just dropped his flashlight," said the Chief.

"Do alligators hunt at night," I asked?

"I don't think so, why?" The Chief was looking at me like I was on the pedestal again, and all of my answers would be wise.

"Well, I didn't see any other flashlights, and no one picked up the one on the ground, so I'm going to rule out the possibility that the guy dropped it because someone living attacked him…assuming it was a man."

I added, "I don't think alligators hunt at night, either, but I know what does."

The Chief looked concerned but not really worried. "Ed, if there are infected dead running around over there, it means we're safe at night, because they can't get here, and they're going to keep anyone else from getting here. I feel bad for whoever that was, but at least they didn't bring the infection over here."

******

The ladies came up from the lower levels toweling their hair dry and wearing really comfortable looking navy blue bathrobes.

"We found these robes in with all of the other clothes. Talk about being well stocked," said Kathy.

Chief Barnes asked, "Leave me any hot water?"

They both laughed and said, "No," at the same time.

The ladies joined me on the couch while the Chief went to take his turn. Since the center control console was in the down position, I was squeezed into a smaller section with Jean. Her fresh smell was making me dizzy, but having her up against my hip and thigh were killing me.

"What is that on the TV screen?" asked Kathy.

"The Chief and I spotted a flashlight moving around over on the beach. That's where a smaller dock is just like the one where we tied up the boat. We think whoever was using the flashlight was attacked by something and dropped the flashlight. It stopped moving, but the batteries haven't run down yet."

Kathy said, "So, you have a camera system around the island. Is it any good at night?"

I reached over to the controls and switched it back to the nine screen grid. Then I selected night vision.

There was an immediate, collective scream from the three of us. I wasn't ashamed to scream and jump because no one cared...not when the camera on the southern tip focused in on a man standing completely still about ten yards away. The green light made it hard to make out all of the details, but he was standing with his left side toward the camera and just staring out toward the ocean.

I think we were all holding our breath and staying completely still just out of reflex. The man wouldn't know we were here just because the camera was pointed at him.

He turned very slowly, first straight toward the camera, then back toward the ocean. We could see that his clothes were ragged and filthy. He was also soaking wet.

A crab was hanging onto his leg just above the left knee. At first I wondered why he didn't brush it off, but Jean said the reason first.

"He's infected, and I think it's the dead variety," she said.

"You're right," I said. "Crabs are bottom feeders, and the more dead you are the more they like you. People use rotten chicken as bait to catch crabs. An infected dead walking around on this island is bound to attract them."

Kathy had a sick look on her face. "I had considered doing some fishing and crabbing from the top of the houseboat. I think I'll pass on that idea now."

Jean asked, "How did it get here? I thought the current would be too swift because the water is so deep between the island and the mainland."

"There's still longshore drift even with the jetties," I said. "I think that's the only explanation. There are a lot of bodies that went into the water north of here. If they go into the water dead, then they won't drown. As long as the current keeps carrying them down the coast, I don't see why they wouldn't get up and walk when they wash up on shore."

The infected dead man began walking toward the ocean and made the turn from the southern tip onto the long stretch of beach facing the Atlantic. He went out of view, and I wanted to know where he went, so I switched to another camera on the grid. He shambled back into view and walked about fifteen or twenty feet up the beach until he tripped over something. When he got back up, the dark shape he had tripped over got up too. There were two of them now.

"Uh, ladies....I don't think there's going to be a reason to go outside alone for a long time, but if we have to go out, we should go out in pairs and be armed."

Chief Barnes came up behind us, looking like a boxer with a towel draped over his head and wearing a bathrobe just like the ladies. "What did I miss?"

"We have a couple of infected dead on the beach. I think they washed up on the beach side, but one had strolled around the southern tip."

He didn't look too concerned, but then again, he hadn't turned on the camera and found one posing for a picture.

"Okay, that's two, but we learned something today," he said.

Kathy answered, "They stay alive in the water, or should I say they stay dead in the water? No, that's not right. They stay dangerous in the water if they are still moving around when they go in."

I said, "We need more sharks."

The Chief said, "They're a fact of life now, so we just need to be careful. I guess we can hope that they walk back out into the water, but we can't assume they will. One thing we can assume is that there will be more on the ocean side. We have a choice, let them wander around out there or go out and neutralize them."

******

There's a lot you can say about being completely safe, but there's one thing you can't say. You can't say that you ever feel completely safe. Over the month that followed the arrival of my new friends, we watched sporadic news broadcasts, we saw more infected dead wash up onto the beach, and we saw plenty of them carried away by sharks.

Some infected dead washed up on the beach and never moved again. When they did, we wanted to know why. We wanted to know what killed them. In one regard, we were always lucky enough to be able to see head wounds, and we knew they had probably been completely dead before they went into the water. We were lucky because we didn't need to go outside to verify it.

One body washed up onto the beach, never moved all day, but was gone the next day. No one saw it leave, but we hopefully chalked it up to a higher than normal tide during a full moon.

Of the news broadcasts, most were just audio, but some were amateur at best. I got a big surprise when the station I had been watching at the beginning came back on the air.

I had the midnight watch and was alternating between outside views and scanning for broadcasts. I had the Internet for a bit, but the bandwidth was so low that I couldn't get pages to load. When I switched to TV broadcasts, I got the same empty newsroom that I had seen dozens of times, but the lights were brighter. A young man with long hair walked into view and sat at the news desk.

"Hi to anyone who might be watching tonight. I have a little bit of news to pass on that probably can't be verified, but I'm going to tell you about it anyway. Oh, by the way, names don't really matter anymore, but you can call me Mike."

I leaned closer and turned up the volume. I didn't really care if it was verified or not. Any news was still news.

Mike continued, "First, for those of you who are wondering about what happened to the news crew, they got word from somewhere that there was a military installation that had managed to keep the zombies, or whatever it is you call them, from getting inside. They sent a helicopter to this station and evacuated them to that installation. Here's the bad news folks; if you're sitting there wondering where that installation is, I can't help you because they didn't tell me. I found a sign they left on this news desk that said they were getting picked up by the military, and that was it. Thanks, right?"

"Ok, the next news story is something I managed to pick up from a shortwave radio broadcast. The guy who was broadcasting said he was a survivor somewhere in a bunker. He said he had been in touch with a US Navy ship off the coast of South Carolina that sank a cruise liner. The Navy said they had been watching the ship for weeks, and that it was still crawling with zombies. They didn't want anyone thinking they could retake the ship, so they sank it."

Mike shuffled some papers as if he was doing a real broadcast.

"Next up is a report that the military has also tried bombing major cities in order to wipe out the spread of infection. Word is that it has not worked so well. If anything, the problem is worse because of collateral damage. That's what the military called it, not me."

"We also have a report."…Mike stopped and looked like he was bothered by something.

"I have a report would be more accurate since there's no one here with me. Reports are coming in that the military has been firing weapons at other military. The Navy has possibly put some cruise missiles into an Army base that was previously considered a safe zone. Sorry, folks. I don't know if it's the same base that evacuated this station."

I didn't hear Jean come into the room, and I was so intent upon what was being said that I jumped a bit.

"Sorry, I didn't mean to startle you," she said.

What startled me was when Jean snuggled up with me on the couch. She did it so naturally that it seemed like we had always been that comfortable with each other. I had a blanket across my legs, so I pulled it over her, too.

"Ummm…this is comfortable," she said. "Can we stay like this for a bit?"

"Sure, it feels nice to me too." What I was thinking was that we could stay like this forever if she wanted.

"You found some news? Anything good?" Jean sounded a bit sleepy.

"No, nothing you'd want to hear. I think the Navy sank that ship you guys were on. That would explain all the infected that washed up on the beach. This guy's news is undoubtedly older than he realizes, so it probably happened a long time ago. Other than that, it really isn't anything we haven't heard on other broadcasts."

Jean's even breathing told me she had dozed off. I was sleepy myself, but I wanted to stay awake for as long as I could and enjoy her warmth against me.

******

"It's definitely a ship, but it's still too far out to tell anything else," I said to the Chief.

I had gone to get him as soon as I saw on one of the camera monitors the sunlight reflect back from something on the horizon. We had agreed that the ocean side of Mud Island was just as dangerous as the side facing the mainland for one reason. Any small ship or boat that was trying to survive at sea for the last month would be trying to find a safe place to come ashore. Fresh water and other supplies would be necessary to their survival, so they would try to come in wherever it looked safe. After all, that's how Jean, Kathy, and the Chief had found safety.

Mud Island would look like a dream come true if they came in close enough to see the northern dock where the houseboat was parked. Since it was well hidden from the mainland and deserted looking, someone in a small boat would have to figure it was a safe haven. Tidal creeks and small inlets away from marinas were much safer than populated areas.

Up and down the coast there were thousands of small boats and cabin cruisers that had made it to safety in the open sea. According to the increasingly rare news reports, they couldn't stay at sea indefinitely, though. Some had tried to seek help from the Navy ships that were patrolling along the Gulf Stream, but the Navy couldn't risk losing more of its numbers to the infected. Those who didn't heed the warnings to stay away were sunk, and as water became increasingly scarce at sea, more of them became too bold with their approach toward naval vessels.

Many of the boats were lost because there were infected on board. Whether they were strangers or family members, it didn't matter. It was happening just as if they had found temporary safety on land. People just weren't willing to turn in their loved ones if they were infected.

Some of them thought they could make it into ports for supplies and then make it back to sea, but they found they either couldn't reach land safely or they couldn't escape a second time.

As small boats encountered each other at sea, the paranoia caused by fears of infection or even piracy caused people to shoot first and ask questions later. On land there were places where people had dug in, and out at sea, every boat had become its own island.

"I don't think they're going to be a threat to us," said the Chief. "They look pretty far out to sea, just barely on the horizon."

"Maybe, Chief, but they are closer than they were before," I said. "I've seen enough ships and boats in the last month to tell that one is coming straight toward the coast."

The Chief studied the image on the screen for a minute and said, "We should have set up a way to tell distance a long time ago, but I think you're right. Is the camera on maximum zoom?"

I checked the controls and answered him that they were at the maximum setting and added, "I'm starting to be able to make out the shape of it, so it must be getting closer."

The Chief leaned closer to the monitor and said, "I see what you mean. Is there something kind of funny about the sides of that thing?"

"That's exactly what I was thinking, Chief. I'm not sure yet, but it's starting to look like it might be a fishing trawler."

The Chief looked at me with a startled expression and asked, "With its nets out? Someone is stupid enough to be fishing out there?"

The thought made me feel a bit queasy, but that's what I was thinking. "Yes, Chief, someone is that stupid."

Jean and Kathy came in together and asked if we had spotted something. Both of us had left the sofa and gotten close to the monitor. We had our faces practically against the glass trying to get a better look.

The Chief said, "Someone has gotten desperate enough to start eating seafood again."

The ladies made a collective sound of disgust and moved up close with us. Jean asked, "Are they coming too close to us?"

"We'll know in a bit," I said, "but even if they do, we don't really have anything to worry about."

Kathy said, "Ed is right. It may be a nuisance having them out there, but it's not like it will hurt us."

Jean said, "What I can't figure is how anyone can eat seafood with all of the bodies out there, or worse yet, how can you drag the nets without scooping up the infected, too?"

All of us were in agreement that there was a likelihood that the net would have squirming fish, shrimp, crabs, and infected dead in it. It was ironically similar to catching a shark. You had to watch out for the teeth.

We watched the ship get closer and closer for the next hour, and it gradually took on the shape that confirmed my first opinion that it was a trawler with its nets out. The spars on the sides that supported the nets were fully extended, and the nets looked like they were heavy with the catch.

Jean finally asked the question that we were all thinking but couldn't quite say. "Why aren't they pulling in the nets?"

Kathy said, "Good question Jean. They look so full that they are slowing the trawler's forward speed."

"That would explain why it has been taking so long to get here," said the Chief.

"It's also coming in at an angle to Mud Island," I said. "If it keeps coming in at that angle, I think it's going to hit the southern jetty."

An hour later, our suspicions were confirmed. There was no living crew trying to steer the ship. There were a few infected dead walking around above decks, but the safety rails were too high for them to fall overboard. We were also fairly sure that the trawler would not be able to miss the jetty at its farthest tip. If it would be just a few yards shorter the drifting trawler would probably miss, but it looked like we were in for a show.

As the trawler came closer, its momentum seemed to slow, and the starboard side turned toward the shore. We watched it moving almost broadside to the shore, and I saw that the ship would barely miss the tip of the jetty, but the starboard nets wouldn't. The current at the tip of the jetty was more swift than it was further out, and it seemed to grab the trawler just as it passed the rocks, pulling it by even faster.

With a spectacular jerk, the nets snagged the rocks of the jetty as if someone had thrown an anchor off the starboard bow. The entire ship seemed to turn on its axis and it rotated one hundred and eighty degrees until it was facing the other side of the jetty......but it didn't stop there. The nets on the port side literally passed the ship, carried by the swift current and the slingshot effect created by the sudden stop of the ship's forward motion.

The end result was the trawler continuing to arc toward the beach on the other side of the southern inlet until it slammed into the bottom on the mainland side, causing it to slant its deck at a steep angle and dump its infected dead crew out onto the sand. At the same time, the net that had passed the rotating trawler followed the same arc and deposited its load on the beach.

We had begun watching from the southern camera, so we had a clear view of the shipwreck, and we were all holding our breath. The net that had caught on the rocks was writhing as its catch tried to free itself, but the sandy area across the southern inlet from Mud Island was a mass of walking or crawling infected dead. There were sharks in the net that had their jaws around the infected that were still trying to crawl away.

I broke the silence in the shelter and said, "I know they couldn't get in here even if they had the combination, but I'm glad that happened on the other side of the inlet."

"Me too," said Kathy. "I can't help but wonder how many times someone on land who thought they were safe had a boatload of those things dumped in their laps."

Jean reached over and took my hand. At first I thought she just wanted someone to hold onto it, but her tug on my arm was about like the trawler net getting snagged on the rocks. I was only vaguely aware of the Chief and Kathy watching as Jean towed me out of the room.

Jean looked back at them and said, "I don't know about you guys, but I need to have Eddy remind me why I'm so grateful to be alive. If not for him, we would still be out there. Besides, he's also going to help me forget what's happening out there, at least for a while."

We were almost to the next room when Kathy yelled, "Be sure to stop at the medical supply room for Uncle Titus' private stock of optimism."

5 DEAD WORLD

While we were having breakfast the next morning, I couldn't help but notice the little grins Kathy was giving Jean. Chief Barnes also seemed a bit more cheerful even for him. When I made eye contact with Jean, I was happy to see the same little grin.

Chief Barnes cleared his throat and said, "I hate to spoil what is obviously a good mood, but I think it might be time for us to find out what's happening on the other side of these walls, especially after the bizarre events with that trawler."

To everyone's credit, no one let their mood be dampened by the Chief's comment. Maybe we all wanted to know what was happening on the other side of the trees and swamps, too.

"Are you thinking of going somewhere in particular?" I asked.

"Yeah, I'm thinking there are plenty of big lakes in South Carolina where we can set down the sea plane. We can circle the lake first, see what's happening around it, and if it looks okay, we land. I'm thinking we play it really safe." The Chief looked at each of us one at a time for a reaction.

I know it seems crazy to leave the safety of the shelter, but I think we all wanted to see what the world looked like.

"When do we go?" I asked.

"Tomorrow morning if no one has any objections. I want everyone to go. For one thing, we may need the fire power, and I don't want someone to be sitting back here waiting and wondering. If something happens to the plane, I think four is a good number to move with."

We exchanged nods of agreement, and I was surprised to see Kathy was still giving those cute little 'knowing' looks to Jean, despite the serious decision we were making.

We spent the day going over our plans. We agreed that we would leave at sunrise with M-16's for the best firepower and a nine millimeter pistol each. We figured that we would be better off with the same weapons because we wouldn't have to carry a wide variety of ammunition. The seaplane had a big enough passenger compartment, so we put together food and water packs, and left room for the inflatable life raft.

Chief Barnes laid out some maps of South Carolina and showed us the first goal. "I figure we can try for Lake Moultrie first. If the weather is good and we don't run into any problems, we might see what it looks like down here." He put his finger on the map indicating a military installation that was labeled Naval Weapons Station. "The Cooper River goes all the way up to here."

"We can check out Lake Moultrie for an emergency landing area, then we can try for the Naval Weapons Station. I spent a lot of time in that area, and the Weapons Station was like a fortress. They have a military prison, bunkers for nuclear weapons left over from the Fleet

148

Ballistic Submarine days, and a nuclear power training school. I'm willing to bet they were able to dig in at this base just because there was so much security in place already."

Once we had our supplies packed and a destination in mind, we had to admit our first goal had to be getting to the plane. We would know in the morning if Mud Island had become Infected Dead Island. Throughout the day there were plenty of the infected dead showing up within the view of cameras, but some would slip into the water and disappear. Others would wander to another part of the island only to be spotted on a different camera. By morning we wouldn't know how bad it was until we went outside.

We also decided that we had to clear our path to the seaplane as quietly as possible, and the armory had a good assortment of handheld weapons that didn't make noise.

Kathy suggested that we should all carry a machete, but she said she had learned at the police academy that it was intended as a tool for clearing brush. She said we should stay together in a group, be sure to swing outward if we got surrounded, and aim for soft body parts. She lectured us about remembering this was not a movie. She said a machete can get stuck in your target if you connect with solid bone, so don't aim for the skull.

Kathy also suggested that we should wear the heavy denim coveralls we had found in storage. She told us that she had noticed the material was thick, and it would probably be hard to bite through. It was agreed we would all wear them as protection, even though we would look like some uniformed group of mercenaries.

Jean looked me in the eyes and said, "Eddy, I had a close call with one of these things on the ship, and I have to tell you time stands still when one almost gets you. Just remember not to lock up. Time doesn't stand still for them."

I had about a dozen different reactions all at once. Jean's eyes were beautiful, it was the first time she had called me Eddy, she was sharing some deep feelings, and a bunch of other stuff.

Chief Barnes said, "Hell, he's locked up right now, Jean."

Kathy was laughing so hard she was crying. I was beet red, but I started laughing too. I don't think my feelings were a secret to anyone, and I could tell Jean felt the same way.

Our evening ended with supper because we all needed sleep to be at our best in the morning. This was going to be our first time out as a team, and if it went well, it wouldn't be our last time. When we were done clearing the dishes, we started saying good night just as we all had been doing for the last month. We had gotten in the habit of giving each other affectionate hugs, and the Chief would slap me on the back or give me a knuckle bump. This time I hugged Kathy and knuckle bumped the Chief, but when I turned to hug Jean she took my hand and started in the direction of the master bedroom.

The Chief said, "You guys be sure to get some rest."

******

Morning came around too soon. Kathy came into the bedroom and said something about saving something for when we got back. That was enough to get us moving. We had to show more self-discipline when we showered than I knew I had, and we found Kathy putting breakfast on the table for all of us. The Chief was watching the camera views to see if there was any activity, especially between the main door and the dock.

"I've got some good news and some more good news," he said. "It looks like a beautiful day out there, and if there are any infected, they learned how to hide."

"That's good news?" Laughed Kathy. "If they start popping out from behind bushes, I'm going to need to pack spare underwear."

We were definitely in good spirits, and breakfast only made it better. When we were all done, I started to clear the dishes, and Kathy said, "Leave them for later, Ed, for good luck."

We gathered at the big vault door, and the Chief opened it without a sound. We had checked the camera view before leaving the living room, and the area had been clear. He leaned out and looked around then signaled with his hand to follow. We had worked out hand signals so we wouldn't have to talk and draw attention to ourselves.

One thing we had noticed while watching the infected roam around was a tendency to take the path of least resistance. Once they were on a path, they tended to stay on the path. We had seen more than one walk straight off the dock because there was nothing to stop them. We had even talked about building a berm on the beach and at the southern tip of the island. If they did as they usually do, the infected would follow the berms until they walked right into the water.

We were counting on the infected either being on the path or not on the dock side of the island at all. Hopefully, none would have strayed from the path into the trees and brush on either side.

The path to the dock was narrow and dark when I saw the island the first time. The foliage was thick and dark enough to almost block out the sun in some places. It was sinister then, but now it was frightening.

The last time I had been out here, there hadn't been any infected dead sharing the island with me......or at least none that I knew of. It could be I was just blissfully ignorant because I hadn't seen any, and because I didn't think there was any way for them to possibly reach the island.

The Chief took the lead followed by Kathy. Jean was next, and I brought up the rear, constantly rotating to make sure nothing came up from behind. We moved fast and quietly, trying not to let any of our gear get caught on branches.

It was only a matter of minutes before we rounded the last turn and could see the big house boat looming on the sea side of the dock. The seaplane and the Boston Whaler were lined up on the other side of the dock. Straight ahead and at the very far end of the dock stood an infected dead.

His back was to us, but you could always tell it was an infected dead instead of a live person even when they were standing still. They never could quite get their hips squared under them, and their shoulders were never even. This one also had at least four blue crabs hanging onto its legs. I hated to think of the number of times I had eaten blue crabs before this all started, and what they had been eating before they were caught.

The Chief raised one hand signaling us to stop. He closed his fist while it was still in the air, so we lowered ourselves to the ground and would stay until he signaled for us to come forward. He pointed at his eyes and then left and right, and that was our signal to keep him covered in case he didn't see something where the dock came ashore.

He moved fast for a big man, and I couldn't hear a single footstep as he quickly closed the distance between him and the infected standing at the end of the dock. I didn't think he was going to be able to stop once he had a full head of steam, but he lowered his right shoulder and connected with the unsuspecting dead man.

There was nothing graceful about the way the infected dead fell, but this one was about as close to graceful as one would ever get. The Chief came to a full stop, but the dead man shot through the air and did a nose dive into the water. Since he couldn't comprehend what was happening, he didn't try to put his hands out in front of him. It was deep enough at the end of the dock for him to disappear from view, and I didn't see his head bob back to the surface. We had reasoned a long time ago that some of them had less air trapped in their bodies, so they sank quicker than others.

The Chief signaled for us to come forward, and we didn't hesitate. We stowed our gear in the plane as quickly as we could, while Chief Barnes hopped into the Boston Whaler and did something under the dash where the ignition was located. Kathy and Jean boarded the plane followed by Chief Barnes as soon as he was done in the boat. I stood by ready to cast off the mooring line.

The plane really was a beautiful piece of work, and according to Chief Barnes, it was extremely reliable and was a de Havilland DHC-3 Otter. It could carry up to ten people, so we had plenty of room for gear or heavy cargo. On the off chance we would run into a survivor or two who was worth bringing back with us, it was at least a possibility.

The plane was yellow and white with a single engine that wasn't extremely fast, but it was powerful and got good range. It was known for its ability to do take offs and landings in a very short area. The side doors aft of the pilot's door made it much easier to cast off from the dock while boarding. The Chief did a quick preflight check and turned the starter switch to the on position. The engine sprang to life without a single stutter.

"Your Uncle Titus must have been a mechanical genius," the Chief yelled over the engine. "This thing purrs like a kitten." He had a broad, satisfied smile on his face as I pushed the plane away from the dock and climbed through the passenger door.

Chief Barnes turned and looked back at me and said, "You realize, of course, we may have run all the way out here to find this thing was all just for show."

"I don't know if that's a good thing or a bad thing," I said. "I did power up the plane once, but that was all. I thought about driving it around like a boat, but I was afraid I'd do something wrong and wind up having to swim back with the sharks."

It really hadn't occurred to me that the plane would power up but not fly, but since the house boat wasn't capable of going anywhere, I don't know why I thought the plane would actually be functional.

Kathy had situated herself in the front passenger seat and had found some headphones. She was connected to a radio, and she was already searching for signals.

"Kathy, don't transmit unless we know it's safe. Once we're in the air, we're going to be a target for anyone with a gun. It isn't easy to hit one of these things with the average rifle, but we don't want to advertise our location," said Chief Barnes.

"Sorry, Chief. I didn't think about that," she answered. "I'll scan for broadcasts, but I won't answer."

Chief Barnes rotated the plane until it was facing straight out to sea and powered up. He was in the air and banking to the right so fast I couldn't believe it.

He leaned toward us and said, "The faster we get away from the area the less likely someone will get a fix on where we came from."

We stayed even with the coast for a few miles and then came back over the dunes and trees at a south westerly course as we also gained altitude. If anyone saw us they would think we came from near this part of the coast instead of Mud Island.

When we reached our cruising altitude, Chief Barnes leaned over and signaled for us to all bring our heads together over a chart. He had marked the routes from Mud Island to Lake Moultrie and from Mud Island to the Naval Weapons Station in Goose Creek.

He pointed at both destinations and said, "It's almost a perfect triangle. Ninety miles to Lake Moultrie, ninety miles from Mud Island to Goose Creek, and ninety miles from Lake Moultrie to Goose Creek. I'd still like to fly towards the lake in case we have to land, but how about skipping the stop at Lake Moultrie and go straight for the main target? We should have more than enough fuel for the round trip."

"It's just a couple of hours one way," he added.

We all nodded our heads in agreement, and he plotted the course toward Goose Creek from Lake Moultrie. I felt a tug at my shirt, and turned to find Jean reaching to pull me back to my seat.

"Don't get the wrong idea, survivor boy," she said playfully. "We have work to do."

Jean pulled two sets of binoculars from her backpack and handed one to me. "We need to be watching out of both sides of the plane."

"Are we looking for anything in particular?" I asked.

"No, Baby, anything moving is worth knowing about, whether it's dead or alive."

I looked at her when she called me 'Baby,' and I got goosebumps. I had been a loner for so long that I didn't even know what to say, but Jean was happy to help me get used to the idea of being around other people, especially her.

She gave me a smile and put the binoculars to her eyes as she leaned toward the right side windows. I did the same out the left side and brought my binoculars into focus.

I immediately realized why Jean had said anything moving would be interesting. Everything I saw was sitting still. There were cars sitting still on roads, and there were dark shapes on and off the roads that had to be bodies, but nothing was moving. Visibility was very good, and the Chief kept the plane steady, so I had time to focus on details. There wasn't anything encouraging to report except the fact that there weren't any infected dead walking around, either.

Jean was the first to spot something moving, and it was close to the halfway point. There was a group of about six infected dead walking down a road. She watched until we were well past them to see if they reacted to the sound of the plane. Either we were too high, or they weren't interested, because they never looked up.

Time went by fast, and soon we were passing the small town of Moncks Corner. With a population of only about ten thousand people, there didn't seem to be any heavy concentrations of the infected. We saw them from both sides of the plane, but the largest group was in the Walmart parking lot.

We already had the discussion about Walmart when we were back in the shelter having a cozy drink around the kitchen table. I had told the others that Uncle Titus had talked about the apocalypse and how everyone would go to Walmart at the last minute because if you needed something, you could get it at Walmart.

Jean had asked, "Did you ever go to Walmart on Black Friday? It's brutal. Can you imagine what it would be like to go there when other customers weren't just trying to kill you, but to eat you?"

I had been to the Walmart we were flying over, and I remembered a lady taking things out of my shopping cart just because she wanted them, and it wasn't even Black Friday.

Now there were groups of the infected at different places around the outside. It looked like a group of them were trapped inside the garden section, and I figured they were going to be there for a long time.

Chief Barnes turned and told us that he was going to follow Highway 52 into Goose Creek and then turn east when we were parallel to the Naval Weapons Station. He said it should give them an idea of how bad it had gotten in the area. Goose Creek was only about forty-thousand people, and it was mostly suburban. The lack of an urban area would have given them at least a fighting chance at survival.

Kathy held up her hand to get everyone's attention. "Everyone listen up," she said. She put the radio on speaker so everyone could hear what was being said.

"Casualties are high, and the infection continues to spread. There is no known cure for being bitten. If you are bitten, and if you love the people you are with, you should do the right thing and off yourself before someone else has to, or even worse, before you bite someone you love."

Chief Barnes said, "Who is that, Kathy?"

"The person broadcasting said he was a pastor at some church. He said he was passing along information for the military, but I don't believe him. From the way he started the broadcast, I doubt the military even exists anymore," she answered.

"What did he say at the start of the broadcast?" I asked.

"He said this was a scourge brought on us by God for passing laws for same sex marriage," she said. "Doesn't sound like someone the military would use as a PR person. If the military was capable of passing along a message, it wouldn't come through this guy."

"Any military broadcasts?" asked Jean.

"No, and my guess would be that they will remain quiet," said Kathy.

"What makes you think the military will stay quiet?" I asked.

Chief Barnes answered for her. "It's only logical, Ed. The military got pushed back into disconnected units. Ships are at sea, bases are overrun, no word from a Commander in Chief, and not enough supplies to be taking in survivors. Not to mention the risk of the infection being able to get inside the places where they have dug in."

"Chief Barnes," I said, "How do we know the military won't fire on us?"

"We don't, Ed, but there's a pretty good chance they might want this plane, so they would rather take it from us than shoot it down. We should be safe while we're in the air. After we land, it's anybody's guess what they will do."

"The preacher and his friends, on the other hand, are more likely to try to bait us in for a closer shot. That's why they want us to think the military is with them," said the Chief.

By this time we had flown down Highway 52 past the town hall and police station. The surrounding area was all crowded with suburban neighborhoods. Two story, three bedroom houses in several designs were on both sides of the highway, and it was so strange to see everything so still.

Some of the houses had burned to the ground. Some fires had spread to neighboring homes and then consumed entire blocks. A few were still smoking, and I couldn't help but wonder what had happened to spark fires a month after everything fell apart. The stories on the ground probably included people who had survived the initial holocaust, only to be flushed out into the open by a shortage of supplies.

South Carolina doesn't typically have basements because the water table is so close to the surface, so people didn't have anywhere to go but up, and people wouldn't have had time to reach the Goose Creek Walmart or the hardware stores dotting the area to load up on supplies. Sooner or later someone would drag their barbecue grill inside their garage and set fire to the house.

It looked like there was still power to most of the area. There were some digital billboards over the intersections where people would have the longest waits at red lights, and the red lights were still working. There were plenty of cars sitting at those intersections, but they didn't go when the lights changed.

As we flew over the most heavily congested intersections, we could only imagine they way it had all played out, but I had seen it first hand in Surfside. It didn't look real, but it was.

There was an ambulance sitting at one intersection, and the back doors were still open. I remembered the EMT's rushing forward to help, only to be forced to turn and run when they became the victims who needed the help.

By the time the Chief banked to the left where Highway 52 met with St. James Avenue, we all felt like we had seen enough. Burned out homes, cars and trucks abandoned in the road, and the endless bodies. The only thing really absent were the infected dead that were conspicuous in their absence. We expected to see them everywhere, but there was nothing moving.

Our answer to where the infected had gone was answered soon enough. As we approached the main entrance of the Naval Weapons Station we saw them. They were everywhere.

The Chief had kept a respectable altitude in order to go unnoticed if possible. Kathy said, "Can you imagine the noise level down there? Must be a couple of thousand at least."

The Chief said to all of us, "In case you're wondering, there are plenty of good places to land on the river. I'm going to fly over the Weapons Station to get there. Kathy is going to be monitoring all channels in case someone tries to hail us. Jean, Ed, I need you two working those binoculars. Try to spot any kind of central command and control."

As we flew above the main road that drives through the heart of the Weapons Station, we saw that it wasn't laid out like a typical military base. The main gate is usually right up front, but to reach the actual restricted part of the base, there was a long straight road.

"Chief," I said as I tapped him on the shoulder, "why isn't there a big gate with concrete barriers or something."

Kathy leaned over to where we could all hear her and said, "Do you notice anything about the horde of infected dead?"

I looked down at Redbank Road which seemed to be straight as an arrow for miles and saw that the dead were spread out, and there were bodies mixed in with those that were still moving forward.

As I watched, Jean said, "Are you guys seeing this? It's like that great wall of infected reaches a specific point and then they drop over dead."

"Someone is shooting them," I said. "And they must be damned good shooters, because the bodies are really piling up."

Chief Barnes said, "Do you see why they don't need a gate, Ed? The infected have to walk a straight line for miles, and those heavy trees along both sides of the road must be jammed up with military snipers. If we were lower, we could probably hear them."

I put my binoculars to my eyes and watched the infected dropping to the ground. To the left and right sides of the road there were clear zones about fifty to one hundred yards wide. Then there were deep ditches, and then there were tall fences. Most of the shambling infected dead just stayed on the road and tried to keep moving forward, but they eventually were dropped by an expertly placed bullet.

Occasionally a pack of them would veer off to the right or left. If any weren't shot by the time they crossed the clearings, the ditches did the rest. None would be able to get out of the ditches to be able to test the fences.

Kathy had been using her headphones again, and her head suddenly popped up from the controls to the radio.

"Joint Command Naval Weapons Station say again," she said into the microphone that curved down in front of her mouth.

We all looked at her with surprise because the Chief had told her not to key up the microphone unless she had to.

Kathy paused as she listened to something in her headset, then she keyed up again.

"JC NWS, our destination is the Cooper River and the pier at Snow Point, over."

She switched on the speaker so we could all hear the response.

"Otter seaplane approaching JC NWS, I repeat, you do not have clearance to land. If you land, you will be fired upon, over."

"NWS we request permission to land and assist with NWS defense. I am a trained Charleston police officer. We have a civilian naval officer and a registered nurse on board. We would be an asset to your defense, over."

Kathy didn't say anything about me because I didn't really have anything going for me except that I owned a survivalist's dream home, a boat, a houseboat, and a seaplane. My skills at video games weren't really worth mentioning.

We all felt like we had the rug yanked out from under us. The military seemed to have taken a good stand at this location, but they weren't taking in guests.

Kathy tried again before they could answer.

"NWS we don't understand. We are infection free and can be of assistance. Please let us land, over."

The voice on the other end of the radio replied coldly, "Otter seaplane, JC NWS cannot support additional civilians at this time. We have weapons targeting your aircraft. When you reach the Cooper River, you will proceed east toward the Wando River. If you change course before you have reached the Wando River, you will be terminated, over and out."

The last three words were like saying there would be no further discussion.

As we passed over the end of Redbank Road, we saw a real military gate, but it wasn't as if they would actually need it. The target rich environment at the other end of the wide road was going to be the stopping point for most of the infected.

We saw the Cooper River up ahead, and Jean said, "Guys, look at this." She pointed southeast of our path toward Snow point, and we saw that the former submarine piers were back in business. There were several warships lined up around tenders, ships that serviced and supplied submarines and destroyers.

Chief Barnes said, "I didn't think this place would fall, so I don't understand why they won't let us land. It wouldn't be too hard to quarantine us until they were sure we were safe."

"Maybe that has something to do with it, Chief."

I pointed more to the northeast of the piers where an armada of private sailboats and power boats were crowded into one area. There were hundreds of them.

"Good God," said Kathy.

Her reaction was pretty much shared by all of us. The boats were littered with bodies, and a few still had infected dead on their decks. We saw a few fall overboard as we approached the middle of the Cooper River.

We were surprised when JC NWS came over the radio again.

"Otter seaplane, this is JC NWS, please be advised that our base has lost the capacity to contain the outbreak of the infection. We are withdrawing to the fleet of naval vessels at Snow Point. We are already limited with regard to our ability to provide assistance."

The radio operator sounded almost apologetic while explaining the circumstances below.

"The civilian vessels you see in the Cooper River are people who tried to seek military protection. Due to the relative isolation of the NWS facilities, we were able to provide shelter and protection, but the infection came over from Daniel Island on the private boats. That area is now known as the Deadhead Yacht Club. We advise that you continue on course as far up the Wando River and beyond as possible. There are no existing safe zones on the South Carolina coast, over and out."

Kathy keyed up one last time, "JC NWS, thank you for the information. Can you provide any further intel with regard to Naval Base at Kings Bay, Georgia or bases near Norfolk, Virginia, over?"

"Otter seaplane, that's a negative. Naval Station Jacksonville is also evacuating, over. Good luck to you and your friends."

Kathy took off the headset and sat it aside. We were passing over marshes and a few minutes later we could see the Wando River ahead. Chief Barnes stayed on a true course, not because he was afraid they would still shoot them down, but because it wouldn't do any good to turn back. The military was probably pulling its snipers away from the trees lining the road, and within a few hours they would be heading out to sea.

It would probably take a few days for the infected dead to walk all the way to the fortified gate, and maybe it would hold for a few more days, but Joint Command Naval Weapons Station had given up because people who had been bitten just weren't willing to do the right thing to keep it from spreading. I imagined many of them were even bitten by loved ones themselves.

******

We followed the Wando River until it became too narrow to land further ahead, and we were all surprised when the Chief gradually turned and brought the plane lower, then lined up for a landing.

The map showed that we were about a half mile up river from the Paradise Island public boat landing, but the Chief was taking us toward a private dock.

Kathy traced her finger along the path that matched ours and said, "You're trying to get us close to Wando Farms Road. Why, Chief?"

"Because someone must've gotten off a lucky shot. We've been losing power since we passed over the Weapons Station. It looks like we're walking from here," said the Chief.

Jean said, "Did anybody else see what I saw in the bunker area of the Naval Weapons Station?"

Kathy turned toward the back seats and said, "Yeah, I saw it, too. There were a lot of infected strolling around by the bunkers. Some of them were in uniform."

The bunkers were lined up in six rows with eight bunkers per row. Forty-eight bunkers originally intended for storage of the ballistic missiles that were shot out of submarines, were perfect to convert to be fallout shelters. The Navy probably evacuated the families who lived on base and stashed them in the bunkers.

It must've looked like a good idea at the time, but they undoubtedly suffered the same fate as all other bases. No one wanted to leave a bitten family member behind.

"I saw women and children wandering around between the bunkers," said Jean. "I also saw military snipers tracking us from the top of that big berm that surrounds the bunkers."

"In that case, I guess it wasn't just a lucky shot," said Chief Barnes.

"You said we have to walk from here, Chief. Any chance of fixing it?" I asked.

"Not much chance at all, Ed. There are a lot of things you can fix with string, but the problems that are related to engine pressure are usually major. If it's just an oil line, we can probably come back and repair it, but we won't know until I get a look at the damage."

I aimed my binoculars toward the tree line beyond the dock. I didn't see anything moving. The good news was that we were not in a populated area. The bad news was that people headed for the rural areas when everything hit the fan on the first day. I guess I was living proof of the thinking that it was safer out in the sticks if they didn't go to the same rural areas. We had heard on a news broadcast that most people tried to reach the mountains.

The dock was a long one that ran from the water right to the trees. It reminded me of my own dock because it seemed to just disappear once it reached the trees.

"Ok, folks. We're going to be pretty exposed as soon as we get out onto the dock. I need a few minutes to see if I can find a bullet hole. That will give us an idea about whether or not we're going to be coming back for the plane," said Chief Barnes.

Kathy jumped out onto the dock and tied us off. As soon as she had the rope in place, she laid prone on the dock and took aim at the trees. Jean laid down next to her and began searching the terrain with her binoculars.

I jumped out onto the left side pontoon and scanned the opposite shoreline. It was all marsh and mudflats, so there wasn't much chance that anything would reach us from that side, but I would be covering the Chief's back in case there were any living people in boats. Right now they were as dangerous as the infected because guns were as common in this area as toothbrushes.

Chief Barnes inspected quickly and found a bullet hole on his first pass.

"We're walking, everyone, but we can come back with some oil and hoses, and I'm pretty sure I can get this thing in the air again. I didn't fly it too far after we got hit, so I didn't burn up any cylinders."

"Movement in the trees," yelled Jean. She pointed for Kathy to see where she had spotted movement. It wasn't far from the end of the dock, and Kathy zeroed in on at least four infected dead. The shambling, jerking way of walking was a dead giveaway that they were infected dead and not living people.

Kathy took aim at the first one but waited to shoot. There was no sense in shooting them from so far away. A missed shot was wasted ammunition.

I went back through the cabin of the plane and laid down next to Kathy and Jean with my rifle aimed down the dock. Kathy said in a low voice, "Hold your fire unless I have a problem, Ed. Unless the woods are full of them, this should be like shooting fish in a barrel. You can help by getting a head count so I know what we're up against."

I laid my rifle aside and got my binoculars out, too. Jean was already scanning other gaps in the trees making sure there weren't more threats. I located the infected at the end of the dock and was surprised by how revolting they looked. They had a variety of injuries and looked like they had all been eaten to some extent.

"More coming up from behind the first row," Kathy. "I count eight, so far."

"Movement on the left," said Jean.

I shifted my binoculars to the left and found what Jean saw. "They're not using the dock," I said. "They're going to try to walk across the mud plain to get to us."

"Good luck with that," said Kathy. She had a really big smile on her face. "They're going to get stuck in the mud, and when the next high tide comes in they're going to have a lot of company. They may go slow by crabs finding them, or they might go fast if the alligators get to them first. The area really has a lot of gators."

The eight infected dead were making progress coming down the dock, but the ones in back were trying to push past the slower moving ones in front. The end result of a little pushing and shoving was that two went over the edge into the mud. They immediately sank deep enough to be stuck.

Kathy centered her crosshairs on the forehead of the infected dead that had pushed his way to the front.

"I'm going to drop Mr. Aggressive, and the others behind him will have to either go around him or trip over him."

She exhaled slowly and squeezed the trigger. Kathy had been a good shot at the police academy, but the rifles they had brought along were great for this kind of shooting. They didn't have much kick, so it was easy to stay on target.

The first of the infected dead fell perfectly in the middle of the dock. There was a neat pile up as the others began falling over each other. Two tumbled over the side and weren't going to be a problem again. The remaining three were trying to get their feet back under them as they crawled over the first one.

Kathy took careful aim and shot the second one. She immediately switched targets and took out one, then the other of the remaining dead. They were piled up in one general area and would serve as an effective barrier if more infected came along. That would give us a chance to unload our gear without being rushed too much.

Jean said, "I'll keep watch while you guys unload. I don't think we have to worry about people ambushing us since there were so many of the infected out here."

We were ready to start walking a few minutes later. The Chief had mapped out the best route to get back to my island. It looked like we were going to be walking a four lane highway most of the way, and there was only one town that would have a population large enough to cause us any concern. It looked like we were facing a sixty to seventy mile trip.

When we walked from the plane to the trees, we stepped carefully over the bodies of the infected that Kathy had shot. The ones that had fallen into the mud and the ones that had walked straight into the mud from the trees were all groaning loudly.

We all started exchanging looks at each other, all thinking the same thing. We needed to get clear of the area before more were drawn to us.

The Chief caught our attention and said, "We're only a little over a mile from Highway 17, but we're less than a mile north of the Paradise Boat Landing. There were probably a lot of people at the landing when the hammer went down. The woods south of here might be full of infected, and we have to get by them to get to our road. If they have been keeping to the road, they may be between us and Highway 17."

"And we just announced our arrival," said Kathy.

The four of us picked up the pace, but we moved quietly with our weapons up. At the end of the dock, we came into a circular clearing and were immediately spotted by another group of the infected.

"Keep moving," said Chief Barnes. "We have to go down Wando Farms Road. We don't have another choice." He sounded more calm than he felt.

We went straight toward the infected, and when we were in a comfortable kill zone, we came up along side each other and took aim. It didn't take seconds, and we were moving again.

Forty yards away we could see a barn, and to the right of that a big house. We veered toward the house, and Jean was the first to put into words what we were all hoping.

"Do you think there's a car?"

"If there is, and if we can find the keys fast enough, we can be back to the shelter by tonight instead of six days," I said.

"Let's get inside the house," said Kathy. "If we can get to the garage from the inside of the house we can look for the keys and be a bit more secure at the same time."

We all ran straight for the back door that was up on a small deck in the corner of an L shaped part of the house. Kathy told us to form up on her and follow her lead. She had been trained on the proper procedures for clearing rooms, and we had no problem letting her training pull us through this. That's why we were such a good combination. "The police officer, the pilot, the nurse, and the video gamer," I thought.

Kathy tried the door knob, and it was unlocked. She didn't waste any time, and she quickly cleared a family room. To the left was a large kitchen and dining room. At the back corner of the kitchen was a door, and she signaled for us to head that way.

When we got to the door, she gave hand signals that positioned us to the left, right and center. She pushed the door open and was ready to shoot immediately, having switched from her rifle to her pistol.

It was the garage, and there was a car, but the garage was literally crowded with infected dead. Kathy got off one shot, dropping the infected nearest to her, but she had no choice but to pull the door shut again.

Another of the infected had gotten close enough to grab her sleeve, and Kathy almost got pulled back into the garage, but she pulled so hard as she slammed the door that she wound up severing the arm of the infected at the elbow. The fingers were clenched shut on her sleeve, so Kathy had half an arm dangling from her wrist, and she was trying to shake it off.

I lunged for the swinging and swaying arm and tried to pull it off of her, and that probably saved my life. In the mayhem that had followed when Kathy opened the door, we hadn't seen the infected woman who had come from the hallway that led back to the bedrooms. We hadn't cleared the rest of the house because we weren't planning on staying. It was supposed to be find a car, find the keys, and hit the road.

The infected woman followed my movement as I went for the swinging arm. I changed directions several times, and so did she. I caught the arm at the exact moment that she grabbed me, and probably at the exact moment that Jean put a bullet through the side of her head.

Once I pulled the arm off of Kathy's sleeve, I turned and heaved it across the kitchen. It was then that I realized what had gone on behind me. I had actually thought Jean had grabbed me from behind instead of an infected dead. I felt faint when I saw what was laying at my feet.

In the meantime, Chief Barnes had moved into position to help Kathy get the door shut and locked. We could hear the infected pushing on the door, and I reminded myself of my mental note that it was safer to be in a room with the door opening outward instead of inward.

I looked at Jean who was still pointing her gun at the infected woman who had almost bitten me. It was the first time I saw real fear on her face, and it was because she knew we had almost lost each other.

"Ok, everyone, we have work to do," said Kathy. "We have to get those things out of the garage. We need to figure out how we're going to do that, but at least we can find the car keys first. Let's clear the rest of the house and see if we can get lucky."

I asked, "What if the keys are in someone's pocket out there in the garage?"

"We'll deal with it if that's how it goes down," she answered.

We formed back up on Kathy again and went toward a main hallway. The first turn on the left was the entry into the living room at the front of the house. It looked as if the residents had just walked out and left.

Kathy led the way toward the first bedroom. The door was open, and it had probably been where the infected woman had come from. A quick check of the room told us it wasn't the master bedroom, so we kept going.

There were two smaller bedrooms, one set up as an office of some sort. Both were closed and empty. The master bedroom was occupied.

As Kathy pushed open the door and stepped into her shooter stance, she saw a foot disappear under a king sized bed. At the same time, she thought she saw movement near the master bath. She kept her gun aimed into the room with her left hand, but she raised her right hand in a fist for us to stop. We all knew she saw something.

Kathy whispered, "The infected don't try to hide."

We all waited for her to make the next move, but I have to admit, I jumped more when she spoke than if she had pulled her trigger.

"Police. Come out from under the bed," she said. "You in the bathroom, get out here, too."

There was a brief pause before a girl's voice said from the bathroom.

"Don't shoot. I'm coming out."

At the same time that she hesitantly came out of the bathroom with her hands up, a man's head appeared from under the bed.

Kathy kept her eyes on them, but she said to us, "For some reason, I thought that would work better. Most people just automatically do what a police officer says when they need help."

The man raised his hands above his head after standing up.

"Please don't shoot," he said. "You can have anything you want. Just take it and let us go."

"Are you bitten?" Kathy asked in an authoritative voice.

They both shook their heads vehemently, obviously aware of the consequences of saying yes. "No, no, we're fine. We've been stuck in here in the bedroom ever since that one zom......thing got inside."

He got stuck on what to call the infected dead, and for a moment it sounded like he was going to say, "Zombie".

Chief Barnes stepped in with Kathy and said, "Strip."

Both of them looked at him like they didn't understand at first, and then the man looked at the woman and back to the Chief.

"If you think you're going to......," he managed to stammer out before the Chief interrupted him.

"Do you think we just plan to have some fun with you two? I've got news for you," he bellowed. "You're not my type."

Jean was grinning a little when she stepped in front of the Chief. She put one hand onto the Chief's massive chest and pushed gently as she said to the man, "From the way you reacted, I'm guessing you two are married?"

They both nodded their heads and edged a little toward each other.

"Yes, we are. Mark and Becky Harrison. This is my parents' house. We don't know what happened here, but we came out here from Charleston to get away from those things. When we got here we found everyone in the house was dead and walking around like that. We trapped them in the garage, but that's where we parked our car, so we couldn't leave."

Jean held up one hand to stop him and said, "We're pressed for time, Mark, so let's get down to business. You cooperate, and maybe you leave here with us. You don't cooperate, and maybe we leave you right here."

Becky Harrison wanted no part of staying in the house and stepped forward. "We'll do whatever you say."

"Then strip," said the Chief.

Jean and Kathy both gave him a withering look, and for the first time I saw who was really in charge in our group. I guess I should have known after the way Kathy had handled the pier in Charleston.

Jean said, "I'm a nurse, and before we go anywhere together, I'm going to examine both of you for bites. If you think it's giving me a thrill, you're wrong. The Chief and Ed can wait in the hallway. Now, do as the man said and strip."

The Chief and I backed into the hallway, but as we did, I said, "Ask them about car keys."

He turned to me and asked, "What kind of idiots would trap them in the garage with their only form of transportation?"

About ten minutes later, Kathy and Jean emerged with the good news that they were bite free. Kathy had holstered her weapon, and she had a set of car keys that fit with the Chevy Suburban in the garage.

"The gas tank is almost empty, but Mark said his father always kept a few five gallon gas cans in the barn. That means we're going to be stuck with going outside, but it beats stopping for gas on the way home if there's a problem and we have to take a long detour," she said.

"We need to figure out how to get the car out of the garage, but we also need to start thinking about what we're going to do if we aren't on the road soon. I don't want to try making it back after it gets dark," said the Chief.

He looked at Mark and Becky and asked, "Other than the infected in the garage, how have things been around here?"

Mark answered, "We were trying to figure out how to do exactly what you just said when that one thing got into the house somehow. Then we got cornered in the bedroom."

"I'm going to go check for open windows," I said. "We might have missed something."

"I'll go with you," said the Chief. "The rest of you stay back here where Kathy can pick your brains about how you would get to the car."

The Chief and I set off on our search and found a sliding glass door that was behind curtains. Because it was on the front of the house and not the back, everyone had assumed it was a set of windows. I slid the door shut and locked it. We both exchanged looks that sheepishly said we were going to have to do better, and that we had been lucky.

When we got back to the master bedroom, everyone was sitting on the bed.

Kathy said, "Mark is a contractor. He says the wiring for the garage door opener can be reached by going through a wall near the door. We can open the garage door, draw them outside, then lower the door again."

"Sounds like a good plan," said the Chief, "but first we need to get the gas from the barn. While we're doing that, someone figure out how we can lure them out of the garage."

"How do you plan to get to the barn?" asked Jean.

"I think we have to make a run for the barn. Two of us can carry gas cans while two can provide cover," said Kathy.

I said, "Wait a minute, Kathy. What are we going to do with them while we're getting the gas? We don't know them well enough just to believe they're going to open the door when we get back." Mark looked like he was going to say something, but Kathy cut him off.

"Mark's going with us," she said. "As a matter of fact, he's in the lead since he knows the fastest way in and out of the barn. He also knows where the gas is. When we get back, Becky will open the door."

We gathered at the back door and got ready to make the run.

Kathy said in a low voice, "Mark will be in the lead without a gun, so Chief and I will flank him. We're not trying for quiet, we're trying for fast, but we're also not going to shoot unless we have to. Everyone get your machetes out, and we'll switch to pistols if it gets populated. Any questions?"

"One last thing," she said. "We don't have to kill these things. We only have to incapacitate them long enough for us to get by them, going out and coming back."

Kathy pulled open the door, and Mark slipped quietly onto the porch. We were still blocked from the view of the barn, so we wouldn't know until we rounded the corner if it was going to be good or bad. We could see the trees back in the direction of the dock, and the nearest infected we could see was at least fifty yards away.

When we rounded the corner we only had about thirty or forty yards to go, but there were at least six infected between us and the barn. Kathy and the Chief moved slightly ahead of Mark, and with precision I didn't believe possible, they took out the legs of the infected.

Kathy called back to us in a voice just loud enough for us to hear, "We go around them on the way back."

Jean and I gave the infected dead a wide berth as we went by. They were all reaching for us and snapping their jaws.

Mark pulled up even with Kathy and the Chief and led them to a single door. The larger barn doors were on the other side of the barn and would draw much more attention if they were opened.

Chief Barnes asked, "Are there any in the barn?"

"I don't have a clue," answered Mark, "but the barn is one big room, so there's no place to hide. If anything is in there, at least we'll know as soon as we get in there with it."

Kathy stepped up and moved Mark to the side. Now that they were at the barn, he didn't need to be in the lead. She pushed the door wide open but held back without going in. All she could see going from a bright sunny day into the barn was total darkness.

Kathy said back over her shoulder, "We could have used a flashlight."

"I have one," said Jean. Everyone looked at her with the same look.

"What?" She said. It seemed our group had a knack for looking innocent.

Despite the fact we were barely concealed along the side of a barn in the middle of nowhere, facing the prospect of a terrible death at any moment, we all smiled and shared one of those rare moments that can only come from the bond that forms between people who have their backs against the wall. All except Mark who was looking at us as if we were nuts.

Jean passed the flashlight to Kathy. She clicked it on, and it put out a surprising amount of light for its size. Kathy traded her machete in for her gun and pointed the flashlight along the barrel of the gun. She eased into the darkness listening for movement.

There was a tense moment when Mark fell over a body on the floor. He landed awkwardly on top of the body and tried to scramble away. As he did, he was making a crying, panicked sound. We all rushed in with our machetes poised to strike at whatever was attacking him, and in the glow of the flashlight it really looked like the body on the floor was trying to bite him. We probably each hit it twice before we realized it was dead. Kathy kept circling trying to get off a clean shot.

When the noise all died down, the Chief pulled Mark free from the body. He picked him up and got his hand over Mark's mouth trying to get him to be quiet.

The Chief said to him in serious voice. "If you bite me, I'll snap your neck. Now, shut up."

There was a big John Deere mower in the garage. There was also something that looked like a gas powered garden tiller, and off to one side was a row of five gallon gas cans. I grabbed one and the Chief let go of Mark to scoop up another. Everyone else did the same, so we had five cans total. That would be a lot more than we needed, but we were already learning that more was better than less. There wasn't any reason to hang around, so we made it back out the door without a word.

Nothing got in our way as we ran back, and we gave a wide berth to the group of disabled infected that had been dropped by Kathy and the Chief on the way to the barn. They had managed to crawl a short distance toward the barn, but we had no problem getting around them.

Becky was watching as we approached and timed her opening of the door perfectly. Kathy didn't look like she even had to break stride. I was the last one through this time, and Becky closed and locked the door just as fast.

The next step in our plan was to cut through the sheetrock to get to the wiring that controlled the garage door. The missing ingredient was how to draw the infected out of the garage.

Mark suggested that the infected would wander out on their own. Without telling Mark and Becky about how we had watched the infected stand stock still for hours on our closed circuit TV system, we just told them we knew for fact that an open door wasn't necessarily enough incentive to get them to move.

Becky followed Mark's suggestion by saying a boat horn would be loud enough to draw them outside. The four of us stared at her as if she was an alien.

"How have you two survived since this all started?" asked Kathy. "Do you think we want to make enough noise to draw every infected dead within miles to the driveway?"

"There's really only one way," I said. "I'll go out the front door, run past the open garage doors, and circle the house. I'll come in through the back door. As soon as the last one clears the garage into the driveway, you guys can drop the doors and load the car. I'll go right through the house to the car."

Jean got around in front of me and asked, "Are you crazy. What makes you think we're going to let you commit suicide for the rest of us?"

I thought she looked adorable in her coveralls with a rifle on her back and a pistol on her hip.

"No, he's right," said Kathy. "When I was on the dock in Charleston trying to think of a way to get everyone onto the ship before the mobs of infected broke through, I knew it had to be something crazy. We don't want to draw them out with noise, so it has to be a warm body."

Jean grimaced, "God, do you have to say it like that?"

Kathy looked at each of us one at a time.

"Ed looks like the only one of us who could run fast enough if he has to, but I have a suggestion, Ed."

She had that look on her face that we had come to expect. She was a natural at tactics and had proven it repeatedly since the first day of the infection.

"Ed, instead of running around to the back of the house, do you think you could run straight down Wando Farms Road? We don't know if they will keep following you once you go around the corner of the house. They might follow you to the corner and then turn around and come back."

I may have spent too much time playing video games, but I wasn't in terrible shape, so I said, "I think I can manage that. You said it's only a mile or two?"

"Yes," said the Chief. "The road is straight, so they would be able to see you for a long time. We can load the car and catch up with you long before you reach Highway 17."

Jean wasn't happy about the plan, but no one could come up with anything better. The only thing left to do was cut the hole in the sheetrock and find the wiring for the garage doors.

Mark carefully located the right spot and slowly pushed the sharpest kitchen knife into the sheetrock, being careful not to make any noise or to cut the wires.

Jean asked, "How are we going to know if all of the infected actually leave the garage? I mean, some of them may not be interested."

I tried to joke about it and commented that any infected dead in its right mind would want to eat me.

"Not funny," said Jean.

Mark said, "I thought of that already. I can put a small hole into the sheetrock on the garage wall that should give us enough of a view to see them leave."

"But not the entire view of the garage, right?" Jean obviously didn't want me to be the bait for this part.

Kathy put her foot down and said, "Jean, we don't have much choice. Anything else would be too noisy. We're going to have all of our gear and the gas cans ready to go. Once they go out the door after Ed, we aren't even going to waste time shutting the doors. If any are still in the garage when we go out through that door, we'll put them down. Now, let's do this."

Now that the decision was final, everyone got into position ready to do their jobs. Once Mark got the doors going up, he would quietly make the hole for them to see through. The noise from the doors would probably start drawing them away from the door to the house.

From my vantage point at the front door, I could see the garage doors. The infected didn't have a lot of mobility, so they would probably wait until the doors were high enough before they would walk out. If any crawled out before the doors were higher, I figured I could avoid them long enough to draw the attention of the others.

Kathy stuck her head around the corner and said, "We're ready in here. You okay?"

"Let's do this," I said.

She gave me her most reassuring smile. I tried to give her one back, but both of us knew it was weak looking. She disappeared again, and I got ready to open the front door.

It seemed like an eternity, but the garage doors started going up with a rattle. I could see the feet of the infected as the doors rose higher, then the knees were visible. They began gathering at the opening as both doors went up at the same time. I didn't see any trying to crawl under the doors, which was a relief.

Inside the house, Kathy was at the door with her gun in her left hand and the machete in her right. She would quietly disable if she could, and she would shoot to kill if she had to.

Behind Kathy was the Chief. He had both of the gasoline cans in his hands. The plan was that he would open the rear door of the big Suburban, load the cans, and then move to the driver side, open the passenger door as he went by it, and then get in the driver seat.

Jean and Becky were both loaded down with gear and fuel and would follow on the heels of the Chief. Jean would drop her gear if Kathy needed help with stragglers, and Becky was told not to stop for anything. Follow the Chief, load the gear and go around to the passenger door on the driver side.

Mark's part of the plan was to grab the last of the gear and follow Jean and Becky through the door. Plan B was for Mark to start lowering the doors if anything went wrong, and they couldn't contain the infected.

When the doors were high enough, the first of the infected began to wander outside into the sunlight. It was now or never, so I yanked open the door and ran straight past the garage. Almost as one, the infected flowed out after me.

I almost ran straight into one that was coming around the far side of the house. If I had been looking back at the infected to see if they were still following, I would have.

Frankly, I was too afraid to look back, and unless these infected could sprint, I was going to outrun them. My heart was pounding so hard, and I had so much adrenaline pumping through my body that I felt like I could run all the way back to Mud Island. It crossed my mind that I was going to have a heart attack and drop over. My friends would drive up in the Suburban and find me on the pavement being chewed on by a group of slow infected dead.

Back in the garage, Kathy had heard Mark saying it was all clear, but she expected to find at least one or two of the infected hanging around inside the doors. She dove into the garage with her machete raised, but she could see the last of the infected disappearing down the driveway following Ed. For a moment she didn't know what to do, then something clicked and she went into motion.

The Chief was already in the driver seat. Becky was in her seat behind him, and Mark was just finishing putting the last of the gear into the back of the Suburban and closing the door. By some miracle, they were making it look easy.

Everyone's heart stopped, and Kathy felt her mouth go dry when the Chief turned the ignition key. The engine turned over, but it didn't start. That was the one thing they had all taken for granted.

I was still running fast but starting to slow down. There was a stitch in my side that I knew would only get worse as I ran, so I slowed my pace just a bit. I looked back and saw a small army of the infected dead following me.

I had a good buffer between myself and them, so I stopped to watch and catch my breath. I was pretty sure I should be seeing the Suburban come out of the garage by now, but there was nothing happening back there. From my angle, I couldn't see inside the garage doors, so I had no idea if they were having to go to plan B, or if they would be appearing at any moment.

I turned around to see if I could tell how far I was from Highway 17. My heart almost went ahead with the heart attack when I saw that the infected were on the road ahead of me, too.

Back in the garage, the Chief looked at the ignition like he could will the engine to start, and maybe he could, because the engine jumped to life when he turned it again. As soon as it started, the Chief threw it into drive and shot out of the garage.

I was only vaguely aware of the sound of the engine. I was busy trying to gauge the speed of the groups of infected to see which would reach me first. When the Suburban reached the first group of infected dead, the Chief just drove around them and pulled right up next to me. I looked at the big vehicle as if I wasn't sure what to do.

Jean leaned out of the back passenger door and said, "Hey, sexy. Want to go for a ride?"

I didn't need to be asked again and gratefully climbed inside with her. The Chief hit the gas, and we were on our way.

******

A quick check of the map confirmed we were only about sixty miles from home, and almost all of it was on the four lane highway. We would be forced to drive slowly in the places where we couldn't see too far ahead and in the small towns, but it would only be two hours of driving if we averaged thirty miles per hour. After the tension of the last hour, I was glad to melt against Jean in the back seat.

Everyone was quiet for what seemed like forever. I think everyone went into their own private world for a bit. We all had to digest what had happened.

Our new members of the group had the sense to keep quiet, too. I think they were trying to figure out where they stood with the rest of us. We gave them jobs to do, but we didn't give them weapons, and we weren't exactly sharing information with them.

I think our group felt like we would know more about them by the time we reached our turn to Mud Island. If the right things weren't said and done in the next two hours, we could always give them the car and a few supplies when we reached the spot where the road ended. They would never be able to come back and figure out where we went.

Highway 17 was a mess in some places and clear in others. We came to our first traffic jam only five miles into the trip. About a hundred cars were lined up behind an accident that had probably stopped people from escaping the area.

Everyone who saw the news and the attacks in the Charleston area had an idea of where they wanted to be. Some were probably just trying to go anywhere but closer to the deaths, and some might have been trying to reach relatives. People like Mark and Becky Harrison.

The Chief began easing onto the grass median to get past the rows of cars. Most of them were side by side like they were lined up to start the pace lap in a stock car race. As we got closer to the front the cars were pointed toward the sides of the road, and some were already in the grass. Those drivers could see what was ahead, and they had tried to get around it.

The front pile up was the wreck and all the trimmings, just like what I had seen on the first day in Surfside. Police cars, fire engines, and EMT trucks dominated the scene, but the bodies were what stunned us the most. Despite the level of decay, the causes of death were obvious. There were none still walking around, but the infected that had walked away were still out there somewhere.

We were all scanning the trees on both sides of the highway as the Chief cautiously passed the last of the accident and pulled back onto the blacktop. The road was clear ahead, and he accelerated again. We passed a few bodies of people who had probably tried to run from the infected. As a matter of fact, there was something odd about how they all seemed to make it only so far.

"Anyone else seeing something wrong with this picture?" I asked.

Kathy, Jean, and the Chief all said, "Yes," at the same time.

Kathy finished the answer for the group.

"They ran but didn't get away. Why?"

We wanted to get back to Mud Island, but we also wanted to know what had happened. It could be information useful to our own survival. The Chief stopped just beyond the last of the bodies, and we piled out to get a closer look.

Some were face down and had bite marks, but none had been eaten. They had bullet entry wounds on their chests and heads, but all of them had been shot as they ran forward. These were not infected dead. They had been shot to keep them from coming forward.

Kathy said, "I'm going to venture a guess that there was a defensive line across the road to keep these people from coming north. They shot the first vehicles, the rescue vehicles joined the party, and the people on the blockade stood their ground."

Jean asked, "Do you think we need to worry about running into them?"

"No," said Chief Barnes. "This was a long time ago."

"What makes you so sure the same people aren't waiting for someone like us up the road?" I asked.

"Think about it for a minute, Ed. We've seen a military installation armed to the teeth go under to the infected. It gets inside behind your lines no matter how hard you try to keep it out. If the military can't keep this thing out, some militia isn't going to."

The four of us hadn't been away from the Suburban for more than three minutes, and we turned as one when we heard the engine start to turn over. Three of us were paralyzed by the sound, but the Chief had moved fast for a big man.

He reached the driver's side door and pulled it open. In one smooth move he had Mark by the hair and yanked him out of the car and into the median.

"I wasn't doing anything," yelled Mark. "I was only trying to keep the engine running in case we had to get away from here fast." Mark knew his life was on the line. His plea was reasonable, but his guilt was obvious. He was trying to leave us behind. "You heard it yourself," he said. "The car wouldn't start again. We're screwed."

"No, we're not screwed, meathead, but you are. I didn't know if we could trust you, so I pulled an ignition wire off as we got out. I left the keys to see if you would jump on the chance to screw us over, and I got my answer." The Chief punctuated his revelation with a punch straight to the middle of Mark's face. It didn't take a second punch.

Becky was screaming and trying to jump on the Chief's back. Kathy's police training came through for her as she grabbed Becky and immobilized her face first on the ground.

Becky joined Mark in their collective begging, but Kathy smacked her on the side of the head and told her to shut up. It wasn't her finest moment given her training, but she was thinking about how they would have just driven away and left them. Becky trailed off into sniffling and sobbing. She was mumbling something about being sorry, but none of us were buying it.

The Chief left Mark where he was and went back to the open car door. He leaned in and reconnected the ignition wires then tested it by turning the key. It immediately started, and we got back in.

"You can't leave us here with nothing," yelled Mark. "We helped you."

Jean lowered her window further and said to them both, "We would have gotten out of that house without your help, you jerk."

The Chief added, "A favor is only as good as what you have done for us lately, man, and what you've done lately really stinks. You two are on your own."

We drove away with Mark half-heartedly running behind us and Becky on her knees in the grass. She looked like she was praying, but I think she was still begging. I don't think either of them were aware of the two or three dozen infected dead that were emerging from the trees. We could have saved them in time, but I looked around at the faces of my companions, and I wasn't seeing mercy.

My moment of guilt was more for the realization that Jean and I had the whole back seat to ourselves than for leaving them behind to die, and I had no doubt they were going to die. We didn't waste any time getting comfortable, and for at least a while, the world felt right again.

We drove without another incident for a long time. There were plenty of accidents and plenty of bodies, but nothing indicated any of the scenes had played out recently. Most of the time there were trees lining both sides of the road, and they weren't just window dressing with communities hidden behind them. This part of South Carolina was mostly state parks, national forests, and flood plains.

The bridges over the South Santee River and the North Santee River were the biggest concern for the Chief. He asked me to show Kathy and Jean on the map.

"It's the one place I would put a trap if I had a need to do so," said the Chief.

Both bridges were long enough to defend, and there was a straight stretch of marshland and woods between the two rivers. There was nowhere to go if you were trapped in between. We approached the first bridge at about fifty miles per hour, and all four of us were nervous but ready. Three of us had windows down and weapons in position.

We crested the highest point on the bridge and saw nothing but clear road ahead. The Chief put his foot down on the gas and we rocketed up to eighty. I think he wanted to put this part of the trip behind us as quickly as possible.

We made it over the first bridge and rapidly covered the distance between the two bridges. It looked like we were going to rocket over the second bridge, but the Chief slammed on the brakes so hard that we almost fell off the back seat. Chief Barnes turned the wheel and eased us over to the center and then he brought us to a stop just below the top of the bridge.

He leaned over the center console and said to the rest of us, "I would make someone believe they were home free by not having anyone on the first bridge, but I would have a spotter way off to the left or right side of the second bridge. Right now, if someone is on the other side, they're wondering where we went because they can't see the center of the bridge."

"We can't just sit here," said Kathy.

"I know, but we can get a look at what's over there first. If it's a small enough group, we probably have enough firepower to handle them," he answered.

We all got out and ran crouched over until we were close to the top the bridge, then we crawled the rest of the way. The Chief signaled for the rest of us to wait while he eased himself the last couple of feet. He held out a hand with two fingers up, and crawled backward toward us.

"These guys are stupid," he said. "They're actually walking up the bridge. They're already within range for me to drop them, but there's no way a sniper could be in position to hit us because we're so high."

Kathy said, "Take them out or let them walk all the way first?"

Chief Barnes smiled. "I'm thinking we let them walk all the way and then disarm them and see what we can learn. They're either totally dumb, or they have an army so big that we're not getting through unless they let us."

"How are we going to know which it is even if we capture them," asked Jean? "They could lie."

"We'll cross that bridge when we come to it," said the Chief.

Kathy, Jean, and I let out a collective groan at the bad pun because he said it with such a straight face.

"What?" He asked. There was that innocent look again.

None of us dignified him with an answer, so he gave us a look that said, "Whatever," and crawled back to the crest of the bridge.

Even though we were below the Chief and flat to the ground, we could tell how it played out. The Chief eased his M-16 to his shoulder and said to the approaching men, "Put your weapons on the ground, your hands on your heads, and come on up."

One of them answered loud enough for us to hear, "There are over a hundred of us at the bottom of the bridge."

The Chief answered them, "And you were expendable? Now, I told you what to do, and I expect you to do it."

Within about a minute the two men came into view of the rest of us. They paused when they saw three more M-16's aimed at them, but the Chief said, "Keep walking until you're all the way over the top."

We kept our guns on them until they were well past us and out of view from the other side.

The Chief said, "Talk to them Kathy. I'll keep watch for any friends they may have."

Once again, the two men seemed surprised by the handoff of authority. Kathy told them to sit but to keep their hands on their heads. They did as they were told, and I circled around behind them. Jean moved to a position behind Kathy.

Both men were middle aged, somewhere around forty-five. The one to Kathy's left spoke first and said, "You all seem to work well together. Want to join up with us?"

"No, but thanks for the offer," said Kathy. "We're just passing through."

The one who had spoken first looked at the other. I was thinking they had seen their share of people drive over the bridge, but we were the first to stop. This was new behavior to them, and they were unsure of themselves.

Kathy said, "Here's the deal, gentlemen. All we want is to be on our way. If we don't leave soon, we're spending the night on this bridge. If we spend the night here, I'm throwing you over the rail."

I saw them exchanging looks again, and there seemed to be an unspoken decision. The one who had asked us to join them said, "Okay, we don't have a hundred guns at the bottom of the bridge, but we have enough. What we want is to keep infected from coming into our area."

"We're not getting naked for you if that's what you're asking for," said Kathy. "Let me introduce myself. I'm Officer McGinley from the Charleston PD. I know things have really changed in the last month, but you probably don't know just how much. We just came from Goose Creek, and the Naval Weapons Station has been overrun. All we want is to pass through."

"So," said the man, "you're Kathy McGinley?" He asked her as if he knew her name. "If you're Kathy McGinley, how the hell did you get to Goose Creek. The last time we saw you, you were sailing away into the sunset on a cruise ship."

It was our turn to be uncertain, but I knew what was going on since I saw the news broadcasts from a place not too far from here. I couldn't have been the only survivor watching as the drama played out at the cruise terminal.

"Kathy," I said. "They were watching the same channel I was. They saw you on TV."

One turned halfway to me and asked, "What channel was that?"

"I don't know," I said. "I'm not from this area, and the man doing the news didn't give the station's call letters. They were too busy trying to stay alive."

He studied me for a moment and said, "One more question. What happened at the station?"

"No idea," I answered. "I haven't tuned in for a long time." I wasn't going to tell him about the last time I saw the station on the air because I didn't know if it was safe for them to know that I had been holed up somewhere in the area.

He turned back toward Kathy who asked him, "Satisfied?"

"I'm not sure what you mean," he said. "Satisfied by what?"

"You know what happened in Charleston, and I think you know I'm telling you the truth, but I can't really prove it," she said.

The man who hadn't spoken yet said, "You don't look like the lady they interviewed on the ship."

"And that would be because I wouldn't give the reporter an interview," said Kathy. "I could have known that from watching the broadcasts, but that lady right there was a nurse on that ship, and the big guy up there was a Chief on board, too." She gestured toward Jean and the Chief.

The first guy asked again, "So, how did you wind up in Goose Creek, and then up here on this bridge? You never answered before."

"It's a long story, and there's nothing in it that would prove to you who I am, so why bother?"

"What happened to the ship?" He asked.

"You know what happened," she said. "The same thing happened that happens everywhere, but when it happens on a ship, things get bad in a hurry. We got off in time." Kathy didn't clarify how I fit into the picture. It was better to let them assume I was a passenger.

"If you know what happens," said the spokesman, "then you know why we can't just let you pass through."

Kathy was smart, and she showed it with her next question. "If any of us in this little group has been bitten, would we let them tag along, or would we take care of the problem ourselves?"

The other guy asked, "Why does that prove anything, lady?"

"It doesn't prove a thing," she said. "It just shows that we understand your dilemma. Now, you have to decide if you're going to let us pass through."

They didn't look like they were ready to make the hard decision, and the spokesman asked, "If we say we will, you're just going to let us go?"

Jean answered before Kathy could, "What choice do we have? There are still good people alive in this world, and killing you wouldn't be our first choice."

Kathy moved up closer to them, probably so they could see her eyes when she spoke.

"Put your hands down. You're arms must be getting tired."

They both gratefully brought their hands down. The man who had done most of the talking asked if he could reach into his pocket. With me still behind them and Jean keeping a close eye on them, Kathy just nodded.

He pulled out a small radio and slowly put it up to his face.

"Jason, this is Hampton. We're going to be riding back. Tell everyone to stand down and let the vehicle pass. They'll drop us off after we cross the Waccamaw River. Tell all check points it's a green Suburban, and Kathy McGinley of the Charleston PD is with us."

We were all caught off guard by the sudden generosity. An escort to the other side of the Waccamaw River meant we would be protected crossing three more bridges as well as going through a city without getting shot at. Georgetown wasn't big, but there were plenty of guns. Hunting deer was a way of life here, so there would be scopes and good shooters.

We were also surprised at the extent of the recognition given to Kathy. The people of this area considered her to be a hero.

Kathy said, "You control Georgetown?"

"Yes," said Hampton, "but only because we were lucky. The infected poured south from Surfside toward Pawley's Island, and we retreated to the bridge over the Waccamaw River."

"But how did you get control of a whole town?" I asked. "We all know what's happening. People get bitten, and relatives don't turn them in. Next thing you know, someone else gets bitten."

"That's what happened on the ship," Kathy added.

Hampton lowered his eyes to his hands and then looked up at Kathy.

"It's what she said about there being good people left in the world. It's only a matter of time before someone gets through with the infection, or there's already someone inside our lines who has it but isn't telling. That's more likely the case, so to answer your question, I have no illusion that we have control over a whole town, but we can try. Right? Until that time, we need to remember to be good people."

Kathy called out to the Chief that we were loading up, so he came back down to us. "Your people must want you to come back in one piece. Nothing has moved down there," he said.

He held out his hand to Hampton and helped him from the pavement.

"I'm Chief Joshua Barnes, that's Jean and Ed's behind you. It appears you know Kathy."

"Only by reputation," said Hampton. "That was one of the only broadcasts along the coast, and everyone saw what she did. It's a shame that it didn't turn out better. Any other survivors?"

"Not that we know of," said Kathy. "When it went to hell, it went fast. If not for the Chief, I wouldn't have made it out."

"This is Ward," said Hampton. "He's been with me since this started. He may be more skeptical than I am, but he's a good guy." Ward grunted at the comment, but he gave everyone a half smile.

We shook hands all around and headed for the car. We weren't far from Mud Island, but we all wanted to be back before the sun went down. It was hard to believe it had only been since that morning that we loaded up the seaplane and set out for the Naval Weapons Station.

There was plenty of room in the car, and I couldn't sense any tension for the first time today. With escorts, we would be to the end of the road by Mud Island in no time.

******

When we passed the guards at the bottom of the bridge there were mostly friendly waves. Some of the people actually yelled at Kathy and asked for her to look their way so they could get a picture. Kathy looked at Hampton, and he shrugged his shoulders at her as if to say, "What did you expect?"

"Did you think I was the only one who saw the broadcasts, Officer McGinley? Hell, there's more than one family going around telling people they had relatives on that ship. Fact is, we'll never know, will we?"

Jean asked, "How many people do you figure you have in this town, Hampton?"

"Georgetown had a population of about nine thousand before that day when everything went crazy, but that includes everyone who was at work when it happened. A lot of people were at their jobs in Pawley's Island, Surfside, and Myrtle Beach. Being a weekday meant folks weren't home when people started biting people, and families started trying to evacuate at the same time people started trying to get home from work," said Hampton.

"When the infected started pouring down from Surfside, a lot of them were people who lived in Georgetown and got caught up in the traffic jams. Those who got out of their cars and started walking got into trouble when they couldn't get away from the big herds of the infected," he added.

I asked, "Hampton, where were these traffic jams?" I was secretly dreading that we were going to be blocked on Highway 17 and be forced to walk part of the way.

"We sent out some of our best people to have a look, and just shy of Simmonsville the road is pretty much blocked. They said too many people had tried to cross over to the North side of the highway, and that caused a traffic jam in the median and all of the lanes. We decided that the best thing to do was to leave it alone. It's not a great barrier, but it will slow down trouble from that direction, living or dead," he said.

I liked Hampton and trusted him, but I didn't want to give away the fact that we weren't going all the way to Simmonsville. He might be trustworthy, but if he said something to the wrong person, word might get around.

If Georgetown fell apart the same way everywhere else did, more than a few people might get the idea that we could take them in. If I was correct, our turn toward the island would be less than a mile before the traffic jam Hampton was talking about. That meant we also reaped the benefit of another barrier from the North.

We passed the small town airport, took a small bridge over a smaller river that I didn't see the name of, then reached downtown Georgetown. The road took a sharp turn toward the East and went straight at the ocean. Along both sides of the road we saw people boarding up homes and businesses. The population of this small town was preparing for a siege.

Word hadn't spread this far, so people didn't know there was a celebrity in the car. Most didn't even look in our direction, and none bothered to wave. I figured we would find out soon enough what they were waiting for, but I was surprised that the stream of infected dead hadn't made it to this area yet.

Kathy asked Hampton, "Is that our bridge up ahead?"

He answered, "No, that's the first bridge over the Great Pee Dee River, then we'll come to the second bridge over the Waccamaw River. If we get a large horde like the one you described at the Naval Weapons Station, we're going to drop the Waccamaw bridge and fall back to the one over the Great Pee Dee. We already have the charges in place. Our scouts have told us there's a real mess above the big traffic jam, but it hasn't overflowed yet."

Before we had completely crossed the bridge over the Great Pee Dee River, we could see the Waccamaw bridge. I think we were all just a bit excited to be getting so near to our home, but I felt bad for Hampton. While we would be safe in our shelter, this area was going to be the next to go. From what we had seen, dropping the first bridge would buy them some time, and dropping the second bridge was going to buy them even more, but the result was inevitable. The infection was probably already on the wrong side of the bridges.

A couple of hundred yards past the end of the Waccamaw bridge was a solid line of trees, and the highway changed from being two lanes back to four with a wide grassy median.

Hampton motioned for the Chief to pull over to the side of the road where a group of men had set up a check point. They had hunting rifles with scopes aimed down the road, and a few of the men had set up deer stands to use as watch towers. It looked like a good set up because a horde in the numbers that had overrun the Weapons Station would be restricted to the road.

Tidal plains expanded outward on both sides of the road, and in each direction the big mud flats would prove fatal to a horde of any size. The snipers could shoot down the center of the road, and with any luck the log jam of bodies would cause the infected to be forced to go around and out into the mud flats. If the area didn't have a drought, the infected would be getting stuck in the mud like they had walked onto a big sheet of fly paper.

If there was a heavy rain followed by flooding, the infected would probably be washed downriver and out to sea. Those that weren't washed away would be alligator and crab bait.

Hampton and Ward piled out of the Suburban, and we all wished them luck. For a group that didn't have a shelter, it looked like they had at least a small chance of survival, but what the hordes of infected couldn't do to them was probably something easily accomplished by the few infected who were already behind their lines.

Chief Barnes leaned out of his window and said in a low voice to Hampton, "Take my advice and start a house to house search now while you can. You have enough firepower, and you know the biggest threat is that relatives don't want to let go. You also need to know what resources you have within the area you control."

Hampton understood why the Chief didn't want the others to hear him. If they did, they could easily take matters into their own hands. They couldn't stop anything if Hampton lost control.

"I'll think about it, Chief. It's probably already too late, but you know that airport you saw back there? There are a couple of dozen small planes ready to leave on a moment's notice. At least some people will make it out. We need to figure out where it will be safe to go, but we've been sending out some flights to see if there are any other clear areas. We'll just have to wait this out the best we can."

Hampton gave the Chief a last handshake and backed away from the Suburban. The Chief put the car in drive, and we headed for the tree line. We had plenty of room to spread out inside the big vehicle, but Jean and I were sharing the space behind the driver seat. Kathy kept giving us approving looks, and there was a strong feeling of camaraderie and family amongst the four of us.

It didn't take us long to figure out that we were a lot closer to our turn off than we had realized. Only about three miles further up Highway 17, I saw a sign that said we were one mile from Simmonsville. The road was clear, thanks to Hampton's people, so we were moving fast and almost missed our turn. I saw the little roadside stand where the old lady had been selling her sweetgrass baskets, and Chief Barnes made the turn.

The Suburban had no trouble handling the dirt and gravel road at a pretty high speed, and it really felt like I was going home. The sunlight was blocked out by the trees, and within a few minutes I could see the jeep I had left parked at the end of the road.

The Chef brought the Suburban to a sliding stop, and no one needed to be told to get out. All four doors flew open at the same time, and we piled out dragging our gear behind us. We were almost there, and we could almost smell the salt air from the ocean......but there was another smell.

We gathered on the driver side of the Suburban and got down into a tight circle. Kathy asked in a whisper, "Anyone else recognize that smell?"

"I guess we all know what it is," I said, "but where it's coming from is the real question."

"Being at sea a long time has its advantages," said the Chief. "You learn to tell the direction of the wind from the slightest breeze. My best guess would be that the infected from Pawley's Island have been washing ashore and crossing through these marshes, and at the same time they've been being forced around the log jam on Highway 17 into this area."

"They had to go somewhere," said Kathy, "but are you thinking what I'm thinking? The reason it stinks so bad is because so many of them are getting stuck out here. Besides the alligators, there's a damn lot of mud and other things to get hung up on."

Jean was the one with the observation that scared us all.

"How do we know they haven't already made it over this road? I mean, we could have them all around us by now."

"There isn't much we can do about that now," I said. "We can go on through to the beach, or we can go back. If we go back, we have a horde of infected dead stuck behind a big roadblock, and we have a town that will probably die from within. And even if we keep going past Georgetown, where to from there?"

As a group we decided we should make our way through to the island as quietly as possible. We did some quick planning and agreed that we would have the whole infected population on us in a hurry if we started shooting, so we all kept our rifles on our backs and pistols holstered. Machetes had to be the weapon of choice unless we lost control of the situation.

We stashed any extra gear we could do without in the car, and we took only a small amount of food and water. I had told the others a long time ago about the night I had spent in a tree, and I told them we should consider it an option if we run into too many infected. The problem was that we would most likely have more than one or two hanging around this time.

Since I had been through the area several times before, I took the lead. I knew that I wouldn't have to chop away any brush or undergrowth to get to the beach. Jean fell in behind me followed by Kathy and then the Chief. We moved quietly and fast, but the smell was almost overpowering in some places.

I held up one hand to stop when I saw movement in the thick bushes just a few feet ahead of me. Behind me, everybody went into a crouch to await the all clear signal.

When I got lower to the ground, I saw the feet of an infected dead only about three yards away. I couldn't tell immediately if it was a male or female, but I could tell it was an infected dead because it was only wearing one shoe, and the bare foot was missing two of the middle toes.

It tried to walk forward, but it appeared to be stuck on something. I motioned for the others to stay where they were, and then I circled left to get a better look from behind. I saw that it had managed to get one arm stuck between two small trees, and it didn't have the sense to realize it was only the elbow that was keeping it in place. If it would straighten the arm and the lift it upward, it would come free, but it just kept trying to pull it out.

I held one finger to my lips and then motioned the others to follow me in a slow arc around the infected. It didn't seem to hear us, but we had a long way to go if we were going to be forced off course again.

When I got us back to where we needed to be, I saw the tracks on the damp ground that told me something had pushed through the trees and undergrowth not long before us. I signaled for the others to come closer and whispered to them that we had company, and it could be several of the infected. Whatever had passed through ahead of us was big enough to leave a path.

I whispered, "We can follow the path right to the beach if they kept moving in that direction, but the downside is they are likely to still be there. If they are, we probably have to take them out."

Kathy asked, "Want me to move out in front, Ed? If it comes down to fast hand to hand contact, I might be a little better prepared for it."

I couldn't argue with Kathy about that. I had seen her moving on TV, and she knew what she was doing. I may be able to outrun the infected on a flat paved road, but on a sandy beach we probably would be forced to deal with them on uneven ground. They may also be spread out, and blocking our way. Since going back the way we had come was not an option, we would have to face them head on.

The Chief moved up into second place in line with Jean behind him. I was in back to be sure nothing caught us by surprise. The idea was for us to sneak up on them, not the other way around.

I couldn't hear Kathy moving because she was just so good at what she does, and for a big man, the Chief was impressively quiet. Jean was so small that she could probably walk on potato chips quietly. I was looking over my shoulder so much that I was worried about running into Jean or going in the wrong direction.

Just like the first time I had come to Mud Island, I was surprised by how quickly we got to the beach. The trees had given the impression that it was much later in the day because the sun was in the West, but the last thing we wanted to do was to be on the mainland after dark. Whatever was between us and the island had to be removed.

As we cleared the trees and became fully exposed on the beach, we found ourselves behind six of the infected dead. All six were in an advanced state of decay, and the smell was overwhelming. They were all facing away from us toward the water. One had walked into the water and was still moving forward.

Kathy held out her hand and whispered for us to wait. It was obvious that she wanted us to give the infected a chance to wade out too far, and the first one didn't disappoint us. The drop off was so steep that one moment he was only knee deep, and the next moment he was gone. That didn't deter the remaining infected who were all walking toward the water.

A second one made it to the water and disappeared, but that was when our luck ran out. We had followed at a safe distance, hoping beyond hope that all of them would walk out into the water, but another six came wandering out of the trees to our right. They saw us, and when they became agitated and started to groan, the others turned around to face us.

Ten was still better than twelve, but I thought to myself it would have been nice to see more go into the water and be grabbed by either the current or sharks.

I no sooner had the thought when Kathy and the Chief both did the unthinkable and charged straight at the first group of four. It hadn't occurred to me, but they were all close enough to the water for Kathy and the Chief to see an easy way to dispose of them. They simply pushed them in. The first two were literally launched out into the water. Since Kathy and Chief Barnes didn't have momentum on their side for the remaining two, it took a bit more finesse to send them swimming. That didn't prove to be a problem because the infected dead don't seem to have great balance.

Kathy did some sort of trip and flip move that sent hers somersaulting into the water. The Chief grabbed his, turned it around to face the water, and then gave it a really hard shove. It went face first into the water with hardly a splash.

Jean and I had turned to face the six that had come out of the trees. I remembered what we had been taught about not trying to bury the machete in the infected or it might get stuck, but it was really hard to hold back. I got control of myself and swung low at the knee, and the infected hit the ground. I moved to the next one immediately because the first one wasn't going anywhere.

This one had turned toward Jean who was in the process of going for the knees the same way I had with mine. This time I had an inspiration and swung even lower and slightly from the back. The machete neatly sliced through the Achilles tendon of the infected's right foot, and his next step caused him to fall flat on his face.

I thought Kathy had come up on my left, and I turned to ask her if she had seen that, but instead of seeing the pretty blond hair, I had a tall infected dead opening his mouth and aiming for my face. All I could see or smell was that fetid mouth, but that was probably what saved me. I recoiled from the smell and literally fell out of its way.

The infected that had zeroed in on me fell over my legs, and Jean came out of nowhere to bring her blade down across the back of its neck. The head didn't come completely off, but it was close. She stayed by me until I was back on my feet, but when I looked around for another target, I saw that Kathy and the Chief had mopped up the last of them.

We all broke for the dock together, and the Chief was yanking the big yellow bag open as he ran. As soon as he was on the dock, he pulled the cord that set off the inflation device. It was amazing how quickly the raft was in the water and capable of taking on passengers. No one was shy about getting aboard and grabbing paddles.

It wasn't long before the current began moving us along, and we were steering more than paddling. The dock seemed to be pulling away from us, and we saw at least another dozen of the infected struggling free of the underbrush. One managed to walk out onto the dock without falling over the side, but it was no surprise when it just walked right off the end.

Jean started looking me over with a worried look and asked, "Did anyone get bitten?"

We all answered quickly that we hadn't, but no one hesitated when she said, "Everyone get naked, and I mean now." Everyone immediately stripped to their underwear, and I was a bit ashamed that seeing Jean undress was a bit nicer than it should have been under the circumstances.

We took turns checking each other for bites, and we were all relieved to pronounce each other as being clear of injuries. Jean winked at me when she checked me over and whispered, "Save it for later, stud."

Even in the fading light, I was pretty sure that everyone saw how red I had turned. The tension rolled away from us as we rounded the corner at the southern tip of Mud Island, and when we all looked at each other, the Chief started to laugh. As usual, it was as infectious as the diseased dead walking around on the beach, and we all started laughing along with him. I saw him and Kathy exchange that knowing look again, and they both started to paddle us toward the shore of our island. Jean took advantage of them having their backs to us and snuggled up close to me.

Behind us at the dock, there was a crowd of the infected. I glanced back only once because I couldn't stand to see that sight again. There were too many to count. That meant we had come incredibly close to dying, but it also meant we would be having more of them wash up on the island than usual.

I said to no one in particular, "If there are that many in really thick woods, how many are there getting around the log jam by Simmonsville?"

The Chief turned and looked back toward the dock. He seemed to be trying to figure out how many there were, but he was thinking about something else.

He said, "Too bad we can't contact Hampton. If as many of those things are getting around the blockade to the north as there are to the south, they should drop that bridge now."

I said, "Think about it. Highway 17 is going to act like a funnel when they start meeting back up again further down the coast."

"Maybe," said Kathy, "but with any luck a good portion of them will walk into the ocean, and the horde on the other end will lose a few to the Waccamaw River."

Jean put the punctuation on the conversation when she said, "In the meantime, we're going to get inside the shelter and stay there until they all walk into the ocean or a river."

******

The sun went down before we could get far enough around the southern tip of Mud Island, but there was enough light from the moon for us to see the beach. We didn't need to go to the end of the jetty because the beach was wide where the jetty reached Mud Island. We were able to beach the raft, carry it a few yards, and then get back in the water. I reminded the others that we should watch out for infected dead that might be hidden by shadows like the one that we had watched trip another infected.

No one had to say anything about being quiet. Other than the soft brush of the water lapping at the shoreline, it seemed like there was no sound at all. Any noise would probably carry a long way, and we didn't want anything to hear us, living or dead.

I think all four of us had this movie playing inside our minds where we pulled the raft up onto the beach and slipped inside the shelter. The problem was that there wasn't a clear path from the beach to the shelter door. We knew we would make too much noise if we just punched a hole through the heavy trees and underbrush, but we also didn't want to make a new path for someone else to find. Our best option was to quietly follow the shoreline until we reached the northern dock.

We whispered softly to each other so we were all in agreement with the plan, and we basically felt like fifteen or twenty more minutes was worth the effort. It had been a long day with some close calls, and we didn't want to mess things up now that we were on our own doorstep.

I know we were all hoping the dock would be clear of the infected, but none of us expected to see the houseboat lit up like a Christmas tree. Against the dark background of the shoreline on the mainland, the houseboat stood out in stark contrast. Literally every light had been turned on, and it sounded like a party was in progress.

As soon as the houseboat had come into view, we started paddling toward deeper water. Whoever the morons were who had moved in while we were gone, we didn't want to get to know them. Either they were too stupid to realize how dangerous it was to advertise their location, or they were very confident that it didn't matter. Whatever they were thinking, we didn't need to talk it over to know the neighborhood had gone downhill.

Once we were far enough from shore to be reasonably sure we wouldn't be spotted, the Chief dropped a small anchor over the side, and we all got as low as we could in the raft. Kathy laid out over the end facing the houseboat with a pair of binoculars.

"I don't see anyone on watch," she said. "As a matter of fact whoever these people are, they aren't worried about anyone or anything noticing them. That tells me they probably have some serious firepower."

The Chief laid forward next to her and took the binoculars. "Looks the same to me, Kathy. They must figure with the door shut, the infected can't get in, and they won't show up in large enough numbers to worry about anyway. That leaves people as the only threat, and they either have security we can't see, or they aren't worried about other people. I don't know which is scarier."

From the raft the houseboat was so bright that it was almost blinding. If someone on board looked out over the water, they wouldn't even be able to see the raft because their eyes wouldn't be accustomed to the darkness.

"How many people can you see?" I asked,

"Hard to tell," answered the Chief. "They're moving around so much that they must be drinking and having a real party."

Jean asked, "Do you think they found the shelter?"

"Doesn't really matter," I said. "They wouldn't be able to get inside if they did find it. I'd prefer that they haven't found it because we don't want them watching the door, but as long as we have another way in, they can't get to us."

My three friends and fellow survivors all turned and looked at me like I had just beamed into the raft from somewhere. No one spoke for a full minute, and then I understood. I had forgotten to tell them about the emergency exits.

"Oh, man......I'm so sorry, guys. Seriously, it's not like I've been trying to keep something from you. I just forgot because the emergency exits are so hard to see." I must have looked pretty guilty since I figured out why they were giving me blank stares all by myself.

"Back up just a bit, Ed," said the Chief.

Kathy added, "Yeah, hit rewind, Ed. What are you talking about?"

Jean didn't say anything, but she had her arms crossed over her chest and was looking at me with a mock frown.

"There are at least three emergency exits that lead to the master bedroom. There could be more, but I only checked to see where three of them come out." I sounded a bit defensive, but then I saw the smiles slowly start to appear on their faces.

"Do any of them come out where they won't see us?" The Chief asked.

"As a matter of fact, Chief, all three of them are far enough from the northern dock for us to get in unseen. The one on the southern tip of the island is probably the easiest to get to because it comes out right at the beginning of the tree line," I said.

Kathy asked, "What kind of lock does the door have?"

"Combination lock, just like the front door," I said. "The combination is the reverse of the front door because they're meant to be escape exits. My uncle had an ironic sense of humor."

Jean chuckled and said, "I wonder what Uncle Titus would say about us using them to escape into the shelter."

"He would kick our butts for leaving in the first place," I said.

"Well, let's get going," said the Chief. "We've had a long day, and I can't wait to get in front of the TV and dial up that hidden camera in the houseboat."

"Not to mention just being safer than we are floating around out here," said Jean. "Where do we go, Eddy?" She had a way of saying my name that was so hot.

Kathy said, "I'd tell you two to get a room, but since that's exactly what you plan to do, I'd just be wasting my breath."

Even in the dark I was pretty sure they could see me blushing again, so I turned around and started looking for the anchor line. As soon as I had it out of the water, Kathy and the Chief started paddling quietly back the way we had come.

It only took about fifteen minutes to reach the southern tip of the island for the second time tonight. I pointed toward the right place to beach the raft, and they steered toward it.

Kathy asked, "How can you find it in the dark like this?"

"I recognize this spot," said the Chief. "Isn't there a camera pointed right at us?"

"Yeah, there is," Chief. "My uncle figured if you need to escape, it would be a good idea to get a peek outside first. I found a landmark in the view of each camera so I can line up with where the escape hatch is."

As we pulled the raft ashore, I said, "We need to either drag it into the trees or set it adrift. The tunnel inside the hatch is going to be a tight fit for the Chief, so I don't think we'll be able to get the raft through."

Jean said, "There's always a chance our new tenants searched the island after they got here. If they take a second look and find the raft, they're going to know someone came onto the island. They may not be able to get to us, but it would be better if they weren't looking in the first place."

"I agree," said Kathy. "If they spot the raft adrift on the other side of the inlet, they won't think someone got off over here first. Give me a hand, Chief."

The two of them towed the raft back into the water and started to give it a shove, but the Chief stopped and looked back at me.

"Hey, Ed. Before I ditch our only ride out of here, how about opening the door first."

"Makes sense to me," I said. I turned toward the trees and then looked across the water for my landmark. I spotted one tree that stood out and then zeroed in on the camera location.

I walked up to the trees, and slipped my hands under the lip of the turf that marked where the beach ended and the trees began. When I lifted, it exposed a narrow shaft with a smooth steel hatch a few feet down. I hung down into the shaft and spun the combination lock. As soon as I pulled the handle to the unlocked position and opened the door, I gave the Chief a thumbs up signal.

Kathy and the Chief gave the raft a hard push away from the beach. We all watched for a minute as the raft glided away, then I motioned Jean forward and helped her into the tunnel.

"When you get to the bottom of the shaft, there will be a lever on the door. When you pull the lever, a spring loaded hinge will lift the door upward just like a hatch-back on a car," I said.

She gave me a quick kiss and then dropped over the edge into the tunnel. Kathy followed behind her, and then the Chief. Just for a laugh he tried to give me a kiss first.

"Ugh, Chief. I'd rather kiss an infected dead," I said.

He answered, "I'm so hurt." He dropped down through the tunnel, but I could hear him laughing the entire time. I followed the Chief and squeezed into the gap between the camouflaged turf and the hatch. Once I pulled it into place, the hatch was no longer visible. The only evidence that there had been people on the beach would be the footprints we left, and they could have been from the infected dead.

6 GOING HOME

We had all agreed it was time to look at the outside world, but we had mistakenly believed there would be some form of resistance to the spread of the infection. Mankind couldn't simply give up without a fight. Someone had to be winning against this thing, but we hadn't been given a clue where to look.

What we had found instead of resistance was people waiting for their turn to die. The world we had known wasn't dead yet, but it was definitely dying everywhere we looked. There were small battles being fought on the highways and in the homes, and there were large battles being fought at military installations and at sea. Small or large, they were all being lost.

There's no way to describe how it felt to be back home. Even with the squatters on our doorstep, we were at least safe again. No one could sneak up on us, and nothing was waiting around the next corner to bite us.

When I reached the bottom of the Emergency Exit, only Jean was waiting for me, and she looked utterly exhausted. I had no doubt that it was as much mental fatigue as it was physical. Jean was tough, but she was more petite than the rest of us so no one would blame her for being tired.

"Kathy and the Chief went up to the living area to check out what's happening in the house boat," she said. "I think I'd like to rest a bit before dealing with more problems."

I made sure the hatch was sealed then took her in my arms. "This isn't really a big problem, Jean. They're out there, and we're in here. At least we know about them. They don't even know we're here."

"I know, Eddy, but right now I feel like they just need the right can opener to be able to get inside." Jean was frowning and looked defeated.

Jean obviously didn't know my uncle as well as I did. When he said no one could get in, he meant there wasn't a can opener that could force the lid off of this can. For one thing, they were a mile away. They also would serve as another way of keeping the infected from walking around on their end of the island.

"Jean, try to think of them as if they were another layer of protection, kind of like putting a really mean dog in your yard. They're going to be busy enough with trying to survive out there in the house boat. Even if they explore the island enough to find the entrance to the shelter, remember what my uncle told me. This place could survive a nuclear bomb or a tidal wave, and those guys out there are probably fresh out of nuclear bombs."

Despite her worries, I felt her relax against me, and she had a nice smile on her face where the frown had been. When I tilted her head up with my hand under her chin, she brightened a bit more.

"I guess I'm just tired," she said. "We saw more in one day than we've seen in the last month. It's one thing to watch it on a TV screen and another to see it in person. We're lucky we made it back in one piece."

"I don't think it was all luck," I said. "We made a pretty good team out there." I gave her a kiss and a big hug.

"Go join the others before they come looking for you. I'm going to get some rest," she said.

I gave her another quick hug and headed upstairs to where Kathy and the Chief were studying the views from several cameras. They had both stopped at the refrigerator and grabbed cold beers. They must've been expecting me to join them because there was a third beer waiting for me.

Kathy looked up as I came in and asked, "How's Jean?"

"She's just tired," I said. "She's also worried that we aren't safe with the new tenants up there." I nodded toward the TV and asked, "What do we know so far."

Without looking up, the Chief said, "We know there are at least eight of them. There are five men and three women......no children, thank God."

I sat down on a chair next to the sofa and leaned in to get a closer look. The Chief had the grid view open. One rectangle was the view from the hidden camera inside the house boat. Five of the people were in the field of vision. I found the other three outside on the dock. They were drinking from bottles that looked like beer and whiskey, and they were smoking something that must have been pot because they passed it around.

Kathy said, "The world goes to hell in a hand cart, but we still get the same deadbeats you can find on any street corner on a Friday night."

"I'm not too worried about them," I said. "They don't think like survivalists, so the fact that they've survived this long is more of an accident than brains. I'd be willing to bet they had larger numbers before, and these are the misfits who lasted."

Kathy moved closer to the screen that showed the trio on the dock. She seemed to be studying something she had spotted.

"What is it?" Asked the Chief. "See something?"

"Yeah, look at this guy's belt in back." She put her finger on the spot she wanted them to see. "What's that look like to you?"

"It's hard to tell in this light," said the Chief, "but is that a set of handcuffs?"

"They don't look like police officers," said Kathy, "so I'm thinking these guys helped themselves to some gear along the way from wherever they started. Those shotguns look like police issue, too."

The Chief said, "If you're saying you don't think it's a good idea for us to invite our new neighbors over for supper, Kathy, I was already thinking the same thing."

"Hang on a second," I said. "I don't think my uncle put the house boat out there with the expectation that anyone who moved into it was bad, and I'm not saying these guys look like friendly neighbors, but we have to go with the real possibility that one day some good people are going to move in. When they do, we're going to be faced with the decision to help them or to leave them to whatever comes next."

"So you think your uncle wanted you to play god?" Asked the Chief.

"No, of course not. I'm just saying what if they had been good people and we just left them out there? Then along comes a group of bad people. Would we just stay in here and watch the bad people kill the good people?"

I probably sounded more sanctimonious than I intended, but at the back of my mind was the thought that I didn't turn my back on the Chief, Kathy, and Jean when they showed up.

"Chief, what if I had not gone out there to target practice that day? You guys wouldn't have spotted me, so you would have kept rowing for shore. If you had kept going in a straight line, you would have eventually spotted the house boat. You would have moved in and thought you were pretty safe, but we already know what else is out there. These people don't know it yet, but their days are numbered."

Kathy could see that this was the first time the Chief and I looked like we were squaring off with each other, so she stepped in and said, "Hey you two. Keep it friendly, okay? I don't think Eddy's talking about baking them a cake, Chief."

The Chief and I both looked a little embarrassed, especially since we were disputing a hypothetical situation. If my friends had landed on the island and found the house boat, I was sure that I couldn't have left them out there. The house boat was probably safer than most places, but the obvious threat was from people like this group that was in there now. They looked like they wouldn't have asked Kathy, Jean, or the Chief if there was room at the inn.

"Point taken," said the Chief. "If we see someone move into the house boat that looks like good people, we'll find a way to decide if we should help them or ignore them. Until that time, I think we've already made a decision about these animals."

"Agreed," I said. "Chief, it didn't take long for me to decide about you three, and if Hampton had set up house out there, we would probably bring him in. Like we said when we were trying to get back to Mud Island, there's got to be some good people out there."

Kathy said, "Now that you two are ready to give each other bro-hugs, or whatever it is you guys like to do, what are we going to do about these guys? I don't think it's a good idea to let them stay."

The Chief was stroking his beard and looked like he was thinking of a plan, but he surprised us both when he said, "Nothing, is probably our best option. I think we should let this play out a bit so we can learn from it."

"Learn what?" I asked. I didn't have a clue about how we could get the squatters to move out, but doing nothing seemed like we were just hoping it would all work out for us.

"I think we should wait to see how bad it gets out there for them, not us," said the Chief. "Come into the kitchen and let me show you something."

The Chief brought out one of our big rolled maps we had discovered in our supplies and spread it on the table. He weighted the corners then started drawing and explaining at the same time.

"Here's Mud Island," he said as he labeled our location. "Here's Simmonsville, Pawley's Island, and Surfside. Further south we have Georgetown."

He looked at us as if we were already understanding why he felt the need to give us a picture to look at. When he saw two blank stares that basically said, "So what and thanks for the tour," he went on by adding arrows to the map.

"For some reason, everything seems to be moving south, but I think it's just dumb luck. We chose to move northward and then planned to let the current bring us ashore. We only did that because it was better than letting the current drag us all the way back to Charleston harbor. I think the infected dead and the people who are trying to survive are only moving along the path of least resistance. There's probably an army of living and dead fanning out in all directions from every city, but along the coastline it just seems like they're all coming this way."

"Makes sense, Chief, but what are you trying to tell us?" I asked.

"I'm trying to tell you that it's far from over, Ed."

Kathy said, "Tell us something we don't know, Chief."

I thought he Chief looked really frustrated, as if he was trying to write a book named Zombie Apocalypse Survival for Dummies, and he couldn't dumb it down any further. He was even a bit more red than usual.

"Okay, let me put it this way," he said. "Sooner or later the infected dead that are heading south are going to collide with the ones coming north, and in between them will be the living who are running south and the living who are running north. Never mind that we also have some going east and west, just not as many because of natural barriers."

The lights came on for Kathy and me at the same time. The ocean had everything blocked to the East, and we had already witnessed that there were dangerous things out there that would be coming ashore over time. Rivers to our west were creating a natural barrier because they generally ran north and south in this part of the country. The living were smart enough to block bridges just as they were in Georgetown, and the infected tended to try to walk on water, so as long as the living didn't get caught in between, they were going to survive a bit longer.

The Chief continued when he saw that we were understanding.

"Until we run out of people, we're going to have the living and the infected arriving on Mud Island. That means we're going to be playing god for a long time, my friends."

I felt a bit naive for asking what I was thinking, but I had to know what the Chief and Kathy would say. So, I asked, "Do you think it would be possible for someone to live out there in the house boat with a little help from us?"

We weren't strangers to philosophical discussions and hypothetical situations. After a month of sitting in front of the TV with the Chief, sipping on adult beverages, and talking about what could have caused the infection, we had covered plenty of scenarios. This one was new, though. We knew that sooner or later someone would take up residence in the house boat, but it was a foregone conclusion that when it happened, we would just make sure they never learned of our existence. It had never gotten far enough in conversation for us to have to consider that we were sentencing the occupants to death just by laying low. Sooner or later they would run out of supplies and die when they tried to get more. Either that, or they would die when the next occupants came along.

We also never considered what would happen if we got a bunch of derelicts in the house boat like this group. Other survivors, good people like Hampton might show up, and this group would probably feed them to the sharks.

"So," Kathy said, "we need to find a way to evict our tenants, right?"

"It would seem to be the logical choice," said the Chief.

I asked, "What are we talking about here? You know we won't be able to scare them off, so there's only one other thing we can do, but there's a difference between killing the infected and killing the living."

Kathy said, "Chief, in law enforcement they teach you about ethics, not how to bust heads. We're talking about doing something to get rid of these guys when they haven't even done anything yet."

"Yet may be the operative word, Kathy. We don't know what they've done already."

In the end, we agreed that we should at least sleep on the idea, and maybe we could find a way to get them to move on. The way they were consuming the supplies on the house boat, it didn't look like they would be able to last more than a few days before they had to go to the mainland to restock, and we were curious about how they planned to do that.

Kathy and I had assumed they would use the Boston Whaler, but we learned from the Chief that he had rearranged the wires under the dash. If he had just disconnected them, anyone with half a brain would have reconnected them and taken the boat. If the current tenants of the house boat had tried to start the boat, it probably never occurred to them to switch the wires to their proper connections.

The question of how they had gotten to the house boat was a mystery, because no raft or other boat could be seen on the TV screens. Our position in the raft when we first discovered the men gave us a good view of the side of the house boat facing the ocean, and there was nothing tied up alongside that could have gotten them there. We had a feeling it was going to be interesting watching what they did when they needed to make a supply run.

******

Jean was the one watching the camera feeds three days later when the drama started on the house boat. Everything seemed normal, or as normal as it could be with eight armed men and women sharing limited supplies that included alcohol and tobacco.

The Chief had identified one member of the group as the leader and passed it along to the others. He was bigger than the others and tended to walk around without a shirt, showing off his muscles and tattoos. He even had tattoos on his bald head. He was quick tempered and had pistol whipped a couple of the men. They didn't even put up a fight.

Jean called to the rest of us where we were in the kitchen cleaning up after a civilized breakfast. "Hey, guys. You might want to see this. The boss has a guy by the hair and is dragging him to the end of the dock."

We all gathered around and watched as the other men followed behind the boss and the man who had apparently broken some rule. We couldn't hear what they were saying, but it was obvious that the guy was pleading with the boss. They got to the end of the dock, and the boss pointed at the water. The other guy was shaking his head back and forth and looked like he was begging not to go into the water. The boss only listened for a minute before he ordered two of the other men to take over.

The boss stepped off to one side, and one of the others handed him an empty whiskey bottle, which he held up for the others to see. That must have been the rule he broke. After another few minutes of deliberations, the boss reached his verdict and made a motion toward the water with his hand. The two men who were standing ready didn't hesitate. They picked up the pleading man and literally launched him into the northern inlet.

We all knew how fast the current was at the end of the dock, so the Chief brought the other camera views up on the screen. We spotted the man trying to swim with the current instead of against it back to the dock. If he had tried to do that, he would probably have drowned in less than a minute.

We tracked him with the cameras as he rounded the bend in our personal moat and could no longer be seen from the dock. The remaining seven men and women were filing back into the house boat because there wasn't anything left to see. They probably assumed he had already drowned.

The absence of sharks in the water that separated Mud Island from the mainland probably meant they were getting plenty to eat without coming this close to the coast. If they had been around, the man would never have made it to the southern tip. The current carried him close enough to shore for him to make it across the water. He stood up on the sandy beach that was on the side opposite from the southern jetty.

We watched as he looked across the sand at the trawler that had been wrecked when its nets snagged the rocks. He was so surprised to see the boat on its side on the beach that he didn't see what was coming out of the trees toward him. There were too many to count, and the infected were on him before he could make it back into the water. We switched off the camera because there was no reason to watch what we knew was happening.

It was really a sobering thought to us all that we had passed through the southern inlet only a few nights earlier. We had coasted within a few yards of an army of the infected without knowing it. We had assumed they were there in the trees but not in such large numbers.

We checked the camera in the house boat and saw that there was more activity. The men and women were going out onto the dock, but this time they were carrying every rope they could find. They were then tying the ropes together to make one long rope.

"Wait a minute," said the Chief. "Don't tell me they threw that one guy in so they could test the current."

Jean asked, "Why would they do that?"

The Chief said, "So they would know whether or not they could use the current to reach the mainland. I think they're going to tie a rope to the Whaler and try to use it as a ferry. That may be how they got here in the first place if they came across in a raft or something from the northern jetty. They can't go back that way because the current is too strong, so they're going to try either from the mainland side of the island or from the southern tip."

We all looked at each other with the sudden realization that they were about to solve our problem for us, especially if the morons all got into the boat together. They couldn't see where their former friend had made it ashore by the southern jetty, so they didn't know what was waiting over there.

Kathy said, "Hey, guys. They're easing the Whaler way from the dock letting rope play out from it like a kite. Two guys are in the boat and five are on shore."

Once again we switched from one view to the other and watched as the group of men guided the Boston Whaler around the island. It was almost two miles of labor for the five men on shore to keep the boat from pulling away too fast, and they were beginning to get worn out. Sweat was dripping from their faces, and their hands were beginning to slip on the rope.

The boss didn't want to take the chance that they wouldn't be able to guide the boat all the way to the southern tip and began ordering the men to pull the boat back to the island. After a long struggle against the current, they managed to get the Whaler to shore and tied off to a tree.

"So much for kite flying in this current," said Kathy. "I wonder what they're going to try next."

"They're probably wishing they had that other man right now," I said.

That earned a laugh from the rest of my friends. When you got down to it, this was some of the best entertainment we'd had in a long time.

Jean said, "Too bad the house boat won't start up. It would be fun to drive it away while they are trying to get into the ferry business. Then again, they probably thought they were going to be able to drive it to shore when they moved in."

After several minutes of arm waving and bickering, they seemed to have come to a decision about something. The rope looked like it might be just long enough for them to leave it tied to the big tree where it already was. To our astonishment, they all got into the boat together and let the rope out fast. The end result was that they got past the center of the moat before the current really got them too far off course to the South.

As the rope grew taut, the Whaler began to swing like a pendulum toward the curving shoreline of the mainland, but not quite in view of the southern tip......the place where the eighth man had washed ashore. Instead, the boat came ashore almost half-way between the mainland dock and the southern inlet.

Kathy asked the rest of us, "Haven't we seen this movie already?"

The Chief said, "Except this time the seven stooges have guns, and they should at least thin out the infected dead that are about to come out of those trees."

As soon as the Boston Whaler beached, the men and women jumped onto the sand. One of them spotted the mainland dock further up the beach and pointed at it. They all turned long enough to see what he was talking about and missed the grand entrance of the horde of infected dead emerging from the dense trees. When one of them sounded the alarm, it was too late for them to get back into the boat and push it free of the shore.

If they had stayed in the boat long enough, they probably could have pulled hard enough on the rope to reach the shelf under the water where the infected couldn't follow, but that was their biggest mistake.

Without discipline they fired at the infected at point blank range, not aiming for the heads. They would go down, but precious ammunition was wasted before their boss got them under control. One by one they ran out of bullets and began swinging their rifles like baseball bats, and one by one they disappeared under the teeth of the infected.

The Chief said, "Well, the good news is that our tenants have moved out. The bad news is that it looks like the other end of the rope is tied to the boat."

"Why is that bad news?" I asked.

Kathy answered for the Chief, "Because we have to go out there and pull it back."

******

Uncle Titus was a true genius. Among the many crates stored in the lower levels of the shelter was one with the words Gas Powered Winch stenciled on the side. It might be a bit noisy, but it would get the boat back to the dock faster than the four of us pulling it against the tide. It also solved our problem of navigating the oyster beds that lined the banks on that side of the island.

Our tenants probably didn't plan the time of day when they tried to cross with the boat, but the tide was high enough where they tied the rope to the tree for them not to get hung up on the oysters. Now that the tide was going back out, there was no way we could cross the oyster beds without cutting ourselves to shreds.

We could have waited until the next high tide, but we didn't want to tempt fate. Although chances were slim that someone would be able to make it through the gauntlet of infected roaming around in the trees on the far shore, we didn't want someone else to use the boat as a ferry and cross over to Mud Island.

The plan was to attach the rope to the winch and then to draw the Whaler away from the opposite shore until it was more or less in the center of the inlet. Then we would move the winch back toward the dock, reel it in a bit more, and then repeat the process. If all went well, we would have the boat tied up to the dock in no more than an hour.

Kathy and Jean kept watch while the Chief and I worked as quickly as we could. As soon as the boat was free of the sandy beach, the current tried to pull the boat toward the southern tip of the island, but the Chief had the winch running at top speed for the crucial few minutes we needed to keep the boat's momentum from taking it too far.

It took closer to two hours than the one we expected, but we eventually got the boat back where it belonged.

The Chief said, "Now all we need is to go get the plane, and we'll be back in good shape."

I thought he was kidding at first, but there wasn't his usual half smile on his face that always appeared when he was in a joking mood. My mouth was open, though.

"Better close your mouth before you catch a bug," said the Chief.

"You must be kidding, Chief. We just got back, and you already want to try for the plane?"

"I was thinking," he said. "We almost lost the boat, and we need it to be able to get the plane back. I don't know about you, but I don't plan to try going through Georgetown to get back to Wando Farms Road. By now I imagine they have their hands full with the horde that was being funneled down Highway 17 from Simmonsville."

"But why do we have to go back for it now, Chief? Why can't we hole up and give it a rest at least for a few weeks?" I asked.

"Several reasons," he answered. "First, strategically the plane gives us an edge. I don't know why I didn't think of it before, but we could drive the boat out to deeper water and anchor it. There's less chance of losing it to someone at sea than someone on land. We could fly back to the island and then fly out to get the boat when we need it. I also want to paint it black so it won't be so easy to see."

"That's only one good reason for going now, Chief. I don't know about you, but I would be happy to just hide in the shelter for another month."

"Well," he said, "I have a nagging feeling that the longer we wait the more likely it is that someone else will find the plane first."

"Have you mentioned it to Jean and Kathy?" I asked.

"Not yet, but I'm planning to today," he answered.

"Well, don't expect it to go so great, Chief. They look like they feel a little ragged. I know I do."

Once we had the Whaler tied to the dock, we felt like we had accomplished something major. It looked like it belonged where it was. Standing there looking at it, I realized it was a major tool for our survival.

"You know, Chief, if Uncle Titus was here, I would bet that he would say his one regret was not building some sort of hideaway for the boat."

The Chief got that big smile back that was missing over the last couple of hours and said, "Sounds like a British spy movie, Ed. We come speeding back to the island, a big door opens, and we disappear into the island. The bad guys come zooming around the island after us just after the door shuts."

"Doesn't sound so far fetched when you put it that way, Chief."

That got us both laughing just as Kathy and Jean came down the dock.

"What's so funny?" Asked Jean.

"The Chief and I were just working on an idea about how we could build a garage for the boat so no one will find it." Just saying it caused us to start laughing even harder.

Kathy was smiling, but she said, "That's a good idea. Why's it so funny?"

The Chief and I kept laughing for a few seconds, but we saw she was serious, and it gradually sank in that her mind was working on something. Jean was also looking at her expectantly.

"Kathy, you have everyone's attention. What are you thinking?" asked Jean.

"I'm thinking we could do it with the winch and a little hard labor. You know that hatch on the southern tip? We could make it bigger, put the winch inside, and then use it to drag the boat in. I think our only problem is making it a smooth drag for the hull, and we could solve that problem just by getting a boat trailer out here."

Kathy was a planner, and she could do it on the fly. We knew that she could think things through in a hurry because of what she did in Charleston at the terminal, but there wasn't one of us with a clue of how she planned to get a trailer to the island.

"Chief," she said, "as much as I would like to stay here forever after our last trip, do you think the plane is big enough to carry a boat trailer strapped to its bottom?"

The Chief looked thoughtful for a moment and answered, "We don't need a big trailer because we're not planning to tow it on a highway, so we could go smaller than normal. Yeah, Kathy, I think we could strap a small boat trailer to the bottom of the Otter without it affecting the take offs and landings."

Jean and I were like spectators watching cliff divers. They were making us nervous just talking.

"I don't want to break up your fun," I said, "but are you planning on landing the plane at a boat store to pick up a trailer?"

The Chief was looking at Kathy with a totally mischievous look as he answered me. "We don't need a boat store, Ed. There's a whole boat landing full of trailers only a few hundred yards from where we left the plane."

My fellow spectator, Jean, was as uncomfortable as I was, and she tried to come to my aid by asking, "Is there any reason we can't wait a few weeks to do this? I mean, we could do the grunt work here on the island first. Then we could maybe try for the plane."

"Jean, take a look at the calendar," said the Chief. "Have you noticed the weather is getting cooler? That's because it's the last week of October. I've been amazed that we didn't get any tropical storms this year, but I'm sure as hell not complaining. I think we need to do it while we can. It doesn't really get cold here, but it gets cold enough that I'd rather do this before the temperature starts to drop. Warm sand is easier to dig by hand than cold, wet sand."

That silenced the spectators. Jean and I were both looking at our feet in resignation, while the Chief and Kathy were smiling at each other like two kids who just got told they were going to Disney World.

"Okay," I said. "If we're going to do this, let's hear the rest of the plan. For starters, the woods are crawling with the infected. We made it back once, but making it out through those woods and then through Georgetown won't be so easy a second time."

"We won't be going back through Georgetown," said the Chief, "but we will need to at least go back to the cars for the gas cans. We're going to use the boat to get back to the plane, so we'll need plenty of fuel for the round trip."

The Chief looked over at me and Jean with real concern on his face. What he and Kathy were saying made perfect sense, but it didn't mean it was going to be easy. As a matter of fact, it was far more dangerous than our first excursion down to Goose Creek.

Kathy said, "Let's take a couple of days to plan the trip, and we can talk out every detail. Whatever the risks might be, we can try to anticipate them. Pardon the pun, but we were winging it on the last trip."

As always, our group seemed to have a knack for bad puns, but they were usually delivered with a straight face and fair amount of innocence. Kathy pointing out it was a pun was a sign that she knew we were once again jumping from the frying pan into the fire.

******

Over the next two days, we laid out our plan with much more care than anything we had done so far, and every aspect of it was dangerous. Getting to the cars for the gas cans was definitely going to be a daylight operation, and we decided we would half empty the cans rather than to try to carry full cans of fuel through the dense brush. They were heavy, and we needed the Chief to help with any infected dead on the beach. We could always refill them from our vast supply of fuel provided by Uncle Titus.

Kathy, always the strategist, suggested that we might be able to buy some time by creating a diversion. We decided to at least try to move the Jeep half way to Highway 17 and set it on fire. We would all hide inside the Suburban for at least an hour to allow as many of the infected to be drawn away from the trees as possible, then we would make a break for the island. We were hoping there would be enough distraction to the noise and fire that we could slip right past any that were still inside the trees when we made our run back to the island.

Jean contributed to the planning by suggesting that we carry along anything we could find to blacken the insides of the windows of the Suburban. The plan wouldn't work so well if we found ourselves trapped inside the Suburban with infected dead crawling all over it. We settled on the lightest and fastest method to cover the windows, duct tape and black plastic garbage bags, which we had in large supply.

We dug through the cases of supplies in the lower levels and found spray paint. The Chief commented that Uncle Titus must have just walked into a hardware store and said, "I'll take everything." There were several shades of brown and green, so we all got busy painting everything above the waterline of the Boston Whaler including the chrome. It was quick work because it didn't have to be pretty. We used colors with a flat finish so there would be no reflection, and the end result was a well camouflaged boat.

The Chief spent some time up under the dash of the Whaler installing a hidden dead switch. If they had to incapacitate the boat again, any of them could do so in a hurry without swapping wires around.

Evenings and nights inside the shelter were comfortable but serious. We got plenty of rest and food so we could be as healthy as possible for what was sure to be a difficult trip. Each of us had plans to think of, and mine was the redesign of the southern hatch over the emergency exit. I had to make it big enough to hold a boat and trailer, and that meant a lot of work.

Jean came to my rescue when she reminded us all there was a gas powered garden tiller in the barn back at the farm by the plane. The tiller was small enough to bring back in the boat or the plane. The Chief said he didn't think the Otter would have any problem with the weight of the boat trailer and the tiller if they had to do it. It depended on the size and weight of the trailer.

As Jean pointed out, the tiller would be able to chew up the beach easily enough for them to cut a ditch from the water to the trees and then dig out the underground garage where it would be hidden. We agreed that we wouldn't wait a single day when we got back before beginning construction, and with that agreement came a sense of optimism. We were planning proactively on the determined assumption that we would all make it back together.

As we planned our strategies, we gathered together enough supplies for a trip that could take up to a week. We decided that we would leave at sunrise and travel straight out to sea until we were far enough out to not be heard from the shore. The last thing we needed was to be shot at by crazy people who would shoot at us for no other reason than to shoot at people who have a boat.

We also decided that if we saw anyone else on the water, we would try to keep plenty of distance between us. If we had to, we would drop anchor and wait until nightfall and then sneak by under the cover of darkness. If the weather was on our side, we could go south or go further out to sea. We would only travel a straight line if we were able to.

Over supper of the second night, we laid a map of the coast out on the table. The only way to reach the plane by water was to go back to Charleston harbor. The map showed a direct route down Highway 17 would only be about seventy miles. On a day with no traffic, we could be there in just over an hour, but by water we were planning on no better than two days.

If we reached Charleston harbor without incident, we would still have to navigate the area that had become a virtual nightmare in the first days of the attacks. The harbor had been clogged by hundreds of boats of all sizes, and there was no guarantee the harbor was even clear. If it wasn't, we would have two choices. We could go back to Mud Island, or we could travel an additional twenty miles further down the coast and come in the back door to the harbor.

The Chief showed us on the map that we could pass Morris Island and Folly Island then enter the Stono River. From there we would follow the snaking Stono River until it met with Wappoo Creek. Despite its name, it was wide enough to move barges, and we would be able to follow it all the way to the Ashley River. From there it was only a matter of minutes before we would pass Castle Pinckney.

I thought back to the news broadcast from the Atlantic Spirit and shuddered when I remembered the people stranded there. I couldn't imagine the desperation they must have felt as I watched from the safety of an island barely an hour away on any normal day.

"The obvious downside of this detour is that we will be much closer to shore for a long time," said the Chief. "Anyone with a rifle and the urge to shoot someone will have an easy target to hit."

"Chief," Kathy said, "I grew up in Charleston, so I learned about the Stono River when we studied the Civil War in high school, and there are some choke points, but most of it is wild. It was the only way to get into the harbor without going by the Union blockade, but it was never really developed because of the marshes. Where it isn't wild, it's not heavily populated, and where it is populated there will be plenty of infected dead. Most of the area is too rural for any chance there was a successful resistance to the spread of infection."

The Chief asked, "What about these bridges, Kathy. I count three. Are we likely to have any problems getting by them?"

"The first one is a low draw bridge that they converted to a fixed span when they quit using the Stono

River for heavy traffic," she said. "The only really deep place to cross under the bridge is at the middle, and it is pretty narrow through there." She put her finger on the map to show us where it was. "When we go through here, anyone above with a gun couldn't miss, so we would need to go through at night."

"Any chance of going closer to shore?" asked Jean.

She moved her finger toward the eastern shore and said, "The map shows it gets muddy here, and we could get stuck if we're not careful. Also, the current in the Stono River gets kind of strong. If we try to go through off center, it shouldn't be by too much."

She shifted to the other side of the river to a point just above the bridge.

"Over here is the Stono Marina. They have enough slips for about two hundred or so boats. I would guess the only boats that got out in time were the people who thought a little more quickly than the average person. Most of the boats would be power boats because they don't dredge the Stono, and sailboats draft to deep. That's why I'm worried about the center span. If too many tried to get through at the same time, this could be blocked."

The Chief said, "Okay, so let's plan on going through one span off from the center. We need to take along paddles and long poles in case we have to go through really quiet. What about the second bridge, Kathy?"

"That one is in the Charleston City limits, so I did some ride-alongs over there when I was in training. That one is very narrow, but it's much higher. We still need to go under it at night, but we have two things in our favor. The current is really swift in the direction we will be going, and the bridge is much higher. If we have any luck at all, the drawbridge will be open. If we can ease up to it unseen, we will be relatively safe while we're under it. We need to be careful here."

She put her finger on a spot just before the bridge on the right bank.

"There's a restaurant with a floating dock right here."

"After we pass under the bridge, there's a boat landing on the opposite bank. The good news is that current again. It's so swift there that it would be hard to get blocked. The third bridge is a high fixed span bridge with plenty of room under it. It's called the James Island Expressway, and I'm going to guess that it's a mess because of evacuation day."

She ended her explanation by dragging her finger out of Wappoo Creek and down the Ashley River to the spot we all knew would pass by the Charleston cruise ship terminal.

"That's one place I never thought I would see again," said Jean. "Do we have to go by there? Couldn't we use the other side of the river?"

The Chief said, "We can give it as much room as possible, Jean, but I want to avoid the Yorktown if possible. If any place was likely to seal itself off it was there. They would have been low on supplies, but they would have the proverbial high ground. With weapons, they could have turned it into a fortress by now. I don't want to find out how anyone there treats strangers."

"So," Kathy said, "it's either the short way into Charleston harbor, or the long way around. All we have left to do is make the trip."

******

At sunrise just a few days before the end of October, we left Mud Island again. I was sure Uncle Titus was spinning in his grave. This time we crossed over to the mainland dock armed to the teeth. We decided speed was more important than stealth, so the plan was to give head shots to any infected dead we ran across. We also had the added bonus of two suppressors the Chief found in the armory. He and Kathy were the best shooters, so they equipped the suppressors and took the lead. Jean and I would shoot only if we were outnumbered.

After we tied the loaded boat to the dock we hit the bushes at a run. The leaves had thinned considerably, so we could see farther than before. When we spotted some of the infected, we steered closer to them and took them out to eliminate their threat on the return trip.

A few minutes later we reached the Jeep and the Suburban. There was a moment of panic when I couldn't find the keys to the Jeep, but I sheepishly fished them out of a deep pocket. I got the jeep started and turned around for the short trip toward Highway 17. Kathy and Jean made short work of covering the windows of the Suburban from the inside, and the Chief came with me to provide cover on the way back.

At about the halfway point I stopped the Jeep, and we jumped out to douse it with gasoline. We could see Highway 17 from where we stopped, and what we saw was enough to make us rethink the diversion part of the plan. Highway 17 looked like the straight road across the Naval Weapons Station. It was wall to wall with the infected, and they were walking along Highway 17 as if they knew Georgetown was only a few miles away. There must have been thousands of them.

"What do you say, Chief? Plan B sound good to you?" I sounded like I was out of breath, but it was just a really bad case of nerves.

"Sounds very good to me, Ed. If we light this candle off now, we could get stuck hiding in the Suburban. There are a few that spotted us already, and they've broken away from the pack. Let's get back to the girls."

We got back in the Jeep, and I tried to keep calm as I backed the Jeep away from the horde of undead on the highway ahead. When I had enough distance, I did a three point turn and drove back to the Suburban. The Chief jumped out before I even quit moving.

"What happened?" asked Kathy. "How come you didn't blow up the jeep?"

"Too much company up that way," he answered as he grabbed two full cans of fuel. "We don't even have time to empty these. We've gotta go now."

I grabbed two more cans of fuel, which I found were much heavier than they looked when the Chief carried them. "Sorry about the wasted work on the windows, ladies, but every infected dead in the world is packed onto Highway 17. They saw the Jeep, and some of them are on their way. We have to take our chances with whatever we run into on the way back to the boat."

We made it back with better than a dozen infected dead trying to keep up with us. As we cleared the trees and ran across the beach, Kathy turned and delivered four well aimed shots to the heads of the nearest ones. Then she jumped into the boat with us.

The Chief already had the fuel cans stowed and the engine on. I cast off the mooring lines, and once again, we were on our way toward the southern tip of Mud Island and the open ocean beyond.

The Chief had the engine powered up as if we were still being chased. As usual, some of the infected had walked right out into the water and disappeared. We rounded the southern tip and passed the jetty on the left that had caused the trawler to wreck on the beach. Once we cleared the end of the beach, the Chief only made a slight turn to the Southeast. We needed to be at least a couple of miles offshore to keep from being heard by someone with a rifle.

As we made the turn, I looked back at Mud Island and wondered if we would make it back this time. We had decided not to restock the houseboat. On the off chance that it was occupied again, this time the occupants would be forced to move on in search of supplies and be less likely to stay around. It might be a good stopping off point, but it wouldn't be as tempting as a long term residence.

The sky turned gray, and the wind was much colder than the last time I had taken the boat out. The biggest difference, though, was not the weather. We were a slightly more seasoned group, and we looked the part. If anyone saw us, they would either consider us to be a threat or rescuers. A camouflaged boat with four well armed people dressed in military style clothes would not be a welcome sight to some people. We just had to be careful.

We cruised down the coast, occasionally spotting movement on shore through our binoculars, but never anything that looked alive. The infected we saw on the beaches looked tired, if that was something they experienced. They mostly appeared to be wandering aimlessly, as if they forgot where they were going. If this was a normal world, I would have wondered how someone in a business suit came to be walking along a desolate beach on a barrier island. Since this wasn't a normal world it was obvious that people who looked out of place were people who had tried to escape, only to meet a terrible death without a clue of how to save themselves.

In some places we saw huge flocks of sea gulls feeding on bodies that washed up on the beaches. There were a few sharks, but not as many as we expected. They were probably in warmer water because they were already well fed. I constantly told myself how lucky we were, and I constantly thanked my Uncle Titus for making sure I wouldn't be one of the people wandering around somewhere.

Bulls Bay came up on our right as we made our course correction around Cape Island. Bulls Bay was famous for its oysters, but I didn't think I would ever eat one again. To me the water was tainted now. Poisoned by the shear numbers of infected dead who had disappeared below the surface. I was grateful that I couldn't see any of them mired in the oyster beds that were above the waterline.

"There's a Navy ship ahead just off the port side," said the Chief. "It's further out than we need to be, so they may not bother us. Someone keep some binoculars on them and let me know if they look like they're interested in us."

Jean asked, "Any chance they won't see us, Chief?"

"They already do," he said. "If we see them, they could see us before then."

Kathy laid across the bow with her binoculars aimed toward the ship. "Destroyer, I think," she said. "One of the new ones that doesn't have all those masts and antennas."

"Can you tell if they are making way or if they are anchored?" asked the Chief.

"So far I would have to say neither, Chief. They look like they may be just drifting."

That brought all four of us out of whatever private thoughts we may have been thinking. The Chief throttled back and just let the boat coast for a bit. We all trained our binoculars on the ship. It was pointed toward the coast and roughly parallel with the Isle of Palms.

The sight of a totally still warship bothered all of us because it represented the power of our country, and it seemed that power was gone. There was no doubt in our minds that there were still some ships out there that were carrying on to protect our territory, but seeing even one just sitting still was symbolic of what had been lost.

Kathy studied the ship and said, "The way the decks are laid out on the new warships, there wouldn't be any infected dead walking around where we would see them. They would have all fallen overboard by now."

"Hey, guys," I said. "I think we're forgetting something. The Navy wouldn't let one of its ships get taken over and then leave it just floating out here. Just think about all the classified weapons on one of those ships. The Navy would want that back."

As if on cue, a Zodiac came around the stern of the destroyer, but it didn't turn in our direction. Instead, it appeared to be circling the destroyer from only a few feet away. We watched with fascination as ropes were launched from the Zodiac and armed soldiers climbed to the modern deck that looked more like a floating spaceship than a warship.

The scene playing out on the ship was not something we would see every day, but it was our opportunity to get by without drawing their attention. The Chief pushed the throttle forward again and turned toward the coast. We were passing Sullivan's Island, and we could see the mouth of the Charleston harbor ahead. In minutes we would know if we could take the short trip or if it would be the detour.

Kathy kept her binoculars aimed at the destroyer just in case they decided we were more important than their current mission, but the Navy had probably seen plenty of small boats since the chaos of that first day, and they didn't pay any attention to us.

Fort Sumter came into view, and the Chief eased as close to the channel marker on opposite side of the harbor mouth as he could. I started to ask him why it mattered, but he anticipated the question.

He said, "If I had been stuck here, I would have found a boat, crammed it full of supplies, and made my way to Fort Sumter. It would have been a short term solution at best, but it would have been better than trying to fight my way off of the peninsula. Morris Island is right behind the Fort, but the tidal plains would keep people and the infected from sneaking up on it. If I thought of it, so did someone else, and whoever succeeded in taking Fort Sumter away from the infected dead would be just as dangerous."

No sooner had the words left his mouth when a bullet hit the water not far from the bow of the Boston Whaler. The Chief cut the wheel hard to the right just as a second bullet narrowly missed us again. The sounds of the shots were barely audible, but we could tell the shooter was only taking time to adjust for our forward movement, and the Chief's fast reactions had saved us.

We were dangerously close to shallow water when the Chief came out of his turn, but he was able to get us out of range of the shooter. Without having to discuss our options, we knew we had little choice but to take the detour.

When we had discussed this possibility while making our plans, we talked about trying to coast in at night, but that's exactly what we would be watching for if we were guarding the mouth to the harbor. The Chief had told us that during the night we could expect shooters sitting in boats just waiting for someone like us to sneak in. Of course they could do the same at the mouth of the Stono River, but just like during the Civil War, the back door of the Charleston harbor was more likely to be ignored in favor of the shorter route straight through the harbor. At least that's what we were hoping for.

We passed the jetties at the highest speed we could manage just in case the people guarding the harbor had boats they could send out after us. We also wanted to get more distance between ourselves and the destroyer parked back by Sullivan's Island. We didn't want to be around when they regained control of the ship just because we didn't know what their agenda would be. They could have orders to limit traffic in the area, and we couldn't afford to be turned back.

The coast of Morris Island was deserted. If people had made it to safety there, they had the sense to stay hidden, and there were no infected stumbling around on the beach. Folly Beach was not so lucky.

As we passed the Morris Island Lighthouse, we could see the beach ahead, and it was crowded with the infected. Whatever had gone wrong on the day when people began attacking each other and ripping flesh from other people with their teeth, it must have really gone wrong here. Hundreds of the infected dead were gathered around houses, so it was a fair guess that there were still people holed up inside.

We saw one beachfront house that was built on stilts two stories high, and people were sitting out on the deck of the house drinking beer just as if it was a typical day at the beach. When they spotted us cruising by, they raised their beer bottles in a toast to us. We waved because it just seemed like the polite thing to do, but we exchanged a look with each other that said, "Now we've seen everything."

Only a few blocks later, it was quite the opposite scene but more of what we were used to. Another house on stilts, also surrounded by the infected trying to get in to the occupants, but when the people inside saw us passing by, they rushed outside holding up signs that said HELP US printed in big bold letters. I'm not sure what they thought we could do to help. Maybe they just hoped we would send someone now that we knew they were there.

The entire length of Folly Beach was dotted with the shapes of wrecked people who had become the infected dead. All we could figure was that the beach had been a busy place when the attacks began, or maybe there was a special event that had drawn an unusually large crowd that day.

It was especially heartbreaking to see the children who were wandering aimlessly among the victims. It had become too easy to think of them as infected monsters, but seeing the children brought back their humanity, and I remembered these had once been people.

"The map shows a small island sitting in the mouth of the Stono River where it meets the Folly River," said the Chief. "Let's circle around behind it and wait for nightfall before heading inland."

We reached the end of Folly Island about thirty minutes later. All four of us were quieter and more serious than usual. It seemed that we were all in a much darker mood than the last time we had gone out, and the good humor that had kept us going during the worst of times had disappeared.

"I take it I'm not the only one who's a bit worried about this trip," I said. My timing was never that good, but we were just passing the county park at the end of Folly Island, and the infected dead wandering around the dunes and sandy beaches had heard the sound of our engine. They began wandering our way, and the water was too calm to keep them on shore. It was sad to see so many of them walking into the water, but maybe it was a form of mercy too.

Jean reached out and put her hand on my arm and said, "We're going to be fine, Eddy. We're all a bit scared, but once we get back to Mud Island and get the boat shelter done, we won't have a reason to leave for a long, long time."

"Hey, Chief," said Kathy, "maybe we should put a little more distance between us and the beach."

The Chief must have been thinking the same thing, because he turned the wheel to the left without hesitating, and we became less of a distraction to the dead on the beach. The infected that had already spotted us were still taking a walk out into the surf, but the others seemed intent upon just wandering.

We passed around the end of Folly Island and entered the deep water at the mouth of the Stono River. The overcast sky and the green color of the water made it feel gloomy, which didn't do much for my mood. I guess I was really starting to wonder when our luck would completely run out. When I thought about it, not much we had done outside of the shelter had gone really well. My friends had escaped from an infected ship, and then they found safety with me at the shelter, only to give it up to fly back into the crazy world we had all left behind.

When the plane was damaged and we had to leave it behind, we were lucky again. We could easily have been trapped in Georgetown. Only a few days later the horde of infected had probably swarmed down from Simmonsville. To tell the truth, when we saw them and their unholy parade going down Highway 17, it felt like we should have called off our plan to retrieve the plane.

The Chief went about a hundred yards up the river and then put the Whaler into a wide turn to the right. A small island that was really more of a sandbar with a raised center and scrub brush rose up in front of us, and a small cove was cut into the side facing the mainland. It would be a perfect place to wait for the sun to go down. The Whaler slid easily onto the sand, and we jumped over the bow to pull it forward.

"Shouldn't be a problem to get a small fire going," said Jean. "The temperature is dropping a bit, and I could use a little coffee."

"That makes two of us," said Kathy, "and what is it about riding in a bouncing boat on a cold day that makes me have to pee so bad?"

Kathy ran between me and the Chief and disappeared behind a sand dune so fast that the Chief and I just stared at each other for a moment. Jean was looking at us like she was trying to decide something.

Jean said, "Oh my god, I've been holding it so long that I forgot I had to go." She dropped her backpack and took off for the dunes yelling to Kathy to wait for her.

The Chief asked, "Why do women always have to go pee together, and how long before she remembers the TP is in her backpack?"

We were still laughing when they came back around the dunes together, and maybe that was what we needed. I felt the weight of the world lift from my shoulders because we were a good group. We had each other's backs, and we knew what we were doing. I felt like my down attitude was worse for us than all the dangers ahead, and I mentally kicked myself for not getting my act together sooner. Hopefully, it was just in time.

We built a small fire and heated up our coffee. We had plenty of the food packs Uncle Titus had stored in the shelter, so we decided to eat while we had time. All the choices we brought sounded appetizing, but they all tasted the same to me. I took one labeled beef burrito.

"Are you really going to eat that?" asked the Chief. He was looking at me like he couldn't believe my choice.

"Yeah, why not?" I asked.

He got a big smile on his face and said, "Remind me to dig through that big movie library when we get back to Mud Island. I'll see if there's a copy of Blazing Saddles. The campfire scene made the whole movie worth watching."

Kathy and Jean both got a good case of giggling fits, but I hadn't seen the movie. "Is anybody going to tell me what's so funny?" I asked between their bouts of laughter.

"No, Eddy," said Jean, "it's worth waiting to see for yourself. We'll all watch it together when we get home."

A splash in the water got our attention, and we all drew ours weapons. The sun was getting low, and shadows were starting to make everything look different. We didn't want our campfire to be the only light for miles around, so we finished heating our coffee water and put it out. We also didn't want to be stuck on this little lump of sand overnight, so we decided we would wait the last hour for darkness in the boat.

With our gear stowed again, we pushed off and boarded, then dropped anchor when we were over deeper water. To be less visible, we pulled down dark tarps from where we had them tied above the center canopy over the steering wheel. They blocked out the cold wind that was beginning to kick up, and we were able to rest before starting up river.

Just after darkness as we pulled up the anchor and started up the Stono River. A light rain started, and even though it was annoying to get water down the backs of our necks, it was one way to cover some of the sound we made. It didn't take long for us to reach the first fork in the river, and we turned to the right to stay on course.

"That's the Kiawah River up the left fork," said the Chief. "Nice homes and beachfront property down that river, but they probably didn't do any better than the rest of the islands. They have some security for the private property, but probably just enough to keep looters out when it first started. They would have let anyone onto Kiawah Island who lived there, and you know what that means. Someone inside would have spread the infection."

The river snaked away in front of us, and we stayed as close to the shore as we could. The Chief didn't want to rush because we were likely to find trouble around each turn as we approached the first bridge.

It took almost an hour, but we finally saw the first bridge ahead. We had switched to using our paddles and poles to ease ourselves forward, and the light was really bad, but luckily the shore of the Stono River was more like the big mudbank where we had left the plane. If any infected were out there where we couldn't see them, they were likely to be stuck in the mud for a long time.

The rain was keeping sound from traveling too far. The advantage was that no one would hear us coming. The disadvantage was obvious, and we didn't hear the voices until we were practically on top of them.

A flashlight glared into our eyes just long enough to blind us, but mercifully it was turned off just as quickly. A voice just loud enough to be heard said, "I only need to ask one question. Has anyone in your boat been bitten?"

We were all still a bit blind from the suddenness of the flashlight, but I saw the Chief had one finger on his lips and one pointed at Kathy. He knew someone had at least gotten a look at us, but the light hadn't been on long enough for whoever it was to have done a complete survey. The Chief wanted Kathy to talk us through this one if she could. Maybe her celebrity was still worth mentioning this long after the world had ended.

Kathy understood and said, "No one has been bitten. How do we know the same is true about you?"

"You don't, but it's my job to make sure no one gets by who has been bitten," the voice said from the darkness.

"Exactly how do you know for sure?" asked Kathy. "Do you have some kind of test?"

The owner of the voice laughed quietly. "No, there's no real test, but we have a Psychologist over at the marina, and he told us when we ask the question out here in the dark, bitten people would be more likely to try too hard to convince us they weren't bitten. People who hadn't been bitten would want to know if we were infected. We wouldn't know for sure until it's too late, but we can't shoot everybody who goes by."

"That's good to hear," said Kathy. "What did you mean when you said over at the marina? Did you manage to save people? Did you find a way to seal off the marina?"

"All in good time if you don't mind, Miss. The first thing we need to do is get you safely to the other side of the bridge."

The voice moved closer, and we could make out the outline of a small flat bottomed boat with two men in it.

Both were armed, but neither had their weapons pointed at us, which was a relief.

"I'm John, and my friend here is Dan. Our job is to escort people by the bridge at safe spots."

"Safe spots? What does that mean, and how did you get stuck with the job?" Kathy asked. This was confusing to all of us.

John and Dan could see us a little better close up, and they knew they were seriously outnumbered and outgunned, but they both seemed relaxed. There was no doubt in my mind that they felt like they were in control, and they probably were from what they were saying.

Jean leaned a bit closer to Kathy and said, "Ask them if they are going to let us through?"

"I can hear you okay out here at night, little lady. That's one reason I'm on watch so much. I grew up out here, and I know sounds that aren't supposed to be here. For instance, I bet you didn't know about all those biters less than twenty yards from here." He gestured toward the shore behind us, and we all couldn't stop ourselves from looking.

He chuckled again, "The answer to your question is yes, we will not only let you through, we're going to help you get through. Like I said, it's my job."

The Chief kept his voice low and said, "John, there's a guy up in Georgetown named Hampton. At least there was a guy in Georgetown by that name last time we went through there. Anyway, you remind me of him, and no matter how crappy things get, I hope we keep running into people like you and Hampton."

The Chief pointed at each of us in turn and said, "Our spokesman here has been Kathy, the little lady is Jean, that's Ed, and you can call me Chief. That's what my friends call me, and right now I consider you to be a friend."

"Pleased to meet all of you folks. Now, let me explain what we're doing here. I'm going to escort you to the other side of the bridge. In return we only want to trade information about what's happening out there. If you've been up around Georgetown and lived to tell about it, you might be doing a lot better than most people."

"We'll be glad to tell you what we know," said the Chief, "but I'm confused about why we need an escort just to the other side of the bridge."

"You won't be confused in a few minutes, Chief. We're going to go most of the way through at a crawl, so you won't have any trouble keeping up, but stay right on my stern. If you get around to either side of me, you won't like what happens. We'll stop and talk for a spell after we get up by the bridge."

They powered up a small trolling motor that didn't make much noise, but it made enough to stir up something on the bridge. As we eased up closer to the bridge, the sound grew louder. We hadn't really been able to hear the massive horde we saw marching down Highway 17, but this was what I imagined they would have sounded like if we had gotten closer. The sound was coming from the road that crossed the bridge, and it was getting louder.

John and Dan steered away from the center of the bridge toward one span to the right. In the dim light I could see that the center was clear of debris, so I was curious about why we couldn't go through where the water was deeper. My curiosity was satisfied when the first body hit the water with a loud slap.

Jean let out a low yelp, and as close as I came to screaming like a little girl, I managed to keep from letting it out as a second body hit in the same spot as the first. That one was followed by a third, a fourth, and a fifth. Each one hit the water, got grabbed by the current and pulled downriver.

There was just enough light as we got closer to the bridge to see that the railing of the center span was gone. An accident during the mad rush to safety had opened up a forty to fifty foot section, and the sound of our boat motors was drawing the infected through the gap. The swarm of infected was every bit as large as what we saw on Highway 17, and they started following our sounds as best as they could until bodies were raining over the side.

The railing was still intact on the span where we crossed, and as we were about to reach the bridge, we saw John frantically wave his arm in a forward motion and increase his speed to maximum. The Chief didn't need a second invitation and poured on the throttle. As we passed through, we heard some splashes behind us and knew it has been close. The railing above may still be intact, but with all of the pushing and shoving, there were bound to be some who went over the railing. It was just a good thing that the infected weren't capable of climbing over it.

We coasted up to where John had come to a stop and pulled along side. The Chief tossed him a line, and then he gave both John and Dan a hand to come onto our larger boat. We all looked back in the direction of the bridge and saw it was still raining bodies.

"It will be going on like that for some time," said John.

Dan, who had been quiet up to now added, "We've considered driving back and forth under the bridge to get them worked up so they'll start falling off even more. Most of the time they do it on their own anyway, but when they hear a boat motor go by, they get really worked up."

"This place is a natural disposal site for the infected, but why are they up there to begin with? Why don't they cross the bridge and keep going?" I asked.

"Because they can see the marina," said John. "When everything went down on the first day, we were like everyone else. We thought we needed to get to our boats and get to sea as fast as possible. We were wrong, though. All we needed to do was disconnect the slips from the mainland."

"It's too dark to tell from here, but do you see the main building at the marina?" asked Dan. He pointed toward the dark shadow of the building. "It's on stilts, and all of the slips are connected to it by floating walkways. The only thing connecting the whole mess to the mainland are three walkways, and all three have been removed."

John picked up the rest of the story as soon as Dan took a breath. I got the impression that they were both looking for fresh audiences to explain this to.

"About two hundred yards past the end of the bridge you finally come to the exit from the highway that lets you drive down to the marina. The beggars aren't smart enough to figure that out, so they just keep going back and forth on the bridge. Those that accidentally find the turn and wander down to the marina walk right into the water and get washed away," said John.

True to form it was Dan's turn again. "We keep a watch on the docks just in case one gets lucky, but so far none of them have figured out how to get up onto the walkways after they walk into the water."

"How many people managed to survive on the boats?" asked Kathy.

"We did a head count last week, and we had four hundred and eighty men, women, and children," said John.

"Wow," said Kathy, "that's more than I expected, but how do you feed everyone?"

"That's not a problem yet, but we know we can't live off of what we have forever," said Dan.

The Chief looked like he was trying to process that last comment from Dan, but something wasn't quite right. Almost five hundred people had survived for over a month on what?

"John, how have you been feeding that many people for so long?" asked the Chief. Even in the darkness I could see the Chief shifting his hand toward his holster. He did it so casually that it registered with me, Kathy, and Jean, but our two talkative friends didn't seem to notice. Either that, or they were good at hiding any reaction.

John answered, "Well, we had a bunch of supplies on the boats, but no one thought it would go on for so long, so no one rationed. Then we started sending people across into the restaurant next to the marina, and we got a pretty good haul from there."

"The shark fishing and crabbing is pretty good around here, too," said Dan," and when the tide goes out we still get some shrimp even though the weather is starting to get cooler."

I was willing to bet Jean was going to toss her cookies in the boat because she had one hand over her mouth.

"Crabbing?" she asked, though her hand made it sound pretty muffled.

"Sure," John said, "and we don't even need to use bait or traps. We just hook those stupid biters with a long pole hook and pull them up. They're usually covered with blue crabs, so all we have to do is pick them off. Some of the guys got the idea of putting a rope around the same biters and dropping them back in. That way they don't have to hook a new one each time. The crabs also seem to like the ones that have been in the water longer."

Jean couldn't hold it in, but she did manage to keep it in until she was hanging over the stern.

"Don't lean over too close to the water," said John. "They bob back up to the surface sometimes."

"We won't be staying for supper," said the Chief, "but we can tell you what we know about the rest of the world before we move on." The mention of supper with them brought on a new round of gagging from Jean.

"Is she all right?" asked John. "You sure she hasn't been bitten?"

Kathy said, "She's fine. Probably just had some bad crab." Jean went for round three. "We really appreciate you escorting us under the bridge. We probably would have had some unwelcome guests if not for you. I'm wondering, though. How does everyone feel?"

Our guides probably didn't connect the dots because they said they felt fine. "No one has been bitten," said Dan, and he looked at John as if he expected confirmation.

We spent about an hour telling John and Dan about the Naval Weapons Station, but we didn't give away any details about the plane or Mud Island. We told our stories as if we had gotten our information from other survivors. The Chief was visibly more relaxed, but it took a long time before his hand wasn't sitting on the butt of his gun.

I spent part of the time helping Jean get over her nausea by feeding her crackers and water, but she whispered something about payback being a bitch, and she was good at payback. I was pretty sure she meant Kathy and not me.

Before parting company we asked the men what they knew about the two bridges up ahead, and if they knew anything about what was happening over in the Charleston harbor. They said the Wappoo Creek draw bridge had been raised to prevent more of the infected from coming onto James Island, and it had never been lowered back down. The biggest problem according to them was clean water, but we had a feeling their biggest problem was the going to be the long term effects of eating crabs that had been eating the infected. They were nice enough people, but neither of them had a clue about the food chain.

John told us that more people had come through from the harbor rather than from the ocean as we had, and most said to stay away from Fort Sumter because it had been taken over by some survivalists that felt like the only way to live through an apocalypse was for everyone else to die. We told them that was why we came in through the Stono River, and that we narrowly escaped the mouth of the harbor. They said they would be sure to warn everyone who came through.

They both agreed we wouldn't have any trouble at the drawbridge because there wasn't any need for it to be guarded. The last bridge was a very high fixed span, and there wasn't any reason to expect either shooters or bodies dropping down from above. No other travelers had reported problems there.

We started for the Wappoo Creek at about ten PM and feeling a little better about making it to the harbor. We still didn't know how bad it would be when we reached the spot where the Ashley River and Cooper River met, and where we would have to pass by the cruise terminal. I was sure that was on all of their minds as I studied my three companions.

"Chief? What were you thinking when you asked John how they were keeping so many people fed? I saw you getting ready to pull your gun if you had to," I said.

Kathy said, "He was thinking they were eating the infected, which is just one step away from eating the uninfected."

"Which reminds me," said Jean, "bad crab? Seriously?"

"You looked like you needed to be cheered up, Jean. I was only trying to help," said Kathy.

If there was one thing our little group was really good at, it was looking innocent at someone else's expense. Kathy was keeping a straight face, but the Chief was about to bust a seam because he was holding it in so hard. He was pretending to focus on steering the boat, but I saw him wiping the back of his hand across his eyes.

"So, Chief, is Kathy right about what you were thinking?" I asked.

"Partially," he said. "I was thinking they had already gotten around to eating long pork."

"Long pork?" I asked. "What's that mean?"

"Cover your ears, Jean," he said with a smile aimed at her. Jean didn't smile back.

"That's what cannibal tribes call people, Ed." He said it so naturally that I was wondering if he was pulling my leg, but when I looked at Kathy, she nodded her head as if confirming what he had said.

I was ready to move on from that particular conversation, but I had one other thing nagging at me, so I directed the question and statement at both Kathy and the Chief.

"I noticed that neither of you told John and Dan about what they could expect to happen from the inside," I said, "you know, like you did with Hampton."

"You mean loved ones not telling the others if they were bitten?" asked Kathy. "It would be even worse here, Ed. This group would be likely to dangle you in the water as crab bait if you got bitten."

"I don't give them another month," said the Chief. "Jean, you're a medical person. Did you see anything useful about the effects of eating crabs that had been eating the infected?"

"If I hadn't been so revolted by the thought, Chief, I might have asked them some questions and maybe would have checked their vital signs, but I didn't see anything obvious."

"Are you serious?" asked Kathy. "You would have checked their vital signs? What would you have expected to find?"

"I couldn't say for sure, but before the infected would die, they would get flu-like symptoms, so I would be interested in knowing if any of them have been experiencing swollen lymph glands, fevers, and all the usual things. Honestly," she said, "what really scares the hell out of me is that mutations of viruses occur exactly like this scenario."

I had been more of a spectator up to this point in the conversation, but the implications weren't lost on me.

"Are you saying the people got infected by being bitten, they died and then were eaten by the crabs, which were eaten by unbitten people, and now they will be able to spread the virus without biting someone?" I asked.

"That's a possibility," she said. "The proof is in the very existence of the infection."

The Chief said, "You lost me, Jean."

"Okay, let me explain it like this," said Jean. "Eddy, where did you see your first infected person, and knowing what you know now, how could you tell they were infected?"

"That's easy," I answered. "It was outside a fast food place in Surfside, and knowing what I know now, I know the person was infected because she was trying to bite everyone."

"How did she get infected?" She asked.

"I assume she was bitten by someone. Are you saying she might not have been?"

Kathy answered for her. "The infection had to begin somewhere, Ed, and the question would be how did the very first person who was infected manage to get infected?"

Jean took it the rest of the way and said, "Patient zero may have gotten it from a bite, but what if the bite came from something like a blue crab? I mean, most people can wrap their minds around something like a monkey bite or some other kind of wild animal bite, but what if it was a blue crab. Now we have people eating crabs that weren't previously infected, but those crabs have been chewing on infected tissue. We don't know how this infection will react to being metabolized."

If I had been drinking, Jean had just invented a way to counteract the alcohol, because I couldn't have become more sober.

"We're coming up on the Wappoo Creek drawbridge, folks." The Chief's voice was low but we heard it loud and clear. We had already seen some surprises we hadn't expected at the last bridge.

The Chief said, "Everyone keep low and as close to the bulkheads as possible. If someone sees us, I don't want them to know how many guns we have."

The Boston Whaler was barely coasting forward as we approached the open drawbridge. It was eerie to see the two sections of the bridge pointing toward the sky. It was still overcast, but the light from the moon was filtering through just enough for us to see shadows moving on the fixed spans. There were just enough of them for us to tell they were likely to be infected. Besides, there wasn't much reason to post a watch on an open bridge that had the infected dead on both sides. That would be a good way to get yourself trapped.

It didn't appear that we had to worry about uninvited guests dropping in because the railings were intact on the side we were approaching, but even if they were down, we were going through the middle. There was zero chance of the infected coming over the open spans.

Kathy said in a whisper, "Chief, it looks like there's a gap between the railing and the raised span on each side, but I think something's blocking it."

We all looked for what Kathy was talking about and saw it was true, but it became obvious as we approached that the gaps were blocked by bodies of the infected dead. The arms and legs of some were still moving.

The Chief said, "I have a theory that seems to make some sense. The bridge must've been crowded with the infected when someone raised the thing. Imagine how many of them went sliding back down into a big pile at the bottom. You could fit over two hundred on each span, so they were probably deep enough to keep the ones on the bottom from walking away."

I pictured the bridge operator trapped in the tower over the first fixed span on the right. He or she probably knew there was no way to leave the tower once they were inside, but payback was probably very satisfying. If it had been me, I would have raised the bridge, dumped the infected in a big pile at the bottom, lowered the bridge, waited for the center spans to fill up again, and then raise it again. I would have done it to my heart's content, or maybe even until there was a chance to escape.

I quietly told Jean what I was thinking, and she got a little giggling fit the way she did from time to time. The Chief and Kathy wanted to know what she was giggling about, so she passed it along to them. Before it could get stopped everyone was trying not to laugh. If anyone would have been listening, they would have wondered about the four survivors coasting under the bridge and choking back laughter.

"Ed," said the Chief, "you are one sick individual sometimes, but that's probably why you're alive today."

It felt good knowing that my friends appreciated my sense of humor, although it was a bit warped, but it also felt good that I was probably right about what had happened on the bridge. I silently hoped that the same scenario had played out at every drawbridge in the country, or the whole world.

As we passed under the bridge, we kept our eyes on the other side. We would know in moments if the infected had a way to drop in from above, but even if they could, they wouldn't land in the center. If we had not been watching, we probably wouldn't have noticed the rope ladder hanging from the tower down to the water. It was a relief to know the bridge operator had possibly escaped to a boat waiting below the bridge.

We passed a boat landing on our left and Kathy pointed out the number of trailers that would be just right for our purposes. The Chief agreed and said he had seen even more trailers at the boat landing just south of where we had left the plane.

A familiar groan came from the mass of parked vehicles at the boat landing, and soon it became a chorus of groans. They emerged from the darkness around the cars and were drawn to the low rumble of the boat motor.

Even as their numbers grew, we were drifting away from them, so we watched without compassion as they walked down the sloped concrete of the boat landing and stepped into the swift current of the water that passed under the bridge. John and Dan had said it was swift at this landing, but that was almost an understatement. As the infected entered the water, they appeared to be knocked down and yanked under by some unseen force. Each groaning infected dead was there and gone in a split second.

I think we were all surprised when the Chief put the engine on idle and dropped the anchor. He brought us to a stop about ten yards from the landing.

"We might just be helping someone else to stay alive," he said. "Remember what Dan said about driving back and forth under the bridge just to make more of them fall off? Well, he may be crazy for eating the crabs, but he wasn't wrong about eliminating as many of the infected as possible. If we sit here for about thirty minutes, it might clear this boat landing."

Thirty minutes later the boat landing was quiet, and we had done our part to help get rid of some of the infected. Even though it was a drop in the bucket, it felt good to fight back. It would have taken a lot of bullets and head shots to dispose of that many infected dead.

The Chief raised the anchor and pushed the throttle forward, and the third bridge before reaching Charleston harbor came into view. It seemed like a skyscraper compared to the other bridges because it was so far above us, and it wasn't going to be a problem for us unless the Chief drove us into one of the massive supports.

We watched it pass by above without incident, and the Chief gave us even more speed as we rushed toward the Ashley River. It was dark enough due to the overcast sky hiding most of the moon for the Chief to give us more speed than before. It wasn't long before he put the Whaler in a long turn to our right as we reached the deeper water of the Ashley River.

"I need everyone keeping their eyes forward," said the Chief. "The river is wide enough for us to be less worried about shooting us then before, but I don't want to run into a survivor who may be anchored out here. We may make them mad by throwing out a big wake, but that would be better than cutting them in half."

I was thinking more along the lines of us being a bug on the windshield of something big that could be anchored in the river, but I didn't say it out loud. I just got myself in a position to see up ahead.

The Chief began his second sweeping turn, but this time it was to the left as we reached the mouth of the Cooper River. Even in the dark I could tell that the island coming up on the right was the one where hundreds of people had landed by Castle Pinckney as they escaped from the marina at Patriots Point.

There were no dark shapes wandering around on the narrow island as we sped past as quickly as we could. The old Civil War fort had never been restored, so it was not an attractive place for survivors to fortify, but it was surprising that no one was at least standing guard on the harbor from that spot. We had to pass far too close for comfort, and we all expected to be shot at again.

The cruise terminal came up on our left, and the sight of the dock had a visible effect on my companions.

"We're home," said Kathy. She tried to make it sound like humor, but her voice was empty of any joy. All of us were reliving that day when Kathy had barricaded the infected from entering the terminal long enough for the ship to escape. They were all hopeful at the moment the big cruise ship had pulled away from the dock, but they knew now it had been a horribly doomed effort.

Jean said as we rushed past the dock where the triage tent had been set up, "We had to try, you know. We couldn't have lived with ourselves if we hadn't. It turned into a terrible nightmare for everyone but us, but it was either that or die right here at this dock."

By the time she had finished speaking, we were past the dock and the Chief was aiming for the channel under the Ravenel Bridge, the main connection between Charleston and Mount Pleasant. There were lights on in the USS Yorktown parked at Patriots Point, and it was tempting to investigate, but it was also dangerous. In this new world, we couldn't know if other survivors would be like Hampton and Ward, John and Dan, or the unknown shooters who we were forced to avoid going past Fort Sumter.

We passed under the massive bridge and watched as the lights on the Yorktown receded in the distance. I think we all had a longing to rejoin society, but the cost of admission could be too high.

Jean squeezed my hand and asked what I was thinking. I told her I was wondering how long everyone was going to survive. Hampton's group would probably be overcome by infection from within because someone didn't admit to being bitten. John's group would probably die from within because they were eating the crabs that had been feeding on the infected, and the people on the Yorktown, whoever they were, would probably be attacked by another group of survivors because they were too visible. It would be too easy for rival groups of survivors to think someone else had it better, and they should take what the others have. The group holding Fort Sumter sure seemed to feel that way.

"We may have the best thing going for us because of you, Eddy," she said.

"We might," I answered, "but we should stop leaving Mud Island until things settle down. If we get back in one piece, I'm not leaving again for the rest of my life."

"I think your Uncle did a good thing by building the shelter on Mud Island, but I don't think he had this type of apocalypse in mind," she said. "I think he was thinking more of a war, collapse of society, or a really big natural disaster. The boat, the plane, and the houseboat weren't necessarily supposed to survive the destruction, so he didn't provide for their protection. If he would have thought of it himself, he probably would have done what we're planning to do."

We looked up ahead and saw that we had reached the Wando River. That meant we were probably going to reach the Paradise Boat Landing in just about two hours if all went well, but we still had two more bridges to go. One of them was another monster that was high enough for big shipping traffic to pass under, but the second bridge could be the worst one we would deal with.

None of us had any first hand knowledge of the last bridge, so we had to rely completely on the maps. They showed that the bridge crossing at Highway 41 was low, narrow, and easily a good place for an ambush. At the river's highest stage, it was barely twenty feet from the surface of the water to the pavement on the bridge. There was a low concrete railing, but pictures showed it was such an odd construction that it literally begged someone to fall over it whether they were the living or the infected dead. There would be no way to tell which we would encounter on the bridge until we arrived.

When we were planning this impossible mission to bring back the plane with the trailer strapped to its belly, we had managed to connect to an internet server that was still running long enough to find some digital maps and photos. We zoomed in on this bridge and decided there was no way we were going to try to go under at the middle. The Boston Whaler didn't draft too deep, so the plan was to tie off at the last private dock to the north of the bridge. We would wait for the next high tide, inflate a raft, and then tow the Whaler under the first span closest to that shoreline.

"How are we doing time wise, Chief?" I asked.

He checked his notes and said, "High tide is at three o'clock, Ed, so we should only have about an hour to wait after we find our target dock."

"That's not bad timing," said Kathy. "We should have time to talk about Plan B."

"I think we did Plan B when we were forced to use the back door to Charleston harbor. Are you thinking we need a Plan C," Kathy?

"I'm thinking I don't want to drive the boat back out the way we came, Chief. We know what to expect in some places, but that doesn't mean there weren't some things we missed. There could even be patrols on the water that were just at the right place at the right time as we crossed the harbor. I think it's too risky because of the distance."

The Chief looked like he was mulling it over when Jean asked, "Is there a way to get the boat from this river to the ocean if we drove it on a road? There's going to be plenty of cars at the boat landing. We can strap a trailer to the plane for you to fly out, and we can load the boat on another. If we can get it to the ocean, we would be pretty close to Mud Island."

"You may be onto something, Jean. When we get to our dock, let's take a close look at the maps and see."

I asked, "What about the cars, Chief? Any worries about them not starting?"

"No, I'm not really worried about that, Ed. Have you ever seen someone jump start a car from a plane engine?"

I had to admit, I hadn't ever thought about that, but I wasn't sure if the Chief was kidding or not, so I just smiled. The Chief had that look like the trap was set and he was just waiting for me to take the bait.

We followed the twists and turns of the Wando River until we spotted the last bridge up ahead. It appeared rather suddenly as we came around a large bend in the river. The Chief kept the boat in the center of the river until we were past the Charleston City Boatyard, and then he steered toward the last of seven private docks that jutted out into the river.

I checked the time and saw we had close to an hour to rest as the Chief tied the mooring line from the boat to the dock. It was a very long dock, so we weren't concerned about any infected dead or living people using it to sneak up on us. Even so, I climbed up on the dock and laid down with a rifle pointed straight down its length to the shore.

Behind me the Chief and Kathy huddled under a makeshift shelter in the center of the boat and spread out the maps. The camouflaged tarps they were using would block the light from their flashlights. I would have been happy to have Jean laying next to me on the deck, but she took up a position by my feet facing back out over the boat toward the water. From her spot she could keep an eye on the water on all sides of the boat.

After about thirty minutes Kathy and the Chief emerged from their shelter and climbed up on the dock with us. They huddled close to us and whispered that they had a plan that would get us home by that afternoon.

******

By three AM the tide was high enough for us to leave the dock. We were all a bit rested, but none of us had been hungry enough to bother with a meal. The Chief had inflated the raft and positioned it just a few feet from the bow. We started quietly forward with Jean steering the Whaler since she was the lightest of the four of us. We didn't want it to draft any deeper than it needed to. As a result, it was skimming nicely along the surface.

I was using a long pole to push down on the muddy bottom below us, and the others were paddling. There was a deep groan from somewhere in front of us, and we all froze. The Whaler drifted up to the raft and gave it a slight bump. We all listened and willed our eyes to see just a little bit farther into the darkness.

"There it is," I said. "It looks like just one at about ten o'clock, and it looks like it's stuck in the mud."

Everyone spotted it, and we started forward again, being careful not to let the boat drift sideways toward the infected. It continued to groan and to reach for us. It had this pathetic look on its face like it couldn't believe that we wouldn't come closer.

As we approached the bridge, the Chief made a quiet sound to draw our attention to him. He pointed toward the center of the bridge and mouthed one word, "Watch."

It was totally dark, and it was at least one hundred yards to the center of the bridge, but we strained our eyes in that direction and waited. After what seemed like forever, there was a reddish glow that arced upward, grew brighter, then arced back downward. Someone was smoking a cigarette. We had seen him lift it from hiding down by his side, take a drag, then quickly put it back down again.

I had read somewhere a long time ago about soldiers in combat who didn't believe smoking at night was as dangerous as others led them to believe, and once in a while, someone would test that theory. It was such a sure way to give away your position that the kill shot was usually to the head. All the shooter had to do was wait for the cigarette to glow brighter, and that meant it was between the smoker's lips.

The Chief whispered to us, "The glow of the cigarette will mess with his vision more than he realizes. Just try not to bump into anything like the hull of the boat."

He signaled for us to start forward again, but we kept a close watch on his position. He must have been trying to stay awake because he lit another cigarette as soon as he finished the other. The lighter seemed so bright in the darkness he might as well have shot off a flare.

"Did you see that?" whispered Kathy.

We all stopped and waited so she could tell us what she saw. "Look under the bridge," she said.

We could't see it well, but there was something unmistakably different about the light coming through directly under the middle span. There wasn't much light anywhere, but there was none under the middle span.

"Does that look like a cargo net to you guys?" she asked.

"Wow," I said. "We guessed this one right, didn't we."

As we passed under the span closest to shore, the canopy over the steering wheel cleared the underside of the bridge by mere inches. We all held our breath hoping we were right about how high the boat would be riding, but on the off chance we could see it was going to be too high, we were all prepared to climb on board at the last moment to make it draft deeper.

Once we were back out in the open, there was a moment when light reflected off the water between the bridge and the far shore, and we could see the net more clearly. If we had tried for the middle, we would have been caught in that heavy cargo net, and there would have been no chance to get free.

The Wando River made a ninety degree turn to the left about one hundred yards past the bridge, and just to be safe, we continued to float using paddles and poles until we had made the turn. Starting the engine any sooner would have been an open invitation to get shot on such a quiet night.

After the turn, the Chief signaled for us all to get back into the boat. He quickly deflated the raft far enough to bring it on board and dragged it over the stern. We had already given up one raft when we had set it adrift after returning to Mud Island the last time, and we didn't know if we would need this one again.

"We have less than five miles until we get to the boat landing. We're going to go right past it to the plane and drop me off," said the Chief. "You guys will go back to the boat landing and look for a vehicle that starts and a good trailer to use to haul the boat across to the ocean. Also, try to find a smaller trailer for us to use on Mud Island. Everyone know the plan?"

We all nodded, and the Chief started the boat. If anyone heard it at the bridge, they would hopefully be well upriver before he could raise the alarm.

The next five miles of our trip went by fast, and by four AM we were passing the boat landing. Unlike the boat landing on Wappoo Creek by the open drawbridge, there was no crowd of infected dead. We cruised past the parked cars, boats, and trailers and came to the dock where the plane sat waiting for us. We all felt our spirits lifted by the sight of the Otter and realized two things were true. We weren't totally sure the plane would still be here, and the thought of making it back to the plane seemed more like an impossibility than a probability.

"Is it just me," I asked, "or did anyone else think we had a snowball's chance in hell of making it back to this spot?"

I looked around and saw that my companions were smiling at me. That was all the answer I needed.

"We have work to do," said the Chief. "The faster we get it done, the faster we'll get home." He already had his hands full of the gear he needed for the repairs. "This repair is so easy, I may be back for you before you can get a car running, so make it quick."

We made a quick scan of the mudflats around the plane and saw that they were as wet and unforgiving as they had been before. There were still infected dead stuck in the mud from our last visit, but they were slumped over where they had become stuck. In the darkness before the dawn, we couldn't tell if they were still able to move, but the ones nearest to us had been mostly eaten. Blue crabs clinging to one brought back bad memories, and Jean turned away. She had seen worse things as a nurse, but it was the thought of people eating the crabs that got to her.

We decided the Chief was safe where he was. He was working by flashlight in a part of the engine where the light couldn't be seen from shore. As for the infected, they had a hard time walking a straight line, so it wasn't likely one could reach him while he's standing on a pontoon of an airplane.

Kathy, Jean, and I spun the boat around and headed back for the boat landing. Since Kathy was the best shot, she was armed with a Glock and would stand watch over me while I found a vehicle I could start. Jean would tag along with a flashlight if one was needed.

In a matter of minutes we had the Whaler tied to the dock next to the ramp of the boat landing and were sprinting toward the rows of parked cars. Our plan was simple. We would check every vehicle with a trailer attached to it to see if the keys were in the ignition. If we were unlucky, Kathy had a screwdriver and would break the ignition switch to start the car. We preferred finding keys because there was always a chance that the electronics of the car would get messed up when the ignition switch broke, and we didn't want the car to cut off and refuse to start again.

It was Jean who got the idea that we should check the vehicles that were facing away from the water with the trailers facing toward the water. Her logic was that the boats had been off loaded, but the vehicles weren't parked yet. There were also several with their boats still on the trailers.

The first vehicle was a new dark colored Silverado with the extended crew cab, and we couldn't believe our eyes. The keys were in the ignition. We all looked at each other and smiled.

"Jean, you're a genius," I said.

She answered, "That's what I've been trying to tell you guys for weeks. I'm not just another pretty face."

I gave her a big kiss, and Kathy rolled her eyes before jumping into the driver seat and turning the key. The engine burst into life, and Kathy only kept it running long enough to see if it had enough gas.

"It doesn't get any better than this," she said. "It has a full tank."

I asked, "Hey, is there any reason not to take the boat too?"

"None that I can think of," said Kathy. "If we can find another vehicle that starts and doesn't have a boat on the trailer, we could keep the Boston Whaler. You know why your uncle picked a Whaler don't you?"

I thought back to the first day I saw it and remembered that I was too happy to have the boat. I never gave a thought to why he picked that type boat, but now that I had spent so much time in it, I knew it was because of the shallow draft. It was great in these coastal rivers.

"I think I have an idea of why he picked it, Kathy. Some of these really comfortable cabin cruisers could only travel right down the middle of the rivers where the water is deep. This one on the trailer probably has to go under the bridge at low tide."

"Exactly, but it would be better out on the ocean if we were having to make a run for it. It has about twice as much speed as the Whaler. The biggest advantage would be as a decoy. If we have it parked next to the houseboat, no one would even think to look for the other boat."

"Ok, Jean work your magic again. Where's our next winning vehicle?" I said.

Our next winning vehicle had a body on the ground next to it. When this guy went down, he must have been really swarmed because too much of him was eaten for him to get up and join the others. Jean checked his pockets and fished a set of keys out of the grisly mess.

A quick check of the green F-100 next to the body showed that the guy hadn't made it too far, either. His boat wasn't on the trailer, so odds were that he had put it into the water and gone back to park his car. I looked at what used to be a man and wondered if it had all happened that fast, or if he was so obsessed with obeying the rules that it didn't occur to him to just drop off the boat and leave the truck and trailer on the ramp.

"Whatever," I said. The key fit, and the truck started just as easily as the Silverado. It had three quarters of a tank of gas, which was more than enough to get us where we needed to go.

Jean jumped in with me, and I backed the trailer down the ramp until it was submerged enough to let the Whaler slide onto it. I didn't use the headlights, but the back-up lights and brake lights seemed unnaturally bright against the darkness. I put on the emergency brake and killed the engine.

We all made a mad dash for the Boston Whaler and got it started while Jean threw the mooring line from the dock. Then she turned and ran back to the truck as I jockeyed the Whaler into position.

Kathy was with me in the boat getting ready to jump off as I slipped the boat over the submerged trailer, and it was a sick feeling when I glanced toward Jean and saw that she wasn't alone.

Less than ten feet behind her were three nightmare figures lurching with outstretched arms in her direction. I was in no position to help because I was having to hold the boat in a straight line. Kathy was on the wrong side of the Whaler and was looking down into the water for the right place to land when she jumped. She would never see Jean needed help in time.

With only a faint light of sunrise behind Jean and the three infected, I knew I was going to watch her die. I was so sure of it, that I didn't even understand what happened next or what the sound was behind me.

Three quick pops, and the heads of the infected dead exploded right behind Jean. She screamed and fell in my direction while the head shots propelled the infected the other way.

I saw Kathy leaping over the bow, and when I looked over my left shoulder, the Otter was floating at the end of the dock, and the Chief was standing on the left pontoon with a rifle aimed toward the parking lot. There were three more pops as he shot another three of the infected when they emerged from the dark.

"No time for thinking about it, Ed," he yelled. "You can do that later. Get the boat tied on and follow Kathy. She knows the way. I'll see you at home."

Kathy had gotten Jean off the ground and calmed down a bit, but like the Chief said. We could all think about it later. Close calls had happened, and they would continue to happen. I just didn't want them to happen to Jean.

Kathy pulled a cable with a hook on the end of it from a winch on the trailer and hooked it to the Whaler. I backed off to take up the slack, and she started the motor on the winch. The boat slid easily onto the tracks. Jean had gotten herself together and had jumped in to help. She was strapping down the boat to the trailer before I could hit the ground.

I ran up to the cab of the truck while Jean jumped in from the passenger side. Kathy shut down the motor on the winch and sprinted to the door of her own truck.

When both engines started and the headlights came on, we saw what we had expected from the start. The infected were coming out of the woods in large numbers. With no large predators in the area, there had been nothing to decrease their numbers except the river, and without people on the river they had not been drawn out onto the mudflats the way they had when we had first landed the plane at the dock.

The Chief stood on the pontoon and took some well aimed shots ahead of Kathy. Before they became too thick to drive over with the trucks or the trailers, we needed to get onto the open road.

There was no direct route over to Wando Farms Road, even though it was only a short distance away. There was a marshy inlet between the landing and the farm where we had found the Suburban. That meant a speedy drive down Chandler Road to Highway 17. That was about two miles, but it was mostly straight. Then we made a left onto Highway 17 and drove like maniacs back to Wando Farms Road. We covered the distance at speeds faster than anyone should tow a trailer, but our plan called for good timing.

I never thought I would ever see Wando Farms Road again, and I never thought I would be driving at breakneck speeds back to that barn, but with the sun coming up behind me, that's exactly what I was doing.

I only got a chance to glance over at Jean because I was going so fast, but it was enough for her to say, "Don't worry about me, Ed. I'm ok, and we have a job to do."

While Kathy and I drove to the farm, the Chief stayed behind for a few more minutes shooting at the infected. He revved the engine on the Otter a couple of times and generally made as much noise as possible. Over on Wando Farms Road, the infected dead began to move in the direction of the Paradise Boat Landing. The tide was going back out, so it was leaving behind soft pluff mud that was like quicksand in places.

As the infected reached the ramp at the boat landing and began to slide into the river, the groaning seemed to reach a fever pitch. Some of the infected tried to reach the Chief by walking out onto the dock, but he had let the seaplane drift away from it just far enough to be safe but to keep them tempted.

"The more the merrier," thought the Chief.

He kept up the firing until he guessed the others had made it to Highway 17. Then he jumped into the plane and drove it around the bend and back to the dock nearest to the farmhouse. He shoved a new magazine into his M-16 and charged down the dock like a bull. He remembered they had left a stack of corpses on the dock when they were there before, but small predators and vultures had removed the remains.

His timing was perfect, and he arrived at the barn just as Kathy pulled up. She was just about to unhitch the boat to open the gate on the back of the bed of the Silverado when he yelled not to bother.

We all knew the Chief was strong, but he wheeled the tiller out of the barn and lifted it into the back of the pick up truck by himself. He ran over to Kathy and gave her a big hug then ran for the trees. As he did, he yelled back that he would meet us at the rendezvous.

Kathy wheeled her truck around with me right behind her. A few of the infected had just begun to make it back from the distraction at the boat landing, but they didn't show up on Wando Farms Road until we had already passed by.

******

I didn't know exactly which way we were going to go. I was only sure it wouldn't be through Georgetown. The Chief planned on doing a little reconnaissance over the area to see how Hampton had made out, but he wasn't going to get close enough to take another bullet through the engine. We were lucky the damage wasn't severe the last time. This time it could be enough to bring him down hard and fast.

When we reached the intersection of Wando Farms Rd. and Highway 17, Kathy made a left and headed in the same direction we had gone the last time, but instead of staying on Highway 17 to Georgetown she made a hard right onto Seewee Road and floored the gas again. Because this road put us closer to the coast, I was getting an idea of what she had in mind.

Jean spread out a map and said, "You're going to be coming to Bulls Island Road in about five miles. After you make that turn, get ready to eat her dust again because it's about three miles of fairly straight road with no intersections. If any infected are on the road, I expect she will run over them."

Kathy hardly slowed down for the turn, and I thought she was going to roll the boat, but she got control and was off again. Jean was right that I would be eating dust because that cop could drive.

Jean said, "We may have one other problem."

I didn't want to ask, but I had to. "Is it another boat landing?"

"Worse," she said. "It's a boat landing and a ferry landing. If the ferry was there when everything happened, there could be a lot of infected."

"Well, it has got to be better than trying to go through Georgetown. The pedestrian traffic north of there on Highway 17 is hell."

The good news was the walkway to the ferry was a couple of hundred yards long. The bad news was the railing along the walkway was too high for the infected to fall over. Judging by the number of dead that were milling around on the walkway, someone else must have recently tried to escape by reaching the ferry. If they had escaped we would never know, but they left behind over a hundred groaning, angry, infected dead.

The walkway was just barely wide enough for a vehicle, but on the boat landing end there were big pillars that looked like they could stop a tank. The clear purpose of those pillars was to keep people from driving a vehicle down to the dock. A golf cart might get through, but not a car. Kathy swung her truck around the parking area and came up alongside our Ford.

When she rolled down her window, she said, "There's no way we can shoot all of them, but let me drop off my boat first. After the Chief gets here, I'm going to try to block the walkway to give us enough time to strap the trailer to the bottom of the plane. Give me some cover."

Jean and I went to work shooting the infected that were close to the boat landing but still on the walkway. We were making a big enough pile of them to keep them from reaching the landing, but there were so many that time was going to run out.

The seaplane approached from the North and made a smooth landing near the end of the long walkway to the ferry. The Chief immediately summed up the problem and brought the plane to within a couple of feet of the slip where the ferry was usually docked.

Jean and I stopped shooting as we watched the horde of infected begin to reverse their direction to reach the plane. The infected that were already nearest to him were stopped from falling into the water by the height of the railing, and their fellow dead began crowding against them from behind. It only took about ten minutes for all of them to be packed into the far end of the walkway.

"That railing must be made for real dummies," I said to Jean. "It's holding against a lot of tourists."

She laughed and said, "Let's see how much time the Chief bought us."

Kathy had already backed her boat down the ramp and used her winch to slide it into the water. She signaled for us to help her, and Jean climbed into the boat while I got it free of the cable. Jean started the engine and idled it down to where the seaplane was keeping the infected busy. By this time we were all working together so well that I think we all knew what the other people were doing.

Jean's boat was about twice the size of the Boston Whaler, and it made a lot of noise. As soon as she had it on station next to the seaplane, the Chief eased away from her and lowered his engine noise. Now that the infected were being aggravated by the bigger boat, the seaplane was free to come to the dock.

I saw what Jean was doing, so I got back in the second truck. Kathy managed to dump the tiller out of her truck then drove over to the parking area and lined it up with the walkway. She left it idling there and ran to where I was backing my boat into the water. As soon as it was in far enough, Kathy was sliding it off of the trailer. I jumped on board and got the engine started, then moved it out of the way so the Chief could come toward the ramp.

He brought the plane to a stop facing the ramp with the pontoons on either side of the trailer. He feathered the propeller and jumped into the water to help Kathy. They strapped the trailer to the underside of the plane, and with the help of a bit of buoyancy, the Chief was able to raise it high enough to clear the pontoons. He wanted to carry the tiller back in the larger boat, but Jean was using it to distract the infected. So, he lifted the tiller into the cargo hold of the plane. It sank a bit lower, but he was still satisfied and appreciated the plane even more. If it produced too much drag when he tried to take off or land, it would rip the bottom off of the plane, but he felt like it was a good job, and the plane would handle the entire load.

Satisfied that the trailer was up high enough, the Chief climbed back in the plane and started the engine. He coasted away from the dock and headed for the deeper water. As he passed our boats we could see that big smile back on his face.

I coasted back up to the landing to pick up Kathy, but she was gone. I was immediately panicked because we had done such a good job keeping the horde of infected under control. Then I saw the big Silverado racing toward the end of the walkway with no one behind the wheel. It hit the pillars head on with an incredible crash, but it kept going for a few yards. It came to a stop completely blocking the walkway.

Kathy came strolling up to the boat ramp and said, "I don't think we should eat the seagulls either. It's my guess that it's going to take them a while to stop moving, but the gulls are going to start hanging around this dock for a long time after that."

She climbed into the boat and pushed off at the same time. "Eddy, give me a ride out there to Jean and let me hop over there with her. The girls are going to take that big boat for a test drive."

"With pleasure," I said. "Let's go home."

After pulling alongside the other boat, Kathy jumped over, and they were off. We went up the waterway that separates Bulls Bay from the mainland until we reached the town of McClellanville, then we found a deep enough channel to head for the ocean. It was smoother traveling along the coast in the channel, but the banks were too close on both sides, and I was going to worry about being shot at until we were home.

After we reached deeper water, we were only two hours from Mud Island, but the girls got there much faster than me. I could still hear the whooping and hollering as they began to leave me behind. I was happy for them because it felt good to be going faster even in the Boston Whaler.

As I came around the jetty at the southern tip of the island, the Chief already had the trailer and the tiller unloaded. He was busy covering them with tree branches to keep them hidden until we could come back out to build our boat garage.

The Chief gave me a wave and signaled for me to just keep going, so I throttled up and sped for the dock at the other end of Mud Island. As I pulled up to the dock, Jean tossed me a mooring line and Kathy grabbed a rail to guide me in. I thought for a moment about the first time I had docked in this same spot and was amazed that I considered it to be home so much more now than ever before.

7 GUESTS

We could tell we only had a few weeks before the weather would begin to get cold, and the days outside would be limited due to the cold wind blowing off of the ocean. So, there would be no time to rest and recover. The best I could hope for was a long evening in the hot tub with Jean and then a good night of sleep.

It always seemed like I was the last one to get up in the mornings, but once again the smell of fresh coffee, bacon, and scrambled eggs pulled me from a deep sleep.

I had been dreaming about riding in the boat on the way back to Mud Island. That was the one thing that was fun on our trip. As the smell of food pulled me to a higher level of consciousness, the memories came back in a flash. There were people in control of the Charleston harbor who had no regard for the lives of others. They would shoot you just because they could.

There were people who had survived just because they were in the right place at the right time. The people living in the marina on the Stono River wouldn't last a day when the other people, the shooters, finally decided to expand their territory, but would they be there when the others arrived? Probably not, because they were eating something they had eaten their entire lives. To them a blue crab was just a blue crab, no matter what it ate. I had no doubt that Jean was right. They would get sick and die from eating the crabs that had been eating the infected.

There were people who had turned to laying traps for travelers, and if not for good planning on our part, we would have been caught in that trap when we reached the bridge on Highway 41. What they would have done with us was anyone's guess.

Then there was the military. We knew they were still out there, but we couldn't turn to them for help. They were still fighting for control of their own infrastructure, and they wouldn't be able to help us with ours until they were in one piece again. The big question about them would be whether they respected our right to continue as we were, or if they would be no different from the shooters in Charleston harbor. So, there was no trust for the military, and we would avoid them for as long as we could.

We had met some good people and some people who showed they couldn't be trusted. My thoughts seemed to reach only a few miles down the road to Georgetown when I would wonder what the world was going to become. My hope for Hampton and his friends was that they would see the end coming in time to make it to the planes they had loaded and ready at the small airport. It was inevitable that their fall would come from within because they controlled their borders but not what was within their borders.

Then there were the infected dead. They outnumbered the living. That much was obvious, and it seemed they were still increasing their numbers. If they tended to be lingering in large groups around places like boat landings, it was probably because that's where the living were still finding a way to escape. Just as we had succeeded in taking boats and trailers out from under the very noses of the infected, there were far more people who failed and joined the hordes that roamed around looking for fresh victims.

As I finally sat up from my half awake and half asleep reverie, I had one last thought. If this was life on the coast where water was a way to delay death if not totally escape it, what was it like in the heart of the country? What happened where people had gathered in malls where they knew there would be supplies behind chain gates. If there had been pockets of survivors, would they fall from within just as Georgetown probably had, or would they fall from attacks by other survivors who would want to take what they had?

Malls, hospitals, schools, fallout shelters, military bases, ships at sea, and even private homes. They had all been places where people went to get away from this deadly infection, but none had the advantages of Mud Island.

Jean came into the bedroom and saw that I was already awake. This was one advantage of Mud Island that the other places certainly didn't have. The world had ended, but I wound up with a girlfriend.

"Are you ready to join us for breakfast, sleepy head?" she asked.

"The food smells wonderful," I said, "but I would pass on it if you stayed here with me." I gave her my best sexy grin, which wasn't saying much.

"That would be my first choice too, my dear, but we have important work to do. Come and get some breakfast, and maybe we can get some alone time this evening." Jean gave me a little wink and headed for the kitchen.

Five minutes later I passed through the kitchen, and Kathy handed me a plate of food and a steaming hot coffee. She also gave me a little peck on the cheek that made me blush a bit.

"Hands off, Kathy," said Jean from across the room. "He's spoken for."

"I just can't help myself," said Kathy. "He's been such an animal out on the road."

Kathy may have been kidding, but I was starting to feel like our group wasn't just lucky. We were planning, we were improvising, and we were doing. I just hoped we weren't going to plan or do anything in the near future.

"Hey, Chief," I said. He was sitting at the kitchen counter with his own cup of coffee and plate of food. "Anything good to report this morning?"

"Good morning, Ed," he said between bites. "We hit the jackpot yesterday, if that's what you mean by good news."

"Yesterday?" I asked. "I hit the jackpot last night, but how did we hit the jackpot yesterday?"

That earned me a chorus of boos, but I got an appreciative look from Jean.

"Rub it in," said the Chief. "Did you hear about the boat Kathy picked at the boat landing?"

"What about it?" I asked.

"It was well stocked," said Kathy. "If you're going to pick a boat to steal, pick one that's loaded with things you need."

They were all looking at me with anticipation, and I felt like I was about to get an early Christmas.

"Is anyone going to tell me, or do I have to negotiate for my share of the booty?"

This time I got the chorus of boos and a poke on the arm from Jean.

"Do you do that on purpose, or does it just come naturally to you, and if you act like you don't know what I'm talking about, I'm going to cut you off," said Jean.

This time I just grinned because I was busted.

"Okay, what's in the boat that I'm going to get excited about?" I asked.

The Chief reached down to the floor and lifted a large box up onto the counter. I took a peak inside and couldn't believe my eyes. It was the second best collection of video games I had ever seen. The best collection was the one I left sitting on the counter in the game store. There were also several sets of game controllers and two different consoles.

Kathy said, "Ed, you think it's a given that you'll beat everyone here at those games, but don't count on it."

I was so stunned I almost forgot my food, but Jean reminded me to eat before I could play.

The Chief said, "How long do you think it's going to take us to finish the boat garage, Ed?"

"With no interruptions from unwanted guests, I think we can do it in one to two days. All we need to do is dig out the area around the hatch, give it some extra support for the material we use to hide it. The tiller should tear up the beach pretty fast, so getting the boat into the hideaway isn't going to be a big project," I said.

"There's one modification to the plan I'd like to suggest," said Kathy. "If someone finds the boat, we don't want them to find the escape hatch, too. We need to make it look like the only thing under there is the boat."

"That's no problem," said the Chief. "Has anyone given any thought to the ditch itself? If I was walking down the beach, and I came across a ditch like we plan to dig, I would naturally follow it right up to the trees."

"I've got an idea for that, Chief. Which would pull over a tree the quickest, a boat, a winch, or the plane?" I asked.

"Depends on the tree," he said. "If it's a dead tree, I imagine any of them could."

"Well, I'm thinking we could pull a dead tree down over the end of the ditch after we have the boat inside. As long as it isn't a tree we can't move again but big enough to look like it wasn't put there, it should disguise the hideaway nicely."

******

We finished our breakfast and went back to the dock by the houseboat. We had decided to restock it with a smaller supply of food than before. That way, unwelcome tenants wouldn't stay as long before having to leave. Kathy and Jean took over with that project while the Chief and I loaded the bigger, more powerful boat with our construction supplies.

Thirty minutes later we were starting the tiller and cutting a ditch from the water to the tree line where the hatch was hidden. The Chief took over with the tiller while I went up and began cutting away the turf in large sections. The idea was to put them back in a way that they wouldn't be too heavy, but they would look like natural turf. It was a bit sandy, but Mud Island was appropriately named. It had enough wet ground for our purposes.

By the time I had cut away the brush and the turf, the Chief had a fair ditch from the water to the hatch. We weren't worried about water filling the ditch, because it was like any beach. The water never stayed long.

The Chief and I began using the tiller to excavate a section of the tree line that was deep enough to hold the trailer and the Boston Whaler. It was back breaking work, but we had the hole dug in only two hours.

Our next job was to hide it all, and Uncle Titus had left enough materials in the storage area of the shelter for that. We hauled a load of two by fours to our newly dug hole and built a roof into the tree line. It was so solid that we were amazed how well the turf fit back into place over it. We didn't even need to drop any trees over the top of it to hide it from the top. Someone could walk right over the top of it without even knowing it was there. It would look just like a place in the tree line that had a sharp drop down to the beach because it was a bit higher.

"We're ahead of schedule," said the Chief, "probably because we haven't had any unwanted guests."

We both looked across the inlet toward the trawler and the strip of beach by the trees. While we worked, there had been a steady stream of infected dead trying to reach us. One by one they had walked into the water and disappeared into the swift current.

"I know," I said. "This has been a lot like anchoring next to that boat landing and baiting them into the water. We may be making these woods just a bit safer than before, and at this pace we'll be done tonight."

We crafted a wooden lid and then cut out another section of turf of the same size. We carried it together back down to the hatch that led to the emergency escape and placed it over the hole. It would be hidden unless someone chose to dig in that exact spot. If someone found the boat, there would be no reason for them to expect an escape hatch to be located underneath it in the same place. Even if they found the hatch, there would be no chance at all that they would be able to enter the shelter through it.

Our last chore was to get the boat onto the trailer and then tow it up to the hideaway, and luck was on our side. The tide was out when we slid the trailer into the water, but it began to come in as we moved the boat into place above it. With a little help from the water at just the right time, the boat and trailer glided with the tide into our ditch and right into its new garage.

We lowered the turf of the tree line that was to act as the door to the hideaway and were pleasantly surprised at how well it was hidden, and the best part was the way the tide was smoothing out the sand on the beach.

"Give it a day, and it will be nothing more than a big groove in the sand. In a week it will be gone," said the Chief.

Living proof of the power of the tide was how much sand had built up on the trawler that had wrecked on the other side of the jetty. It would take years for it to be buried, but they could already see the changes to the terrain around it.

We had seen the infected on that part of the beach all day, but the number had begun to dwindle. As we watched the area south of the wrecked trawler, we saw one stumbling down the beach in our direction. It looked like it was already snapping its jaws open and shut in anticipation.

"That's what I call an optimist," I said.

The Chief sort of laughed, and we watched in morbid fascination one more time as the infected dead reached the other side of the inlet, walked into the water, and then just disappeared.

"Your uncle was a genius, Ed."

"I don't doubt that, Chief."

The Chief opened our hideaway and dragged the tiller inside. He closed it just as easily as a garage door, and we took a last look at our handiwork. We didn't know when we would need the boat again, but it would be there for us when the time came. If it was left up to me, we would never need it again.

We waded out and boarded the new boat and the Chief drove us back to the northern dock where we found the ladies had done a reasonably good job of making it look like the houseboat had been abandoned for a long time. We told them we had also finished, which produced excited cheers from them both.

Kathy said, "We haven't celebrated for so long, that I'm going to cook a big fancy meal. Afterward we're going to get into that box of video games and find out who the gamers are."

"Women rule," said Jean as she gave Kathy a high five.

"Oh it's going to be like that," said the Chief. "I'll take my man Eddy here, and we'll show the women a thing or two about why women should stick to cooking."

The Chief wasn't nearly a chauvinist, so I knew he was putting on an act to get the friendly rivalry started. With the boat and plane disabled and the houseboat looking abandoned, we carried our tools and supplies back through the woods to the shelter. There was still enough light for us to see through the security cameras, so we did a sweep of the island before settling in for the night.

The fancy meal was a large rack of prime rib that was stored in the big walk-in freezer. Canned vegetables were plentiful, so we added corn, peas, and potatoes. Canned peaches and ice cream were for dessert, and since it was a celebration, the beer was not rationed.

By the time we were all done eating, we were holding our stomachs and groaning like we belonged outside. When I made the observation that we sounded like a bunch of infected, I wasn't met with the usual boos because everyone was a little drunk and actually thought it was a little funny.

We set up the video game console and harassed each other mercilessly as we tried to establish who was the king or queen of the video world. We even played a zombie apocalypse game and ran around shooting zombies. Jean would start screaming to look out every time I let them get too close, like she thought I was going to get bitten for real. She probably would have cried if I had lost the game to the zombies.

Between turns, the Chief drifted over to the short wave radio and slowly scanned the channels. We still had our rule to listen but never broadcast because we didn't want anyone to know our location. He picked up a few signals, but they were all too weak to understand.

We enjoyed each other's company well into the night and finally decided to get some sleep. As a matter of fact there was a general agreement that we would sleep in the next day. It had been a long time since we had taken that luxury. We had finished the work that had taken us back out onto the road for a second time, and as we went to bed, we all vowed that there would be no need for us to leave again. The world was our oyster, and we were safe as long as we stayed on the island.

******

Through our cameras hidden outside, we watched as November went by and December became one day after the next of cold, gray skies and a choppy ocean. We had endless days of reading, movies, video games, and chores, but as a group we didn't neglect the exercise room.

The Chief was an avid weight lifter, Kathy was an all around exercise nut, and Jean loved to run. Of course that's what I loved to do when I was asked. It was probably painfully obvious to everyone that I wasn't high on any kind of exercise, but as the days passed, I really began to look forward to my sessions on the treadmill. Jean watched to see when I was starting to tire out, and she would slow to a stop with me. It wasn't long before she was really ready to stop as I built up a stamina I didn't know I had. The fact was, I was feeling better than I had in my whole life.

When we were pretty sure it was Christmas, Kathy and Jean thawed out a turkey and we had a real feast. The Chief found some DVD's with football games on them, and we watched them as if they were live broadcasts. When Jean said it would be nice if we could bundle up and go out onto the beach and build a fire, it didn't take long to put the idea aside as the wrong thing to do. She admitted she had felt so safe and comfortable that she had forgotten just how dangerous our own island could be.

As we settled in for our nightly video games and movies, the Chief started casually turning the dial through the frequencies on the short wave set. One signal came through so clear that it sounded like it was in the same room with us. The man broadcasting was asking if there were any other survivors out there, and he even said he didn't blame people for not speaking up because there were so many criminals who would be glad to locate a survivor and take what they had.

He said his name was Tom Bergman, and he had managed to stay alive with his little girl, Molly. She was nine years old, and they had lost everyone else, but they still had each other. He said he wouldn't disclose their location, but for the first time in a long time they felt safe, at least from the sick people if not from the criminals. He said they had some supplies that they were rationing, but he hoped to at least make them last a couple more weeks.

Tom Bergman said he would be willing to talk with anyone who wanted to work together to stay alive, but that he would do anything to protect his daughter, so he would only disclose his location after he was sure it was to the right people. He signed off for the night, but he said he would broadcast again tomorrow night at the same time.

When the radio went silent, Kathy said, "I think we should find out where they are and bring them here."

The Chief had always shown a soft heart, but even he was skeptical.

"Kathy, how do you know he has a nine year old daughter, and how do you know it isn't just a trap to flush out other survivors?" he asked.

"I don't know, Chief. He just sounds real," she said.

"I have to agree with the Chief," I said. "We're about to have temperatures near zero out there, and we don't even know where he is. We can't advertise our location, and he isn't going to tell us his."

"So we're just going to leave them out there?" said Jean. "Have we become that immune to death that we can turn our backs on them?"

I felt like hiding my head under something. Jean and I hadn't so much as exchanged cross words with each other since the day we met. I looked at the Chief, and I could see he felt the same way.

The Chief said, "In defense of the men, this conversation might have gone better if it has started with the question of finding them rather than the outright decision to do it."

"What's that mean, Chief? I need to ask if we can help them?" asked Kathy.

"No," he answered. "You need to ask if anyone has a clue of how we can help them. This isn't a 'should we or should we not' problem. It's a 'can we or can't we' problem. Give me an idea of how we can find them without advertising their location to everyone else who's listening. As soon as they say where they are, every nut job left alive will go after them."

It was Kathy's and Jean's turn to hide their heads. The Chief had laid out the problem pretty well. Everything they said on the radio was heard by us and anyone else who was listening. No matter what was said to try to arrange a rendezvous, there was no way to do it privately.

"I'm sorry," said Jean. "I shouldn't have accused you guys of being insensitive or not caring enough to help. You two are probably the finest men I've ever known."

The far away look on Jean's face as she apologized told me she was thinking of the past and maybe of someone she had known. We didn't talk much about our pasts. As a matter of fact, all four of us had been elusive about life before the infection. I wasn't even sure of ages, birthdays, or where they were from. It made me see that we were living for the present, not the past. We wanted to stay alive, and we could worry about the before times when it was possible to do that and stay alive at the same time. All I really knew for sure was that we cared about each other.

Kathy asked, "Would anybody object to bringing them in if there was a way?"

"Do you have a plan?" asked Jean.

"No, I wish I did. I just wanted to be sure that we're all in agreement that there may eventually be someone else who we can rescue. The Chief was right about the real question, but we also need to be clear that we don't intend to turn our backs on people."

"Not everyone is going to be like that couple back at the farm where we had to leave the plane," I said. "We gave them a chance, and they blew it. They would have left us standing there on the road if they could, and they'd also probably be dead by now if they had."

The Chief had been quiet since defending the men, but when he spoke, it was clearly what we were all thinking. There was one thing that we had ignored because it was unthinkable.

"How many children have we seen since this started?" he asked. "The news broadcasts in the last days, our travels along the coast, and Georgetown. We never saw any kids surviving. If we could bring in even one, it would make us feel less guilty about what we have here. It's in our nature to share, but it's in our genes to share with children."

We were all sobered by the thought, and it was getting late, so we drifted off to bed. No one felt like celebrating after the discussion about children. So much had been lost. So many people had died, and so many more would die.

The next morning began with the usual breakfast as a group, but the conversation was subdued. It seemed to be limited to the food tasting good, what day it was, and what the weather was like outside. What we were really thinking about was a little nine year old girl named Molly, and how her dad had kept her alive. We didn't know if it was true or a trap, but we could picture Molly just as if she was standing in front of us.

The day passed with everyone doing their own thing. The Chief was in the armory inspecting and cleaning weapons. Jean was doing an inventory of our supplies, and Kathy was trying her hand at baking bread. I tried playing video games, but for the first time I could remember, I was bored.

I switched to the surveillance cameras and checked the view from the southern tip of the island. We probably had some heavy winds through the night because there was a lot of debris on the beach from the trees. The camera angle was just right for me to inspect the cover over our hidden boat, and I was pleased to see that the ditch we had dug gave the appearance of a run off from the island. There was a trickle of water standing in it from the high tide, so it looked like it belonged there.

I made a mental note to talk with the Chief about dragging some of the bigger trees out onto the beach in a random pattern. They could be a good way to keep people from being too interested in Mud Island, and they would slow down the movement of the infected if they started washing ashore again. Their numbers had steadily decreased, but there was no way to tell when they might start showing up again. This would be an ideal time to get it done.

I turned on the camera that faced the mainland and studied the trees near the dock. There wasn't any movement, but I made another mental note to talk with the Chief about the guns our unwanted tenants had been carrying. I wasn't sure because of the distance and the debris on the beach, but it looked like they were gone. Of course they could also have been covered by sand over the last few weeks.

When I switched to one of the main cameras on the ocean side of the island, I wasn't surprised to see some whitecaps and choppy seas. The sky was overcast, and a winter storm was moving across us. It was like watching a movie because we couldn't even hear what was happening outside.

The camera to the northern tip showed our collection tied to the dock. The boat and the seaplane were bobbing safely on the inland side of the dock, protected from the brunt of the wind by the houseboat.

I only saw it for a split second, but something moved through the air on top of the houseboat. Whatever it was, it was just there and then gone. I was ready to pass it off as just a sea gull, but there it was again. This time I was looking straight at it, but it moved so fast that I still didn't know what it was. One thing for sure, it couldn't be an infected dead, because they didn't move that fast.

I was afraid to blink because that's how fast it came and went from my field of vision. I was focusing so hard on the spot where I saw the movement that my eyes were starting to hurt. When I saw it a third time, I caught a glimpse of something that looked like an arm, but I still wasn't sure what I was seeing.

There was a switch we had discovered by playing with the controls on the center console. It operated a microphone that could be used as an intercom system in the shelter. We hadn't bothered to use it because there was never anything really that big to report that couldn't be done in person, but this seemed like the appropriate time.

I flipped the switch and said, "Testing, testing. Chief, Kathy, Jean? Could you please come to the living room?

There's something on the camera view of the houseboat that I'd like for you to see."

Kathy was the closest, but she arrived with the Chief close on her heels. He knew it had to be important for me to use the intercom.

Jean came up behind him and said, "Dammit, Eddy. I almost peed my pants when you used the intercom."

The Chief said, "Is that all? I almost shot off my foot."

Kathy looked at the two of them and said, "I honestly thought he was going to say something else, but I'd better just leave it at that. Why'd you call for us, Ed?"

"Watch the camera on top of the houseboat," I said.

The three of them started watching, and of course nothing happened. Just as Kathy was starting to ask what they were watching for, there was a blur of motion.

Jean asked, "What was that I just saw?"

"I'm not sure," said the Chief, "but putting two and two together, I think I have an idea."

The blur of motion happened again, and the Chief said, "Yep, that was the backswing of a fishing rod. I think someone is fishing from the top of the houseboat. Ed, switch to the interior camera view."

I reached over and flipped the switch to bring up the camera hidden in the main living area of the houseboat. There were a couple of back packs sitting on the little table that served as the social area in the middle of the main room. Open cans of food were next to the back packs.

"Someone had a little snack before going fishing," I said.

The Chief leaned closer to the screen and said, "What does that look like behind the back packs?"

"Oh my god," said Jean. "That looks just like the microphone cord on that old shortwave radio we have over there." She gestured toward the table where ours was sitting, and we all looked back and forth making the comparison.

There was a collective gasp from our little group as a little girl walked past the table where the back packs were sitting. She passed out of view then returned carrying a bottle of water. She sat down at the table and picked up one of the cans.

"Is that the cutest little girl you've ever seen?" asked Jean.

She had jet black hair that still had plenty of curls, and she was swinging her feet while she ate a can of peaches. Her face was pink, looking like it had been recently scrubbed.

She looked up and smiled in the direction of the door to the houseboat. We had been so intent on watching her that we didn't see the man climb down the ladder from the top of the houseboat. Now he was standing in the room with the little girl, and he held up a fish that he had caught. He held up a bucket of blue crabs in his other hand, and the little girl scrunched up her face at the sight of the crabs trying to climb out of the bucket.

Jean was the first to react, and she was at our short wave radio in a flash. She switched it on and said, "Tom Bergman."

The man in the houseboat sat down the bucket and the fish and moved the back packs out of the way. He keyed the microphone and said, "Who is this?"

The Chief had also moved quickly and stopped Jean from going on.

"Be careful what you say. There may be others listening," he said.

Jean gave him a nod and said into the microphone, "Tom Bergman, don't answer yet, just listen. You can't eat what you just showed your daughter. It's contaminated. Just throw it out and wait to hear back from me."

The man on the screen, obviously Tom Bergman, was more than confused. His head whipped around as he tried to figure out how someone knew his every move. He raised the microphone to his mouth, but Jean stopped him before he could speak.

"No," she said. "Don't say anything. Wait to hear from me."

We watched as the man looked at the crabs and the fish then walked over and picked them up. We couldn't see what he was doing, but it sounded like the door opened and closed. He returned back to his daughter and sat down with his arm around her as protection. He looked like he was waiting for the female voice to tell him what to do next.

Jean asked, "What should we do now?"

"It was probably good that you spoke first, Jean. A man's voice might have been more intimidating," said the Chief. "Tell him you are coming and will be there in exactly one hour."

The Chief turned to me and Kathy and said, "Suit up, super heroes. We're going on a rescue mission. Jean will approach the houseboat alone, but we'll need to check the area to be sure it's clear."

Jean keyed the microphone and said what the Chief told her. She added instructions not to use the radio again. Then she caught up with us as we put on our warm camouflage gear and boots. We all carried rifles and handguns because our least favorite time to be outside was after dark. The sun was low in the West, and it would be dark within the hour.

Less than ten minutes later we were outside and quietly moving on the now familiar path. Even though it was a mile from the shelter to the dock, we were all in good shape and making good time. I honestly thought we could sneak up on an infected dead before it would even hear us coming.

Forty minutes after telling the man to sit tight, we were in position to scan the area around the dock. The overcast sky was blocking out most of the light, and the wind coming over the water was covering all other sounds. We had no choice but to trust our luck.

The lights were out inside the houseboat. Whoever Tom Bergman was, he was smart enough not to advertise his presence. We approached keeping low, covering all directions of possible attack and didn't stop until we were around the door. Jean reached up and tapped on it lightly.

"Tom Bergman, it's me. I'm the lady who spoke to you on the radio." She only spoke as loud as she needed to, but we could hear him move as soon as she spoke. It sounded like he crossed over to one side of the door.

He answered in a hushed voice, "How do I know I can trust you?"

"You don't, but if we had meant you harm, we wouldn't have warned you we were coming," she said.

"You're not alone." It didn't sound like a question, but the man didn't know what to do. He wanted to protect his daughter, but he was cornered. A cornered parent could be dangerous, even by accident.

Kathy moved next to Jean and said through the closed door, "Mr. Bergman. There's no time to explain everything, so listen carefully. There are four of us, and it's not safe out here. We have a safe place for you and your little girl. Put on your warm coats and get your backpacks. Don't worry about anything else. When you are ready, come out and just follow us to safety."

It was quiet for a few moments, but then he answered, "Do I have a choice?"

Kathy said, "Yes, you can stay here in the houseboat for as long as you like. We'll even share our supplies with you, but you will never really be safe. Oh, and one other thing, don't eat the seafood. It may look safe, but it's not."

The man probably had his mind made up even before Kathy answered, because the door opened a few inches before she finished talking. He peered around the corner and looked at our group. We must have looked like a SWAT team on a raid.

"Hi neighbor," I said.

That probably confused him more than anything else, but he squeezed through the door with his back pack and reached behind him to help guide the little girl out onto the dock. She was bundled up in a coat with a big furry hood, but she looked more curious than afraid.

The Chief pointed toward the end of the dock and said, "Follow the ladies. We'll cover the rear and our flanks. We have about a mile to go, but it will be worth your time. I promise."

When we arrived back at the entrance to the shelter, I remembered the day I had met the three people who had become my best friends ever. I dialed in the combination to the big lock on the door, and just before I pulled it open, I turned to the man who was hugging his little girl and said, "I know you have a thousand questions, but I'll answer one now. We have a fresh water supply."

The others all let out a soft chorus of groans, and Jean said, "You're gonna get it when I get you inside, Eddy."

ABOUT THE AUTHOR

Bob Howard (1951-) was born in New Jersey to an Army Sergeant from Ohio and a mother from Romania. He was moved from one Army base to the next, and before he began high school in Huntsville, Alabama he had lived most of his life overseas in Germany and Okinawa with brief stays in Maryland and North Carolina. He credits his imagination to his exposure to different cultures and environments at an early age. He began reading science fiction and fell in love with post apocalyptic novels. He still has an original copy of the first one he read in 1966, The Furies by Keith Edwards. He joined the Navy after high school and continued to move from one base to another, including a submarine base at Holy Loch, Scotland. He eventually stayed in one place when he got stationed in Charleston, South Carolina. He graduated with a BS in Psychology from the College of Charleston and married his wife of 31 years. His son still lives in Charleston, but his daughter has married and made a home in Ohio where the Howard family has its earliest known roots. Through the years he has had one burning passion that he has wanted to fulfill, and through Alive for Now he is getting to live that passion. Creating a book is something so many people want to do but never have the opportunity, and after writing this book he believes the sky is the limit. He plans to write for the rest of his life because it is enjoyable beyond his wildest dreams. As for the zombie genre, he saw Night of the Living Dead when it originally hit the theaters, and until recently it didn't receive the attention it deserves.